SEVERED EMPIRE

QUEENS OF OSIRIS

PHILLIP TOMASSO

Mirror Matter Press

Austin, TX

www.mirrormatterpress.com

November 2016

Cover Art by Jim Agpalza

Book Design by Zach McCain

Text Design by Travis Tarpley

ISBN: 978-0-997837-72-8

This is for my kids, Phillip, Grant, & Raeleigh If not for you
I am nothing

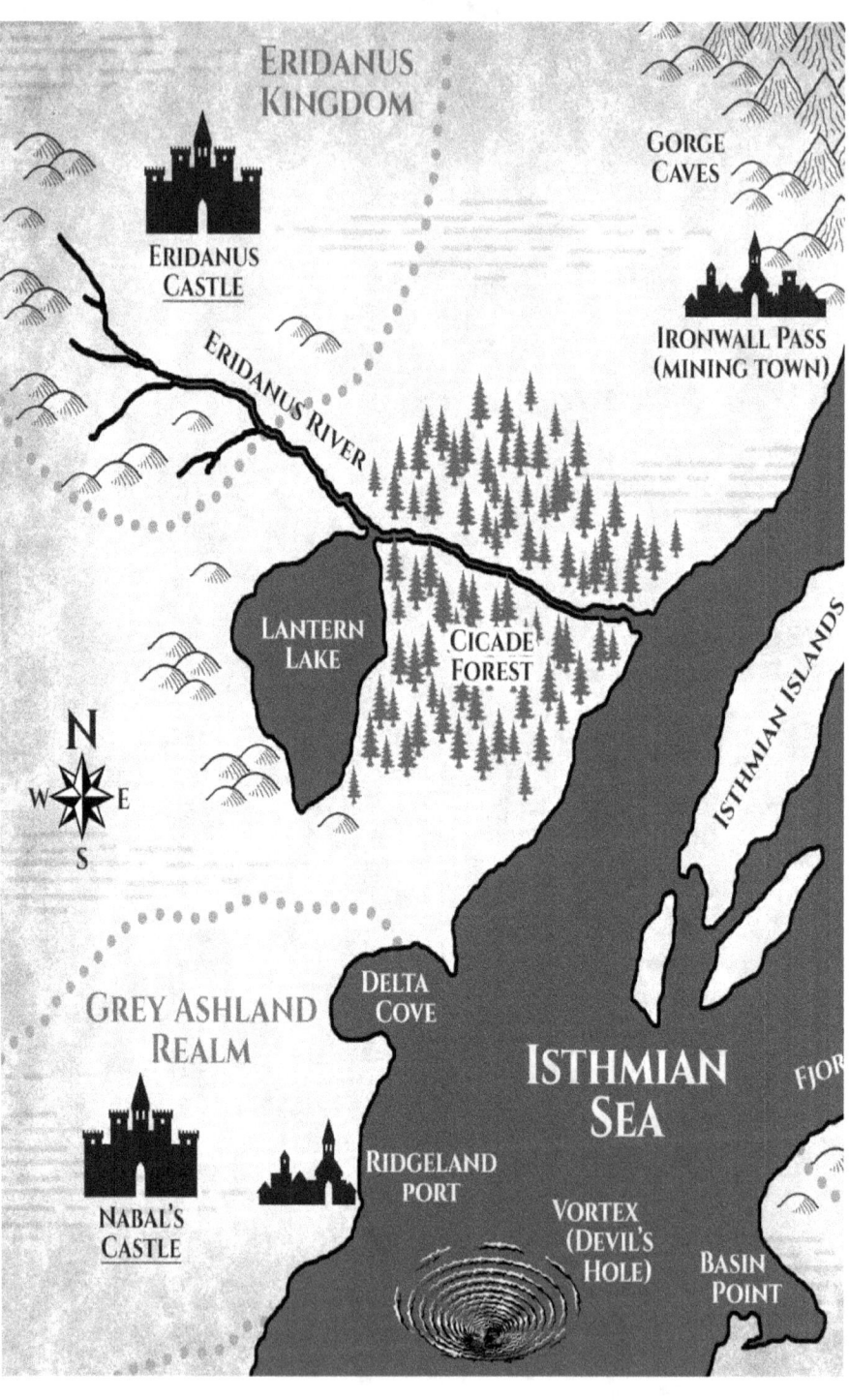

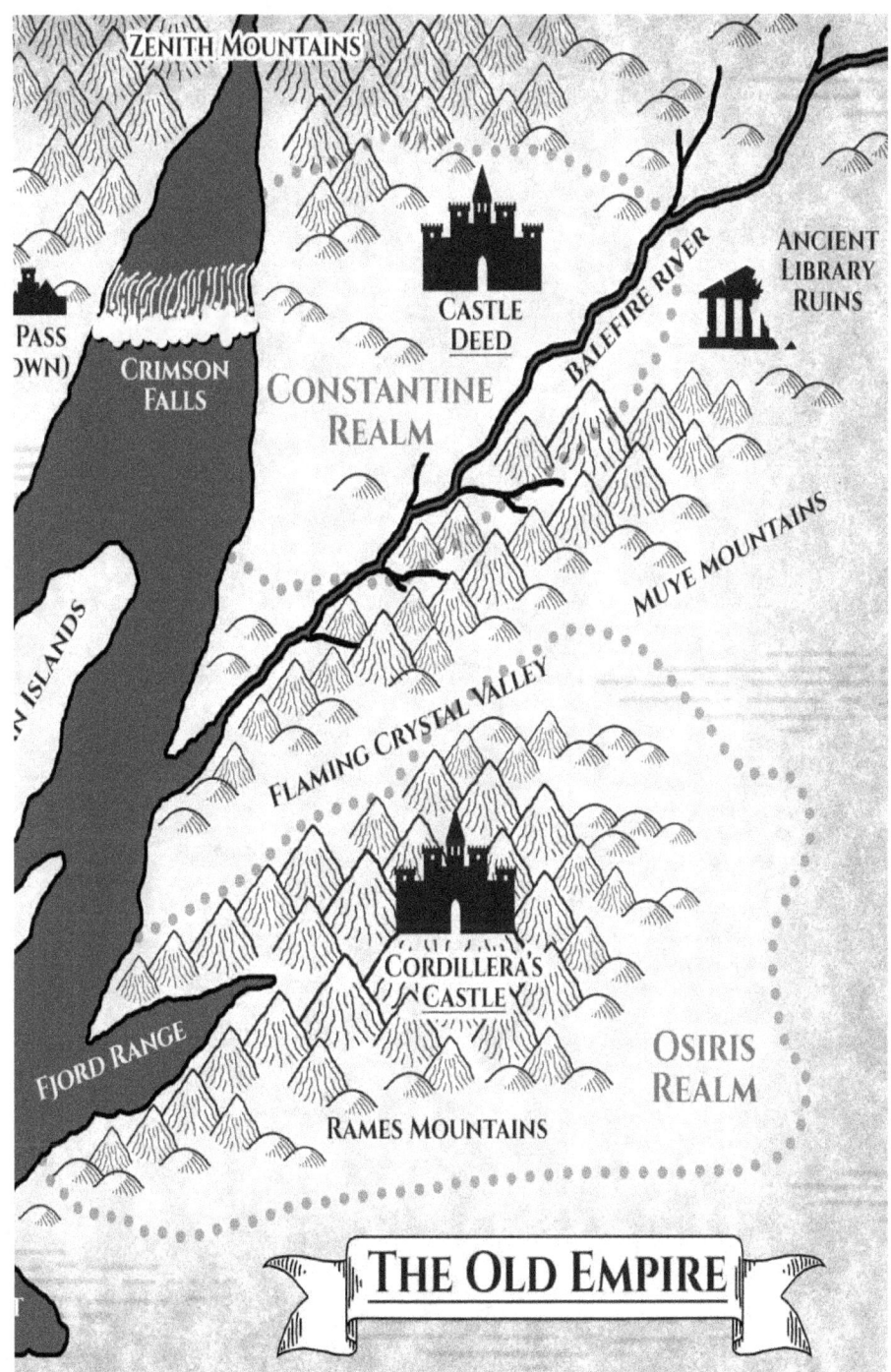

CHAPTER 1

Deidre hummed while she knelt on the rock and scrubbed laundry across the tin rungs on her washboard, but stopped when the hairs on her arms and the back of her neck stood on end. A tingle traced its way down her spine. She shivered when it felt as if now a finger of ice raced back up, and across her shoulders.

She straightened up, the bones in her back cracked like someone had stepped on twigs, and she searched the surroundings. Tall grass, big rocks, and a setting sun impeded her vision. It could have been a nearby animal, but she didn't think so.

It didn't matter. The work in front of her needed completing. She could not return with soiled linens. Whether someone watched her work or not, she had no choice but to continue.

The cold mountain water numbed her fingers. Perpetually bright red hands with dry, cracked skin, and shredded knuckles were the result of her manual labors. Never mind the tight muscles in her lower back which forced her to walk bent forward, or the way her feet swelled at the end of the day when she was finally able to step out of well-worn shoes.

She didn't complain; since the death of her husband, she needed the work. No one would have listened anyway.

Despite having her kids depend on her, she had never felt more invisible.

As the sun set, the day's heat disappeared with the last rays of light. With the last full bushel of her employer's dirty clothing beside her, it would be some time before she could return home and start supper.

She wasn't certain if the tune she hummed had a name. It was a simple melody, really, and if lyrics were associated with it, she was unaware. The humming served a purpose: it kept her mind off her life. Long gone were her carefree days as a child. Sure, there were chores her parents expected she would complete, there would always be chores, but once finished she'd spend the rest of the day playing Kings and Queens with her siblings. They'd slay dragons, hold high court, and the knights often rescued princesses from their sinister captors. And, quite often, princesses rescued knights from ferocious monsters!

If there was an age, or a moment, when she realized she wouldn't grow up and become royalty, she couldn't recall it. For some nearly unforgivable reason her mother had allowed her to live in the fantasy world created by an overactive imagination. The woman let her believe fairytales actually came true to those who wanted happy endings most.

There wasn't anger toward her mother. Just disappointment. Deidre was certain her mother had meant well, and not to be cruel.

She remembered now.

Her mother hummed the same song. Was it something she had done to forge her own mental escape?

Keeping her eyes closed, she ran her employer's skivvies up and down the washboard. Plenty of the filth crusted the fabric, and was quite the challenge to remove. She scrubbed harder, the repetitive motion made her elbows sore, and biceps ache. The long walk home always took a toll on her legs. The veins bulged out on her skin from the ankles up to her knees. The pain was constant. Her knees sometimes refused to bend smoothly—the bone, cartilage and whatever else was behind the cap rubbed together and resulted in an agony beyond words. The only relief came— and it was temporary, at best—when she soaked strips of cloth in salt water and wrapped her legs tight.

She folded the last of the laundry and placed the stack in one of the three baskets beside her.

Groaning, she stood up, and brushed strands of loose hair behind her ear. With hands on her hips she arched her back and strained against stiff muscles. The slight relief was euphoric enough that she sighed with mild pleasure.

In front of her, she saw the reflection of a full moon in a cloudless sky on the placid Isthmian Sea. Silhouetted mountain caps and the Fjord Range marina seemed so small, insignificant, and far away. The Rames behind her were towering and imposing, like cold, rock weights, because she would swear she felt them pressing down on her shoulders, crippling her spine and crushing her soul.

The path to the stream cut narrowly through those same mountains. Loose gravel underfoot made walking dangerous. With crumbled pebbles, ice and snow, countless times she had slipped, and far too often, she fell. For all of her effort, she wore jagged cuts and purple bruises like pigment scars on her arms and the palms of her hands.

She would walk toward the darkness, up the path, and finally toward home. She stopped when the hairs rose once again, and she sensed... *something* was breathing behind her. She narrowed her eyes, and held her breath. It was her fast beating heart making the most noise. The *tha-thud, tha-thud* of the beats pulsed like thunder inside her head.

She turned around, and opened her eyes wider as she searched for any light that might penetrate the swelling darkness.

The shadows moved around her.

If she weren't holding bushels of clean clothing she might have reached out into the black.

There was nothing there. Couldn't be. Nothing more than her imagination getting the better of her.

No. Deidre didn't think anything was there.

She spun around, her back to the shadows, and continued forward. She did her best keeping herself convinced her mind played tricks on her. Cruel, yes, but tricks nonetheless.

"You're tired, and working too hard," she said aloud, shaking her head as if scolding herself. Humming a simple tune, and talking to herself. *This* was how she passed the sunrise to sunset on working days. "If you don't start taking better care, you're going to get sick."

Her kids might not be toddlers anymore, but since the death of their father, they relied on her more and more. Perhaps a bit more than kids their age should, but family didn't turn family away. Ever.

Something shuffled on loose stones behind her.

She stopped, and held her breath.

There was no denying it; this was not her imagination. Something *was* following her.

She could hear it breathing again, and thought she felt its breath spray onto the back of her neck, hot and moist.

Her chin quivered. "Who's there?"

She wasn't prepared to turn around. Not this time. Her bravery for the night was shot. A bit of cowardice spread through her bones, and surged in her veins. The muscles in her stomach twisted into knots. She would run, but with the baskets she'd never make it very far. And she was tired, so tired.

The thing behind her huffed. It sounded like a horse, or bull; an animal.

She took a step forward. It was short, tentative. It was also the only option. Walk away. Just walk away.

When nothing happened, she took another step.

She heard it breathing a little harder, a little heavier. The sound was no closer. Perhaps it didn't intend to give chase?

She walked. Slow. Steady.

Inside, she cringed, expecting something would stab her through the back, or sweep out her legs. She'd drop the laundry. It didn't matter if she lost the job, but she would keep her life. She'd find other work, a better position if she had to.

When something with claws clamped down onto her shoulders, she screamed. The bushels fell out of her hands. The clothing she'd just spent hours cleaning spilled onto the muddy ground. She was pushed forward. She stumbled over the baskets, and fell onto the clothing. She clawed at skivvies as she scrambled forward.

Feet stomped down on either side of her, straddled her above her back. She felt paralyzed, but somehow managed rolling over.

Above, the shadow of her attacker was backlit by a hint of moonlight, letting her see a large blunt object arc over and down.

Throwing up her arms, she deflected the blow. Fingers broke on both hands. Tears poured out of her eyes and rolled down into her ears. When the second blow came, she turned away and, again, raised her arms. The club slammed into forearms. Pain shot through bone as it raced toward her shoulders.

With no defense, no time to prepare, she saw the third swing too late, and the club smashed against the side of her head. Darkness consumed her.

CHAPTER 2

Mykal wore the green cloak Blodwyn had given him. It was long, heavy, and protected him from, among other things, the wintery weather. The falling snow seemed like a perfect reason to skip the day's lessons, but Blodwyn wasn't having it. The morning sun did its best, but most of the rays and all of the heat was absorbed by the surrounding flat grey clouds. His hot breath plumed in front of his face, but did nothing for the frozen hairs inside his nostrils.

Blodwyn stood with his left leg forward, right back, and knees slightly bent. He held his six-foot-long staff balanced out in front of him on the palm of one hand, and the backside of the other. He started slowly, twirling the staff around and around until the staff spun so fast the wind whistled. Mykal could barely see the staff at all. As if the speed of movement wasn't impressive enough, Blodwyn rotated his arms all the way to the left, and back to the front, and then all the way to the right. Any opponent unlucky enough to... well, Mykal didn't even want to think about the consequences.

When Blodwyn slowed the twirling, and then finally stopped, he stood his staff up right in the snow, leaning his weight on the iron and wood compound, and cocked a hip. "Now, you try."

"Me?"

"Your control of the staff is essential in completing your training. The two of you will be like one."

"That sounds a little weird."

"Enough procrastinating."

Mykal shrugged. "Not really procrastinating. Just delaying the looking-like-a-fool part, is all."

Blodwyn laughed. He was a good three inches taller. And while Mykal was all brawn from working his grandfather's farm, and his hair was copper-colored, and unkempt, Blodwyn was more wiry and lithe, and wore his long black hair in a braid that ran down his back. He kept his mustache and beard long, too, and bound by bands.

Mykal sucked in a deep breath, and held it for a moment. He balanced his staff across his hands, as he had seen Blodwyn do, and slowly began rotating the staff around.

And dropped it.

"Don't laugh," Mykal warned.

Blodwyn held up hands. "Wasn't. I assure, I wasn't."

Mykal picked up the staff, along with snow. He shook the snow away, rested the staff in the crook of his arm, and quickly blew into cupped hands before trying again.

"Try closing your eyes," Blodwyn suggested, ever ready for coaching.

"I won't be able to see what I'm doing." Although he protested, Mykal closed his eyes. The staff made it around once, before he dropped it again. "I heard you laugh that time!"

"Got me," Blodwyn said. "This is something I want you practicing any time you have a free moment. I believe it will also bring you a sense of peace. There is a music created that runs through you. It is a very satisfying feeling, a calming one."

Mykal wasn't useless wielding a staff. He wanted to master everything Blodwyn taught him. The man had tremendous patience. He'd dedicated his life to standing by Mykal's side. "I'll practice. You have my word…"

"Shall we duel?" Blodwyn twirled his staff around in his hands, and spun it up and around in one hand and then around, and over the top of his head. It was made of cedar and iron, and nearly six feet long. When he brought it down, he teetered the staff across his back, and into the opposite hand. He stepped forward, and thrust the head of the staff out. He took a step to the side, and drove the other end behind him. As if paddling a canoe, he rotated the staff side-to-side, and around and around, alternating hands. His left, his right. His left, his right. He strode forward.

Mykal grinned, and came at his teacher—his friend—fast.

Long, thin black beard hair ran down to just above the center of Blodwyn's chest. His facial hair consisted of bushy and overgrown eyebrows; the arms of the mustache fell past the corners of his chin, and tied off at the ends with little bits of string; the chin hair was also long and thick, and braided. "The fancy footwork looks lovely."

"Thank you." Mykal repeated his motions, twirling and spinning the staff around. Back when he was nine or ten years of age, he had been tall, stocky. Over time, and now nineteen, his muscles grew from years of working on a farm.

Blodwyn drove his staff forward when the opening was obvious.

Mykal didn't have time to counter.

The head of Blodwyn's staff crashed into his gut, the air raced out of his lungs. "Oomph." Mykal pressed his hand over the spot where he'd been struck.

"Those fancy moves help you?" Blodwyn didn't hide his smirk.

Mykal lowered his hand, and grabbed the staff in a white-knuckle grip. "Oh, it's like that, is it?"

"It's like that." They circled each other with slow, deliberate steps.

The wind howled around them, as if a spectator cheering on the fight.

Blodwyn struck out with his staff. Mykal parried, blocking the blow. The staffs slammed together. Mykal stepped back, spun around, and followed up by bringing the back end of the staff forward.

Blodwyn chopped downward with his staff, knocking Mykal's out of his hands.

The snowfall was heavy. The wind whipped the flakes around in a near-blinding flurry. The tip of Mykal's nose and cheeks were numb. He could barely feel his hands on his staff. He needed a pair of gloves like the ones Blodwyn wore.

Mykal froze for a fraction of a second.

Blodwyn saw an opportunity, and seized it. He twirled the staff over his head, and drove the back end in a stabbing motion toward Mykal's head.

Mykal skirted, rotating his hips and shoulders so his skull wasn't punctured open. He dropped to the ground, and somersaulted away from the next attack, but also away from his staff.

Blodwyn fought relentlessly, and stepped toward Mykal while swinging around the head of his staff.

Mykal swayed back, and then dove forward. He expected to wrap and tackle Blodwyn.

Blodwyn may have been caught off guard, but maintained balance.

Mykal grabbed for Blodwyn's staff, left hand, right.

Blodwyn was faster, spinning his staff away, and out of reach. He stomped his foot forward, between Mykal's legs.

Behind his left leg.

Before Mykal could react, he found himself on his back, in the snow.

Blodwyn stood over him, and the head of the staff at the dip in his throat. "It's like that," he said.

Mykal winked.

Blodwyn levitated into the air. His feet kicked at nothing. His eyes opened nearly too wide, frantically searched for a foothold. "This is not funny!"

Mykal stood up, brushing off snow. As he set his teacher down, he held out his arm, and opened his hand. His staff flew from the ground and into his palm. "Looks like you brought a staff to a wizard fight."

Blodwyn grimaced. "It's important you master using the staff, just as it is important you continue your training in all forms of self-defense. There may come a time when you need more than your magic to save you, or to save someone else."

Mykal knew Blodwyn was right. When the sorcerer, Galatia, had been captured by the Mountain King, she'd been gagged. Her magic was stifled. She needed her words to speak her magic into existence. While he could wield power without words, there could come a time when his magic would be suppressed. "I'm sorry, Wyn. I am. But it's cold. Aren't you freezing out here?"

"When your life depends on it, will the cold stop you from defending yourself?"

"My life doesn't depend on it. Not now, at this moment." Mykal let his teeth chatter as a means of punctuation. "We practice every day. We practiced today, I was just hoping we could cut it a little short, is all. Go inside. Sit by the fire."

Blodwyn's jaw set. His eyes narrowed, brows furrowed. "There will be no sitting by the fire for you. If we end our lesson early, you will begin your studies with your mother."

Blodwyn may have thought he was threatening Mykal. He wasn't. The young man enjoyed reading through the ancient scrolls, manuscripts, and books. The art of magic contained in the pages inspired him. It was not that long ago he'd first learned that he was a wizard. Now, it seemed as if there were just the two of them left. Him, and his mother, Anna.

Although they'd battled magic in a war, and won, there was so much he didn't know about magic. Anna was the perfect teacher. For the last few weeks they'd been studying the magic rituals and customs of natives who had lived on the land long, long ago. They were a people who drew power from nature. Aside from the elements, they found usable magic in the soil, from herbs and roots, flowers, oils, and berries. Magic came to them from the trees, rocks, and rivers. It was fascinating, and Mykal couldn't wait to learn more. So Mykal said, "But sitting by a fire—"

Blodwyn held up a finger. "Ah, ah, ah. Hit the books, kid. Don't argue."

"Fine," Mykal said. He wondered if Blodwyn realized how easily the manipulation worked?

"Wait," Blodwyn said.

Mykal ground his teeth. It was the only way to keep them from clicking together. "What is that?"

In the distance, by the foothills of the Muye Mountains, was the lone shadow of a figure.

"It's not a what," Blodwyn said, squinting against the wind, and snow. "It's a who."

They stood side by side and waited. It seemed as if the person walking toward them stopped, and was now standing still. "Why have they stopped?"

Blodwyn shook his head. "They are walking into the wind. It must be slow going."

"Should we see what they want?"

"That's presumptuous."

"Presumptuous how?" Mykal asked.

"How do you know it is us they want to see?" Blodwyn folded his arms, his staff nestled in the crook.

Mykal looked around. "I think we're at the beginning of a storm."

"It very well might be. It doesn't show signs of letting up any time soon," he agreed.

"At least we can offer that person some shelter until it passes," Mykal said. "And I am not being presumptuous saying that. They may not want shelter, but offering it can't hurt."

Blodwyn nodded. "I don't disagree."

"You don't disagree?" Mykal laughed. "So should I?"

"Should you, what?"

"See if they need a place to get warm. If they crossed the mountains, could be they've been out in the cold for a while now."

"Why not wait until they get here?" Blodwyn asked.

Mykal thought the person walking toward them might avoid the ruins. Like Castle Deed in the Constantine Realm, there were rumors the Library was haunted. He'd witnessed the ghosts in Castle Deed, but so far, he'd not seen any sign of spirits in the library.

They stood silent for several moments. Mykal didn't think the person approaching made much progress. At least when they were training with their staffs, they were moving, keeping the blood going. Exerting energy kept him warm. Plus, he had the cloak. The problem was his face and hands were uncovered. The cold had teeth, and it bit like a rabid dog at any exposed skin.

When the person was closer, Mykal saw the labored steps. "He doesn't look so good."

"Agreed." Blodwyn started toward them, Mykal following behind him.

The person stopped walking, perhaps this time when they noticed Blodwyn and Mykal, and then collapsed into the snow.

Mykal ran ahead. He heard Blodwyn's repeated warnings during instruction replay inside his head. Be mindful of traps. Be aware of your surroundings. Just because something appears obvious, doesn't mean everything has been revealed. If you expect the unexpected, you'll never be caught off guard.

He slowed when he was several yards away from the person.

The person was wrapped in linens that were tattered, torn. They looked useless against the wind, and snow. If this person came from any distance, they could be near dead.

Mykal cautiously closed the distance, and knelt beside them. He set his staff down, and rolled the person onto his back.

Only it wasn't a *he*. It was a *she*.

Her skin was red, and raw, and her lips chapped. Mykal lowered his ear to her mouth. The wind made listening for her breathing too difficult. He placed a hand on her chest. It rose and fell. The rise and fall was quick, shallow. The young girl was not well. She needed someplace warm, and dry. He determined that if she stayed in the cold any longer her life was in jeopardy.

"Wyn! We have to get her inside. She's dying out here!"

Blodwyn was still about twenty yards back. Mykal thought he saw his teacher nod. That was all he needed. He reached for his staff and placed it on top of the woman. Mykal closed his eyes and pictured the library foyer.

The bold blue smoky plume appeared as if out of the snowy ground and encircled them. It swirled as fast as a small tornado around them, and spread upward until they were engulfed in the dense fog.

In the next instant, the two of them were transported. There was a brief moment of disassociation. His mind and body separated. It was jarring, but he was growing somewhat used to this method of travel. He kept his hands on the woman, though. He wasn't sure if someone without magic could be lost between the here's and there's. When his mother used this type of magic they always had held hands. Seemed safer, so he didn't alter the technique.

When the bold blue smoke evaporated, the two of them were safe, and warm; out of the storm, out of the cold, and inside the library.

CHAPTER 3

Two years ago, after the War, Blodwyn, Anna, and Mykal travelled east of the Isthmian Sea. On the north side of the Muye Mountains, and just east of the Constantine Realm, were the old Library Ruins. Most of the main level had been destroyed by time, neglect, and weather. It didn't detract from the overall architecture of the place. Cracked and crumbling steps led to marble pillars that stood like cylindrical guards posted outside the front entrance. Marble was clearly the motif, or theme, throughout. The floors were marble slabs that were only visible after many days of sweeping and washing when they first arrived.

The front foyer was large, with rooms on the left and right. It opened up to the large library with two levels, and a sublevel, as well. On the first floor there were bare, and mostly broken, or missing shelves lining rows of bookcases. The second level was a wrap-around. The staircase was in back. Above was a tall dome ceiling. What windows were still in place were stained glass. Where there were broken or missing windows, Blodwyn and Mykal boarded up over the openings, keeping the elements and wildlife out.

The average person would see the place for what it was. A ruin.

The magic was hidden.

It wasn't a glamour spell.

Around back was a hen house where they cared for chickens, and further back, a small barn where they kept several cows they'd acquired. When it wasn't winter, they planted and harvested a variety of fruits and vegetables.

When they first arrived, Anna showed them into a backroom, off the small kitchen with a stone oven, and past a contained open fire area, where she revealed a secret panel on the corner wall. She depressed it and a door in the flooring opened. A spiral staircase led into the bowels of the library. Below (there was more marble) rolled up scrolls, manuscripts, and books were filled the bookcases. In the lower levels, the ancient materials remained safe and preserved.

Inside the library, in the foyer floor, Mykal called out: "Mother! Mother!"

Mykal pressed his palms against the woman's face. The skin was blistered. She felt like ice. Her skin was both red, burnt from the sun and wind, and blue. He lowered his head and again listened by her mouth for signs of her breathing.

It was faint.

"Mother!" If she was downstairs, she'd never hear him.

He reached out with his mind. He called to her in his thoughts. That magic seemed limitless in the library, more powerful and easier to call upon. She could hear his mind's cry from miles away.

He peeled away the gray garment. Holding it up between fingers he inspected the sewn together rags, and shook his head. Although he didn't know where she'd come from, he knew the distance crossed was too far for mere rags. Winter in the foothills of the Muye were proving more extreme than in Grey Ashland on the southwest side of the Isthmian.

He needed to get her warm. Mykal stood up and removed his cloak. He placed it over her like a blanket, the hood over her feet.

The front doors swung opened.

Wind whipped into the library, bringing with it wisps of snow, and the freezing cold Mykal had just escaped from.

"Wyn, shut the door!"

"You said we had to get her inside," Blodwyn said, turning and using brute strength to force the doors closed against the wind. The hinges creaked. The vacuum created sucked them shut with a bang that echoed.

"We did."

Blodwyn walked over to them. "Wrong. *You* did. When you said we, I just assumed you'd wait for me to get to the two of you. Then we could have jumped from there to here together."

Mykal offered up a failed smile. "*Oops?* Look, I panicked. She's barely breathing."

Blodwyn took a knee by the woman's head. He looked at her, and then up at Mykal with his head tilted to the left.

"What?" Mykal said.

"Pretty young lady." Blodwyn pulled off a glove and touched the back of a hand to her cheek. "I'll start a fire."

"What's that supposed to mean?" Mykal said.

"It means I'll put logs of wood in the hearth and set them on fire."

"No. Not that. I knew what that meant. The comment about her being a pretty young lady. What was that supposed to mean?" Mykal said.

"You hadn't noticed?" There were two hearths. One to the right, and one on the level above, directly over the first.

They shared the same chimney. Blodwyn took logs from the stacks and set them on an iron grate inside the hearth.

Mykal's arm shot forward, blue lightning erupted from his fingers.

The logs burst into flames.

"Help me get her closer," Mykal said.

Blodwyn opened his mouth as if he were about to release a snide comment, but closed it just as quickly. The two of them lifted the woman and brought her in front of the fire. Mykal repositioned his cloak on her, ensuring she was snug. "Do you think she'll be okay?"

"I can't say for sure," Blodwyn said.

Anna said, "Can't say *what* for sure?"

Mykal stood up, and turned around. His mother was dressed in an emerald green dress, her hair in a bun, loose strands draped down in front of her face, and over her ears. They shared the same coppery brown hair color, and while she was tall, and thin, Mykal was built more like his late father. He pointed. "She was coming from the mountains, and collapsed in the snow."

CHAPTER 4

Outside the wind howled. It sounded like packs of wolves racing around the library. Mykal shivered, thankful they were all inside, and warm.

Anna prepared noodle soup in a chicken broth. It cooked in a cauldron over the fire. The woman was awake, wrapped tight in both a blanket and Mykal's cloak. She sat in a chair beside the hearth, and watched everyone closely, but had not yet said a word.

Blodwyn paced back and forth. It unnerved Mykal, but he remained quiet. He stood by one of the stained-glass windows. The reds and greens, yellows and blues made it near impossible to see outside. Mykal didn't need a full moon and clear glass to know the falling flakes accumulated.

When Mykal walked over to the cauldron, the woman eyed him up and down. He offered up a smile that she ignored as she looked away. Anna made it clear no one would ask questions until after the girl had a chance to eat. "Smells like it's about done," Mykal said.

Blodwyn arched an eyebrow, apparently equally anxious about talking with the woman.

The silence was nearly too much for Mykal, and he figured since the soup was about done, what harm could there be in getting the conversation started? He thought he'd concentrate on his tone. He kept his voice quiet, soft, full of empathy. "What were you doing out in the storm? Do you live close by?"

In the two years they'd been at the library, they'd not encountered many other people. Part of Mykal was hungry for the chance of talking with another person. He found both Blodwyn and his mother always focused on his training. While it was appreciated, he knew there had to be more to his new life than just studying, working out, and repetition. He was growing bored. Lonely.

"Mykal!" Anna appeared from the back of the library. She carried a tray with stacked bowls, cups, and spoons.

"Sorry, Mother." Mykal felt like a toddler. As if by reflex after having a hand slapped, he backed away from the hearth, head down, and sighing. It was hard explaining, but the year he spent on the journey across the old empire with his friends, risking his life, and exercising his powers had been some of the most exciting months ever. While the loss of lives, and the scarring from battles during the War were devastating, there was a part of Mykal that craved the action, and dare he think it, the danger. He wasn't sure if he should be troubled for feeling that way, so considered it safer keeping those thoughts to himself.

Anna ladled soup from the cauldron into a bowl. The steam rose into the air. The aroma of her soup filled the first floor of the library.

"You all live here?" the woman asked.

Mykal bit back a grin. It was what he had been waiting for. Answers. He did not want her frightened. She might clam up. Who knew how long they'd have to wait then? Like a few moments ago, he kept his tone of voice soft, calm, and inviting. "We do. Where do you live?"

"I'm looking for someone," she said. Aside from the oval of her face, and fingers sticking out from under the cloak just under her chin, the rest of her was blanketed as if she were a swaddled infant. Her hair was black, eyes green. The wind and sunburn left her cheeks red, but Mykal assumed her skin was quite pasty, and pale, otherwise.

"I was sent to find him."

"Him?" Blodwyn said, as if trying the word out for the first time, and wasn't sure if he pronounced it correctly, or not. "Who sent you?"

Anna handed the woman a bowl filled with soup. "It is very hot. Please be careful."

The woman let her arms snake out, and the cloak lowered, and sagged to just below her shoulders. She repositioned herself, and sat with her feet on the chair, and her knees up. The woman cradled the bowl between her thighs and her chest, lifted the spoon, and blew on it before taking a tentative taste. "This is very good. I'm so hungry. My food ran out a few days ago. Thank you for this."

"Eat, please. There's plenty." Anna tilted her head to the side, and clasped her hands together in front of her. She nodded, lips pursed into a thin smile. "And, you're welcome."

Apparently, beyond impatient with the pleasantries, Blodwyn blurted, "You said you were sent to find someone. Who is it you're looking for?"

The woman set the spoon back into the bowl she held with shaking hands. She tucked her lips into her mouth, and sucked away the salt from the broth. "I was given very specific instructions, and told to find the wizard. He is said to be the most powerful wizard in all of the lands. Although, no one knows what he looks like. It doesn't matter. I've not seen anyone since I started looking. It's probably because of the time of year. If there are people around, they're playing it smart and staying inside," she said, and smiled. "Although, I haven't even passed any villages, or huts, or anything."

Mykal cast a look at Blodwyn, it couldn't have been more obvious if he pointed at his own chest and asked, *Me?*

"And who sent you?" Blodwyn asked.

"Do you know the wizard's name?" Mykal said.

"How are you supposed to find him?"

"What made you come to the Library Ruins?"

"Enough." Anna's arms were stiff, at her sides. "You are throwing questions at her, like someone throwing rocks at a troll! Neither of you is giving her a chance to answer. One question at a time."

Blodwyn said, "Who sent you searching for a wizard?"

"Why, the queens, of course."

A stillness fell over them as Blodwyn, Mykal, and Anna exchanged a questioning look. The woman picked up on the exchange, and crawled back into herself.

Mykal heard *queens*, but figured the young woman was cold still, and a bit delusional.

"What is your name?" Anna used a soft, and gentle tone of voice.

Mykal feared they'd overdone it, and the woman would retreat into silence. He wasn't sure how the situation could be saved. If he didn't say something, who knew how much longer they'd have to wait for answers. He opened his mouth to speak, but before he said a word, she answered: "Geneva."

"Hello, Geneva. I'm Anna," she said.

"It's a pleasure to meet you." Geneva tried more soup. She slurped up a noodle between closed lips. The tail of the noodle whipped about. Hot broth splashed onto her nose, and chin. She wiped away the broth with the back of her hand. "Excuse me. I haven't eaten in a day or two."

"So you've said." Anna bowed. Mykal marveled at his mother's manners. Living on the Isthmian Islands with Voyagers all around, pirates really, he'd never have suspected someone so refined. Although he'd never tell his mother that. She'd most certainly feel insulted. His misconception about the pirates had been proved wrong... in general. "It could explain why you fainted out in the storm. How far *have* you traveled?"

"From Osiris. I live in a mountain village just outside the Cordillera Castle, with most of the queens' subjects," Geneva said.

"That's a long way to travel," Blodwyn said.

Mykal thought about the rags she'd worn. How could she have made it this far with such little protection from the elements? "And why are you looking for this... wizard?"

"I can only discuss the proposition with him," Geneva said. "Those were my instructions."

"And who is the queen of Osiris?" Blodwyn asked.

Mykal would never forget when the Mountain King ruled that realm. Hermon Cordillera had been evil. Although his sinister plan failed, plenty of innocent lives were taken leading up to and during the War. While they were removed from the rest of the old empire, it seemed like they should have *somehow* known a new ruler was already in place in Cordillera.

"Who is queen?" Blodwyn asked softer this time.

"We've two queens." She held up fingers.

"Two, *what?*" Mykal thought he might not have been hearing her correctly.

"Queens." Geneva placed one hand in the other. "I know it's an odd thing. It's been decided that, for now anyway, we'd keep things this way. There is still so much unrest, and tension since the War. The death of King Hermon wasn't the only devastating blow the young princesses received that year. Earlier, they'd lost their mother, as well. Her death was a frightening and odd thing. She asphyxiated, I hear, after a poisonous spider bite." She leaned closer, and whispered, "There was an infestation of the critters, actually. So, since there was no Queen Regent the sisters decided together they'd share the crown. I am sure the royal advisors are ensuring the realm remains intact, and more importantly, safe."

"Cordillera's daughters." Blodwyn's left eye squinted, pronouncing the web of wrinkles by his temple.

Mykal thought Geneva placed a bit too much emphasis on the word *safe*. He wasn't sure anyone else caught it. He couldn't imagine two children in charge of an entire kingdom. If they were anything like their father. . .he shuddered at the thought.

"Queen's Raaheel and Sarah. That's right." Geneva nodded her head as if she were answering a question asked.

"They're just children." Mykal remembered seeing the kids when inside the castle years ago. If he remembered correctly, one dragged around a teddy bear. They were ruling the realm now?

"They are both intelligent, but I've seen them outside having snowball fights, and playing hide-and-go-seek," she said, as if those were horrible crimes rather than just things children did.

"And they've sent you to find a wizard?" Blodwyn asked. "But you can't tell us what it is they want him for?"

She unclasped her hands, and rolled fingers into palms. Although she made fists, she didn't look angry, so much as conflicted. "No. I can only tell the wizard. Once I've found him, that is."

"And why have you come this way? What makes you think the wizard is around here?" Anna asked.

The only people who knew they were studying at the library the last few years were close friends, and family. Altogether, less than ten people. None would have revealed the location, even under the pretense of torture.

"The queens have sent scouts out in nearly all directions searching for him," Geneva said.

"How long are you supposed to spend looking? How far are you expected to travel?" Blodwyn waved a hand back and forth, palm up.

"We're *not* to return until we've found him." Her eyes lowered, and for a moment she seemed more interested in studying the floor. The significance of the statement was clear. If ten people went in ten different directions and none found the supposed wizard being sought, then they had, in effect, been exiled since they would continue walking until they reached the ends of the world. "It's bad. I will tell you that much. I've not given up hope, though. If I don't find him, I am confident one of the others will. I have to believe that. We need his help, desperately."

The queens needed help. He questioned the sincerity of the queens. Perhaps they were genuine in wanting help, but having wasn't convinced of anything yet.

Right now, it was Geneva who mattered most. She deserved a chance to return home.

Blodwyn must have sensed what was coming. His eyes opened a little wider, and he held up a stopping hand that Mykal ignored.

Mykal's eye locked with Anna's, and didn't look away when he said: "I believe I'm the wizard you're searching for."

Geneva smirked. "I promise I will only stay this night. I do not want to be an inconvenience, and in the morning, I'll be on my way. I will share with my queens your generous hospitality."

Mykal cocked a hip, as he shifted his weight from one leg to the other. "I am not sure if you heard me. *I* am the wizard you are looking for."

"I mean no disrespect, but he," Geneva pointed at Blodwyn, "looks more like a wizard than you. We're about the same age if I had to guess. You're just a boy."

She might have prefaced her remark with *no disrespect*, but the disrespect was felt like a paper cut. "Wizard's aren't born old."

"Hey!" Blodwyn warned. "Watch it now."

"No offense." Mykal waved a dismissive hand. "You know what I mean."

"If you're a wizard," a hint of smile curled the corners of her lips, "then prove it."

The left side of Mykal's mouth rose in an uncontainable half-smile. He thrust his hands at the hearth. The fire on the logs grew, flames rose toward the flue. A puff of black smoke rolled out into the library. Happily, Mykal folded his arms, and winked. "What about that?"

Geneva was smiling, too. She looked at Blodwyn, and then at Anna, but shook her head. "What about what? Did I miss it?"

Mykal dropped his arms. "The fire. It was kind of going out. I..." He wiggled his fingers at the logs on the hearth. "...and voila!"

"You... what?" She said.

Blodwyn chuckled, a fist in front of his mouth was unsuccessful in masking the amusement.

Mykal let out an exasperated gasp, and stiffened his arms as he held them so his body was like a T. His hands were balled into fists. He tilted his head back, and with closed eyes *stared* up at the domed ceiling.

Blue energy encircled his fists, lightning spheres that crackled and hummed. His body levitated off the ground, and he lifted into the air several feet. A small wind spun around the library. Autumn leaves, and dust fluttered about. Geneva's hair blew backward, away from her face. The noise level grew. It sounded like the storm outside had entered the building.

"Enough!" Blodwyn shouted. "Levitation, really?"

"Served no purpose, but you have to admit, it looks impressive." Mykal held his position for just a moment longer before lowering himself. The wind calmed. The constant blue spheres engulfing his hands, became a mix of strands like speeding snakes, a single band, and then nothing. He looked at a wide-eyed Geneva. "Well?"

"*You're* the wizard. You *are* the wizard!"

CHAPTER 5

Mykal, Blodwyn, and Anna sat beside the fireplace; Geneva, the center of their attention, sat with her legs extended outward and used the cloak over them like a blanket. Her feet crossed at the ankles, and toes wiggled as if waving at the flames dancing inside the hearth. She kept folded hands in her lap, except for every few minutes when she re-tucked her hair behind her ears.

"I'm not exactly positive when it started happening," Geneva said.

"What started happening?" Mykal said.

Anna touched his arm. "Give her a chance," she said.

Geneva cleared her throat. "People have been going missing."

Mykal almost asked another question, but with effort, stopped himself.

"At first I didn't know any of the people who had disappeared. There are so many scattered little villages in the mountain side, and down in the valley, but because of the inclement weather and dangerous conditions of living on the side of a mountain, well, you just don't get as much opportunity to meet everyone." She arched her eyebrows as she looked from one, to the other, and to the other. Mykal thought she was looking for agreement, so he nodded his head as if he understood.

"Anyway," she continued, "just before I started my search, my Aunt Deidre disappeared. The queens called all of us into court. They addressed us on the seriousness of the matter, sharing all the information they had on the abductions. There were no leads." Geneva took a moment. She pursed her lips, and her fingers twirled together in her lap. "It was almost as if the people ran off during the night. Some people whispered that that was probably what had happened. I'd have agreed, at one point. Until my aunt. She had children. A widow, she'd never have left her kids alone. Never."

"How many people have gone missing total?" Blodwyn asked.

"Fifteen," she answered.

Mykal shook his head, eyes narrowed. "Fifteen?"

"That's right," she said.

"Have any of them been found?" Anna said.

"None," Geneva said. "The queens asked for volunteers. They are seeking the help of a special wizard." She looked at Mykal. "They want your help."

"My help? I don't know anything about finding missing people."

Geneva shook her head from side to side, in a slow, deliberate fashion. "I just saw what you could do. I understand now why they sent all of us looking for you. If anyone can get to the bottom of this, it's someone with your talent."

Mykal regarded Geneva. The people of Osiris were without a king. The oldest queen couldn't be more than thirteen years old. The Cordillera subjects must be in a panic. It was a peculiar situation to say the least. His curiosity grew the more he listened.

Memories of sneaking into the castle in an attempt to save a friend taken prisoner were still fresh in his mind. The pain of having found her tortured corpse in the dungeon couldn't be ignored. The fault was King Hermon Cordillera's, not the queens. Not the peoples.

"Will you do it?" Geneva said. "Will you come back to the castle with me?"

***

Once Geneva fell asleep, curled into a ball on her chair, the others retreated to the lower levels of the library.

Torches were lit as needed. The fear of fire destroying the massive collection of books, manuscripts, and scrolls made taking every precaution necessary. Tapestries lined the halls. Mykal struggled recognizing the difference between a fancy carpet and something worth hanging on a wall, but supposed gold fringes and bulbous corner tassels were sure indicators.

The round table fit eight, but Mykal, Blodwyn and Anna sat clustered close together.

"They must be desperate in Osiris," Blodwyn said.

"Why is that?" Mykal asked.

"For a king or queen to request help from an outside source is something of a double-edged sword. It has to be handled just perfectly. It is partly why magic was outlawed across Rye's empire," he said.

"I thought it had to do with the deaths of King Grandeer's family." Mykal recalled the sorceress, Galatia. She had told them of a time more than two hundred years ago. The king's infant son and wife were ill. No curer could make them well. Desperate, the king called on wizards for help. Responding to the royal call for magic, she'd been hopeful, arriving with nothing but her best intentions. They died, and she was blamed. Her inability to heal the queen and prince caused an uprising against magic. Emperor Henry Rye supported Grandeer's quest to rid the lands of all magic, and backed the king's request for an elite team known as the Watch, to carry out the duties of judge, jury, and executioner.

"It did, in part. You see, Kings, Queens, Lords, and Barons are different from you and me. They are born into a power we'll never experience. You and your mother have so much magic inside of you, but royal blood carries an unparalleled weight of respect, and fear." Blodwyn folded his arms on the dark mahogany. His fingers rhythmically tapped the wood. "There was a time, when Grandeer was young and his father, and his grandfather, called on wizards more regularly than advisors."

"And that was a problem?"

"It became a problem. Every day the king holds court. The subjects wait in line for their chance to plead a case and receive his counsel. They come to the king with land disputes, tales of robbery, arguments over stolen livestock or poisoned livestock, they divulge marriage problems and why divorce should be granted... all of these issues can only be decided on by a king. They are his laws, and subject to his, only his, interpretation. Can you see where I'm going with this?" Blodwyn asked.

Mykal felt foolish, but shook his head regardless.

"When, once in a while, a king called on a wizard for advice it undermined his authority in front of his people. A king would do so when necessary, only when no other options were available. Soon kings noticed subjects bypassing their instructions and going directly to wizards for answers," Blodwyn said, and smiled.

"The kings didn't like that, I take it."

"Wrong." Blodwyn slapped a palm on the table. "They detested it! Royalty cannot help but believe they are better than all other people. They are up here. Everyone else is below them. They love talking just to hear the sound of their own voices. A bloodline should never determine who rules the land. Just because one man is fit to be king does not mean that his son is, or grandson, or great-grandson. I digress. I digress. The point is, once people turned more and more to wizards for help, and the more the wizards actually did to help the people, the angrier kings became. That is why Emperor Rye was not hesitant about decreeing the death of magicians of any kind."

"So what am I supposed to do?" Mykal asked.

"What do you want to do?" Anna said.

"There is an exposure issue," Blodwyn said. "That can't be overlooked. If you return to the Cordillera Castle, word will spread. It won't be long before everyone in the old empire is aware a wizard is once again helping royalty."

Mykal thought about King Nabal. The three of them had left Grey Ashland, left his grandfather and Uncle Quill behind because Nabal threatened imprisonment if he stayed. Although he thanked them for their help during the War, the king still didn't want them anywhere on his land after the fact.

The Osiris Realm was on the east side of the Isthmian Sea, Grey Ashland the west. The castle Geneva was from was south of the Library Ruins, where mountains ranges separated the lands.

"Mykal?" Anna said.

He hadn't realized he'd been quiet for so long. The last thing he wanted to do was respond too fast. The fact he'd grown bored of his life at the library, day in and day out, with just studying and training shouldn't factor into his decision. He couldn't figure out a way of excluding those facts, though. "What good is my magic if I can't help people?"

Anna set her hand over her son's hand. "That's the right answer."

"We don't know what we're getting ourselves into," Blodwyn said. It didn't sound as if he was against the idea of lending a hand to the queens of Cordillera, but neither did he sound hopeful and optimistic.

"Isn't that what we've been working on here? Getting me ready for serving people in need?"

"It is," Blodwyn said.

"Don't you think I'm ready?" Mykal asked.

There was a pregnant pause.

"I do," Anna said.

"As do I," Blodwyn said. "But you're not going alone. I'm going with you."

"I am, also," Anna said.

Mykal smiled. Perhaps the monotony of daily routine wore them equally as thin, and rubbed them just as raw when it came down to emotions. The thought calmed his own insecurities for having craved a little action. "I expected as much."

CHAPTER 6

The next morning, Mykal was up early. After packing a few extra pairs of trousers and tunics, he dressed in a black pair of pants, his cleanest, whitest tunic, and a black vest. Next, he retrieved his sword, and secured it over his shoulder and onto his back. From his growing collection, he filled small vials with herbs, oils, roots, and samples from the different elements he had collected. He placed them in a small brown leather sack, and affixed the drawstrings onto his belt. He was far from experienced as an alchemist, despite numerous lessons with his mother. She'd explained each time that the ingredients combined complimented nature. Each added piece contained a specific root that went to the heart of targeted magic. Overall it was a confusing concept. Little by little he was catching on. Eventually, he'd wrap his mind around the idea of its energy. It was one more discipline, another tool for him to master.

It was better having more, and a variety, of vials than he needed with him, rather than coming up shorthanded. He set his dark green cloak on top of his staff by the front door, next to Blodwyn's things.

He smelled breakfast, and realized his mother must have woken up early, as well. When he rounded the corner into the kitchen, he stopped. Geneva was removing a fresh loaf of bread from a stone oven.

"That smells wonderful."

Geneva's cheeks reddened, and she lowered her eyes. "Thank you. I thought we could wrap it for our trip back to

Osiris. The storm's let up. We must have gotten nearly a foot of fresh snow overnight."

"Bread fresh out of the oven should be eaten while it's still warm." In a cast iron skillet, scrambled eggs cooked over an open flame. She worked a wooden spoon around and around, keeping the eggs from sticking. "And fresh bread with eggs is my favorite breakfast."

"As happy as I am to have found you, I am not looking forward to the walk home," she said.

"I wouldn't worry too much about that." Mykal reached into the skillet and pinched out some eggs he then dropped into his mouth. "We'll be back in Osiris before you know it."

"Something smells good." Blodwyn walked into the kitchen, dressed similarly to Mykal. However, his beard looked freshly trimmed, and tied off. His hair was brushed back, and again, pulled into a tail. "Based on this meal, I believe you must be doing well this morning, Geneva?"

"Very well, thank you."

"Mykal and I will prepare the table," he said. "Is your mother awake yet?"

Mykal frowned. "She doesn't seem to be. I'm sure whatever she's doing she smells the bread. I'll run and get her. It's the only way she'll get a quarter of the food." He clapped a hand on his stomach. "Otherwise, I can't be held responsible for how much I eat."

There were no official bedchambers. The library was not built with the intention of people living inside. With little effort or ingenuity, they had converted smaller rooms off the first floor that once were used as study areas. Mykal built sturdy frames for beds and stuffed mattresses. In place of doors, they hung heavy tapestries found rolled and stacked in a corner on the lower level.

Mykal used the back of a hand to part the tapestry separating his mother's room, and poked his head inside. "Hello? Time to wake up. Geneva has done us the honor of making breakfast."

"I'm awake," she said, her voice hoarse.

Mykal walked in, the tapestry fell closed behind him. The stained-glass window faced west. Very little light found way into the room. Anna was on her side, curled up, and tightly tucked under a blanket. "Are you alright?"

"Just a little tired. I didn't sleep well." She coughed. "Give me a few minutes. I'll be right out."

Mykal knelt next to the bed. Her face looked pale, sweaty. He touched the back of his hand against her forehead. "You have a fever."

"I was fine last night."

"That was then," he said. "Stay here. Don't get out of bed. I'll bring you breakfast."

"I don't think I can eat."

Mykal didn't like the way she looked at him. Her eyes were open, but seemed vacant. It was almost as if she wasn't focusing on him, or on anything at all. "You should try."

"Maybe some tea. I wouldn't mind a cup of tea." She raised the blanket over her mouth, and coughed again. "My throat hurts a bit. Tea will soothe it, I'm sure."

"You rest. I will be right back with some tea."

She lowered the blanket, and sat up.

"What are you doing?" he asked, reached out, and set her pillow between the wall and his mother's back.

"We've travelling to do. I can't spend the day in bed." Her smile quivered at the corner of her lips. Sweat soaked hair stuck against the side of her face. Her lips were chapped.

"You really don't look well," he said. "We're going to postpone the trip."

She waved a dismissive hand. "Don't be silly. I'll be fine."

"Let me get you some tea. Lie back down. We'll discuss this when I get back."

"Who is the parent?" she said, a weak smile followed.

It was something of an odd statement. Their reunion was recent. Mykal was mostly raised by his paternal grandfather, and Blodwyn. Anna had been sent into hiding when she was young. King Nabal's Watch were searching for wizards, and at the time, Mykal had not demonstrated any magical tendencies. Blodwyn called in a favor, and Anna had lived in secret with Voyagers on the Isthmian Islands. "I'll be right back."

Mykal returned to the kitchen.

"What's wrong? You don't look well?" With a used napkin crumpled up on the table, Blodwyn sat leaning back, looking full, and satisfied. The plate in front of him contained a dusting of crumbs from scrambled eggs and bread.

"You ate already?"

"Would have went cold if I waited," Blodwyn said.

"I was gone two, maybe three minutes." Mykal raised his eyebrows in disbelief.

"Exactly. No one likes cold eggs."

"I have more. They're just about ready," Geneva said.

"Where is Anna?" Blodwyn asked.

"She doesn't look well," he said. "I'm going to bring her some tea. I think we need to postpone Osiris for now. She thinks she's still coming. The way she looks, she'll be lucky if she can get out of bed. When she's feeling better we can visit the queens."

"There's water in the kettle, but it's not yet boiled."

Blodwyn sat forward, elbows on the table now. "Does she have a fever?"

"And cold sweats. She said she hadn't slept well. It's more than that, though she is not likely to admit it." A whistle exhaled with a high-pitched scream. Mykal lifted the kettle off of the flame, and poured a cup of hot water. "Let me take this to my mother."

Geneva said, "Does that mean we're not leaving for the castle today?"

"I haven't decided," Mykal said, but thought she looked relieved. He was certain she dreaded going back into the cold. She'd be surprised when she learned how they'd actually travel the distance.

"We can discuss the plans while you eat," Blodwyn said.

"Your eggs will be ready when you get back," Geneva said.

Mykal wasn't sure how he felt having Geneva cooking. She was near dead last night. True, there was no sign of even fatigue this morning, but he didn't think she should be waiting on them. It was a wonderful gesture, and he did appreciate the sentiment. "Why don't you eat those eggs. I will prepare mine after I've tended to my mother. No sense having them get cold."

Blodwyn nodded, as if Mykal had just illustrated the point he'd tried making earlier.

"I couldn't," she said.

Keeping an exuberant eye on Blodwyn, he said, "You can. And you shall. Please, eat. I may be longer than three minutes this time."

***

"Why are you out of bed?"

Anna stood by the window in a floor length, white nightgown. Her hair was pulled back in a ponytail. "I told you I just needed a moment to catch my breath. I'll be fine. You're worrying over nothing."

"I'm not worried," Mykal said, lying. She may not have raised him, but he didn't think the fib fooled her. "I brought you the tea."

She turned, and took the cup cradled in both hands. "Nice and hot. Thank you. Smells wonderful."

Aside from chapped lips and pale-grey skin, her nostrils were red. Her normally vibrant brown eyes looked more like mud. "I do believe you've got yourself a nasty cold, maybe the flu."

"A cold? The flu? Not a chance," she said.

"What?" Mykal said. "You looked like you were just about to say something more."

"Did I?" Anna shook her head, and turned away from him. "Well, I wasn't."

"I want you back in bed," he said. "We're postponing the trip."

"You can't do that."

"You're in no condition for this. I don't want to appear crass, but you look sick. The tea might soothe your throat, but I think a few days in bed is what will make the difference."

Anna offered up a thin smile. "You really are a wonderful son. However, it was once the job of wizards to offer guidance and advice to people when there was no one else they could turn to. I can't remember the last time anyone sought us out for help. The fact that two queens sharing a throne are calling for our assistance is monumental. It could be the turning point we've been waiting for all of these centuries."

"Turning point?"

"A new day when wizards aren't outlaws, and hunted, and executed for no reason other than man's fear of the unknown," she said. Her passion over-powered her illness. The words spoken brought a hint of a sparkle into her eyes. "Your mission to Osiris is the first open invitation bridging the gaps between us and them. Postponing the trip is the last thing we want to do. Can you understand that?"

"I do understand that," Mykal said. "I just don't want you making the—"

Anna held up a hand. "I will stay here. I can see how apprehensive you are. While I assure you I've nothing more than an allergy of some sort, I do have some things to take care of here." She might have tried sounding enthusiastic about missing the trip, but Mykal noticed her disappointment.

"You do? Like what?"

"My business," she said, smiling. "I am quite sure the two of you can handle the queens' request. And you'll represent the wizard community in an honorable fashion. I'm telling you, Mykal, this could very well lead to something wonderful. Mages will no longer live in fear, or stay out of Rye's old empire. You'd most certainly be remembered for that."

"I'm not looking to be remembered," he said. "However, I would love returning home to the farm in Grey Ashland one day."

"It's settled then?"

Mykal said, "You promise you'll stay in bed, and get well? Whatever it is you think you need to do around here can wait until we come home. Deal?"

She handed him her cup. It took a little effort, some moaning, and groaning, but Anna managed climbing back into bed and under the covers. She sat with her back against the wall, and her knees up. "My tea. Thank you. Okay. We have a deal."

Mykal went back into the kitchen. Geneva was sitting at the table eating. Blodwyn's cloak was over a chair, and he wore a sun-yellow apron while he scrambled eggs in the iron skillet.

"Have a seat," Blodwyn said. "These should be ready in a second."

Mykal sat across from Geneva at the table. "Slight change of plans. We're still going to Osiris today."

"She's well?" Blodwyn said.

"She's not. She looks terribly ill, but she didn't want the trip postponed, and I convinced her to stay." Mykal moved back as Blodwyn slid eggs onto his plate. "These look excellent. Thank you."

"Not as tasty as Geneva's, I assure you, but they should fill your belly the same."

"So modest and humble." Mykal forked eggs into his mouth, but didn't chew. "And honest."

Blodwyn gave him a slap on the back of the head.

"It's good, it is. Just teasing," Mykal said, laughing, and chewing. "Is something wrong, Geneva?"

She shook her head. The lie wouldn't fool a child. Mykal cast a curious glance at Blodwyn.

"Aren't you anxious to return home?" Blodwyn asked.

"Your nieces, and nephews—don't they need you?" Mykal wiped his mouth with the cloth napkin.

Geneva lowered first her eyes, and then her head. "I suppose."

Mykal said, "Why don't you want to return?"

"I do want to go home. It's out there that has me worried." An involuntary shudder wracked her shoulders. She hugged her arms around herself. "It's just so terribly cold out there. My whole life I've lived on that mountain. You'd think by now I'd be used to it, would have grown accustomed to long winters. I'm afraid I won't survive another night out in that weather. It took me over a month to get this far. It's so cold, and we can only carry so much food," she said.

"If that's your concern," Mykal said, smiling, "I don't think you have anything to worry about. I can pretty much guarantee we will be back at the Cordillera Castle before you know it."

CHAPTER 7

"Are we ready to go?" Mykal stood in the center of the main floor inside the library. He eyed the back hall. Although he was not comfortable leaving his mother while she was ill, he knew what they planned on doing for the queens was also important.

Geneva walked past Mykal and Blodwyn. She headed toward the front entrance.

"Geneva," Mykal said. She stopped, and looked back. He waved her over. "I think you're going to like this."

She cast one last look at the doors, and sighed as she walked toward them.

Mykal enjoyed holding back the surprise, and letting her curiosity grow. It built suspense. "Take my hand," he said.

Blodwyn reached for one.

Geneva eyed each of them, an eyebrow cocked. There was not a hint of trust visible in that narrowed expression.

"Trust me," he said.

"Trust him," Blodwyn agreed.

She held onto Mykal's hand, and then saw Blodwyn held out his, as well. The three of them formed a circle.

"Ready?" Mykal said, a half smile crept up on his face.

"For what?" Geneva wrinkled her brow.

Without another word, Mykal concentrated on the Cordillera Castle. He saw the structure in his mind's eye. Although he'd only been there once before, there was no forgetting the foreboding sense that consumed his senses. The castle was built into the mountain. There wasn't room for it to spread out over the land, so instead it sprawled out skyward, reaching up to some of the tallest mountain peaks. The foundation sat on a plateau, and backed up and seemed a part of the rise of a separate peak. From a distance the castle blended in perfectly with the rocky terrain. If you didn't know the castle was there, you might never spot it amidst the rocks and low clouds. It was more like something of a nightmarish mirage until the realization of its actual existence confronted visitors.

And then the smoke started. It silently came from the floor, and swirled around them. Geneva's eyes opened wide. She stepped back, almost out of the smoke before Blodwyn and Mykal reeled her back in. Her mouth was shaped like an "O" in surprise, but before she could scream, the three of them were consumed, their feet lifted off of the floor, and they were gone.

When they reappeared, in front of castle gates, the smoke they travelled in was whipped away by harsh northern winds. While the Library Ruins sat on level ground in low lands, the castle was set halfway into the sky. The thin air, and cold temperature was far worse, far more intense, and despite his special cloak, Mykal realized Geneva's initial fears about having to walk the distance were authentic. The curtain wall was a mix of masonry work, and natural mountain protection. Scaling either during an attack made little sense. Mykal knew of a way into the castle from inside the bowels of the mountain, and with magic, but other than those two ways he was pretty confident Cordillera was nearly impenetrable.

There wasn't much flat rock to stand on. Behind them was something of a wide path that cut through the jagged rock. Mykal surmised it led down the Rames toward the Fjord Range, and the Isthmian. From where they stood, with the storm continuing the maelstrom, Mykal couldn't see much beyond a few yards. Fresh falling snow twisted around them. The wind moaned as if a violently ill giant suffered severe abdominal pain after eating one too many villagers during a siege.

Geneva let go of Mykal's and Blodwyn's hands as if they'd caught on fire and burned her skin. She shuffled backwards and looked left, and right, and at them, and then left and right, again. "Wh—what just happened?"

"Why didn't you take us inside?" Blodwyn said. It sounded like he was yelling. He may have been, since it was the only way he could be heard out in the wind.

"How did we get here? Are we back at the castle? Is this the castle?"

Mykal shrugged. "I didn't want to be intrusive. Imagine how that would be perceived if the three of us just popped ourselves inside the front foyer?"

"Can someone answer me? I have no idea what just happened. Was that magic? Did you do that?" Geneva stared at Mykal with an odd expression on her face. Mykal thought it was an unpleasant mix between fear and awe, with a hint more fear. "Of course you did. You really have magic. Your powers are unlimited!"

Mykal felt his chest swell some as he said, "Unlimited? I don't know about that. Are you alright?"

She padded her palms up and down her chest and stomach. "I'm fine. I'm okay. I'm in one piece."

"That's good. Being in one piece is important."

Now she smiled, relieved. Her cheeks were red. It could have been the wind and cold, but Mykal suspected the woman was blushing. She waved her hands up and down. Her smile stretched. It almost looked painful for her cheeks. "That was incredible," Geneva said, and then looked off toward the mountains, toward where the Library Ruins would be. "We just... poof!" Her hands shot into the air, fingers spread wide. "We were there, and now we're here!"

"And, if you don't mind me saying," Blodwyn said, "now we need to get inside because Mykal thought it more polite to deliver us outside of the castle during a storm."

"You don't seem happy with me," Mykal said, snickering.

"I'm cold, Mykal. Cold."

They stood in front of a gatehouse, erected from stone. Two imposing, wide, and tall towers separated the wrought iron gates. Enemies storming the gatehouse would find themselves vulnerable and exposed passing between the towers.

Geneva nodded her head vigorously. She went up to the iron gates and stuck an arm through the bars, and waved it up and down. "There should be guards on duty."

Mykal doubted the claim, but joined Geneva and waved an arm through the bars.

There was a metallic clank. Geneva backed away from the gates, pulling Mykal along with her.

She stood center, Mykal on the right, Blodwyn on her left, as the gates raised. The sound of straining chains, and grinding gears competed with the sound of the wind.

Three sentries exited a guardhouse holding halberds; the staff end was black iron, and the embellished axes on top, with a seven-inch-long spear tips, were highly polished steel.

"The queens are expecting us," Geneva said. She pressed her face between the bars. She might have thought she whispered, but with the raging wind, her voice carried. "He's the wizard!"

The gates opened, the bottoms smoothed over fresh fallen snow. Geneva led them through.

Once past the gates Mykal stopped and strained the muscles in his neck. "I can't see the top of the castle. Know what I wonder? How'd they build something like this? How did they get all of the materials up here?"

Blodwyn, who stood next to Mykal, shook his head. "If I had to guess, magic."

"Do you really think so?"

Blodwyn clapped him on the shoulder. "No. I do not."

Mykal, turned. A sentry stood directly behind him. Mykal hurried after Blodwyn. "Why don't you think so?"

"Because if I had to guess, the construction was completed by the hard work of slaves," Blodwyn said.

"He's right," Geneva said. She walked fast, clearly anxious for the promised warmth that only being inside the castle offered. "The castle was built more than seven hundred centuries ago. I forget who was emperor then. Slavery was very popular."

"I don't recall ever hearing anything about slavery in Grey Ashland," Mykal said.

"Doesn't mean it didn't exist," Blodwyn said. "It's a stain on royal history. They have no qualms ruling as tyrants, starting wars, and such. The slavery thing, no one wants to admit to it. Better to pretend it never happened. Move forward."

"Isn't erasing history dangerous?" Mykal asked.

"It can be. When lessons learned are forgotten they're likely to be repeated," Blodwyn said.

Mykal couldn't take his eyes off the beautiful monstrosity, though. The dark grey bricks nearly matched the mountains around it. The windblown snow made seams between them near invisible. The hint of lit torches burning by windows in the upper levels of the castle reminded Mykal of something.

Dragon eyes.

He remembered the dragon he'd called on for help during the War two years ago.

It was not something he would ever forget.

His skin tingled. It wasn't from the cold. There was something watching them. It was close. Too close, maybe. He scanned the area as best he could. Visibility was limited. He closed his eyes for just a moment, hoping a noise would give the stalker away. The winds howling tainted that plan.

"Mykal," Blodwyn snapped.

"Coming." Mykal quickened his step, his staff poking holes in the snow in front of him, while his boots crunched down, packing the snow tight under his weight. Before they started up‑ stairs that were cut into the mountain, he glanced around one last time. "Right behind you."

He walked, but contacted his mother telepathically. It was something he learned they could do during the war. Their minds were linked, and allowed them the affordability of communication. *Mother, we're here.*

There was a moment of nothing. He strained to hear her response, as if eyes inside his head searched his mind for her presence.

Wonderful! You two be safe. I expect you home and back to your studies as soon as possible.

I don't want to be here any longer than need be, he replied. *How are you feeling?*

I'll live. Don't worry about me.

You rest. I'll be home in no time at all. We'll get you feeling better.

She responded, *Do what needs to get done. I'll be fine.*

Mykal was still several steps behind Blodwyn, and looking around. There was no denying the sensation; they were being watched.

CHAPTER 8

Once inside the castle, Mykal remembered the last time he'd run through the halls. It had been part of a living nightmare. Galatia, close to death, was bound in the dungeon surrounded by the corpses of wizards the Mountain King had murdered. A grandfather he'd never met, his mother's father, was among the strewn-about corpses. A shiver raced up his spine, the muscles in his back spasmed as his shoulders tensed.

"You alright?" Blodwyn whispered. He'd stopped walking, letting Geneva and the sentry at the lead get several feet ahead of them.

"Just memories."

"They're hard to shake. You'll be okay."

Mykal wasn't sure if Blodwyn was asking, or telling him that he'd be okay. He nodded, agreeing, regardless.

The walls were decorated with exotic and exquisite tapestries. It was much different seeing the quality of the work during the day, when natural light streamed through rows of tall, narrow windows. They had looked far more depressing and sinister, when they'd been sneaking through the halls late at night.

Polished wood tables held gold busts. The heads were of men Mykal did not recognize. The ceilings were not nearly as vaulted as inside the keep at King Nabal's castle. He figured it had something to do with Cordillera's structure rising high into the air, with floor on top of floor, on top of floor, as opposed to having the fortification spread out over acres of land.

The main hearth contained a blazing fire. The heat provided was appreciated after even just a few minutes outside. The orange and red flames danced, while the logs inside snapped and crackled. Above the fireplace mantle, two longswords hung mounted crisscrossed.

A tall, thin man in a plush red velvet robe, with patterned gold trim, ambled toward them. His hands were clasped together in front of him. His black hair was cut short, cropped close to his scalp, and his face was shaved clean with the exception of a mustache that ran like a drawn line over the very top of his upper lip, and up to reach under each nostril. Following behind him were two identically dressed women. Their gowns were brown, like deerskin, their feet bare, and their faces covered by veils. Their black hair looked as shiny, as if wet. A single white jewel was affixed on the center of their foreheads. They had dark skin that looked tanned from days spent working in the sun. Long, thick eyelashes framed large, brown eyes.

The man walked past the sentry, and stopped in front of Geneva. While he addressed her, his eyes were clearly taking in Blodwyn and Mykal. "And who have we here?"

Geneva bowed, and introduced herself. The man seemed more annoyed with her recitation, rather than pleased with a response to his question.

"And these oddly-dressed gentlemen?"

Mykal cleared his throat. "We found Geneva unconscious in the storm."

"You're returning her home. That's kind. We thank you." His dismissive manner was off-putting.

"He is a wizard," Geneva interjected.

The man pressed his lips so tightly together that they nearly vanished, and only the hair on his lip was apparent. It was ridiculous, but Mykal refrained from laughing, barely.

"A wizard." He turned his attention toward Blodwyn. "And you? Do you also claim to be a wizard?"

Peripherally, Mykal caught the hint of a smile cross Blodwyn's lips. It wasn't a happy smile, but a dangerous one. The disrespect being shown to them made wanting to help far less appealing. "We were told you needed our help," Mykal said, stepping forward. He wasn't letting the man in front of them bedevil Blodwyn, despite knowing full and well Blodwyn was far more than capable of handling himself in the situation. "And who might *you* be?"

"I'm Gembert, chamberlain to the queens." He tipped his head back, slightly, cocked his head a little to the side. Perhaps not used to being equally disrespected, he seemed unaware how best to proceed from this point forward. "Ma'am, thank you for returning with a wizard. You will be rewarded for your service."

"I'm not looking for reward. Just justice for my family," Geneva said.

"Very well, then. You are excused," Gembert said. With his back now to Geneva he said to Mykal, and Blodwyn: "Leave your things. They will be tended to. And walk with me."

Mykal and Blodwyn set down their small bags packed with some extra clothing. Gembert eyed the bags as if giant roaches had crawled over the burlap.

With that, he turned away. The women that had followed behind him waited for the others to fall in, before following behind them all. Mykal looked back. Geneva stood where she was, looking lost, and a bit afraid. He saw the sentries, completely ignored through the exchange, make their way out into the blustery weather. The wind and snow flashed into the foyer, until the door eventually closed keeping the elements where they belonged.

"Where are we going?" Mykal asked.

Gembert said, "The Long Room. The queens have been in there all morning with Axel, the thane. You'll have to excuse my wary approach. As you may have been informed, everyone is a little on edge lately," the chamberlain said.

Mykal wasn't exactly ready to excuse any behavior just yet, whether the man demanded such, or not. "Several people have gone missing. Geneva explained the unusual circumstances. It's why we've agreed to lend our assistance."

"Who? Ah, yes. Geneva. Let me first extend you a more *gracious* welcome. Your assistance is greatly appreciated. Don't get me wrong. We've had another person go missing during the night. We're not certain the disappearance is directly tied in with the others. However, with how things have been going, it is more than likely related. And since the two of you are strangers," he said, and let the end of his unfinished sentence remain unfinished.

The insinuation was not lost on Mykal. "I can understand your suspicion."

"Who went missing?" Geneva said. Her voice was timid, weak. Mykal barely heard her.

"Baron Richmond, and Baroness Henriette were visiting with the queens. They came around the same time last year, and the year before that, after the untimely death of King Hermon," Gembert said.

Mykal wasn't sure if Gembert recognized him, or if the man was aware of his role in the death of the Mountain King, but thought he detected a hint of sarcasm in the tone of voice.

"Their daughter, Clairece, was visiting the dovecote. That, anyway, was the last place she was seen," he said. "What happened after, is anyone's guess. But I suppose that's why you're here. I'm certain your investigative experience trumps that of any in the queens' guard."

***

Outside the heavy wood doors of the Long Room, Mykal heard arguing from within.

"You were in my room!"

"Was not!"

"That's my dress! You can't deny it. I've been looking for it!"

"Looks better on me than it ever did on you!"

It sounded like a struggle.

Gembert forced a smile. "A moment, please."

He knocked on the door.

Silence answered from the other side.

He knocked a second time. "Enter!"

The Long Room was rather impressive. Colossal windows shaped like gravestone markers climbed the walls behind massive rock pillars. Banners with the Cordillera sigil hung like tapestries between the sections of windows. Knights in full armor and shields bearing identical sigils stood like statues in front of each pillar. A long rectangular table ran through the center of the room. Seated side-by-side at the head of the table at the furthest end of the room were, presumably, the queens.

Heavy wood doors closed behind them with a hollow *ba-bang*. Conversation at the table stopped. Everyone turned and watched as they stood waiting for permission to proceed.

The two women who followed Gembert remained outside of the room.

"Your highnesses," Gembert said, bowing.

The man sitting at the table with the queens pushed back his chair. Wood legs scraped on the stone floor. He stood up and sauntered toward them. Black gloves were folded and tucked inside the belt around his waist. He wore a deep blue vest over a crisp, white tunic. He kept a hand on the hilt of his longsword.

Mykal remembered how Blodwyn had explained that not everyone appreciated the enlistment of a wizard for advisement.

"We're in the middle of something," one of the queens said.

"That is Queen Sarah." Gembert talked out of the side of his mouth so only Blodwyn and Mykal heard. "And that is their thane, Axel."

"They're smaller than I expected. Children." Mykal whispered.

"And yet, they're queens." Blodwyn snapped, speaking with teeth clenched. The warning was clear. Show respect.

Thankfully Gembert was already several steps ahead, and more than likely—hopefully—had missed the small exchange.

"Chamberlain," Axel said. "Is there something I can help you with?"

"I am pleased to announce our search for the wizard is complete." Gembert stood up straight. Once again, his hands were clasped together in front of him. Mykal noticed how white his skin was. It was as if the chamberlain was squeezing his fingers too tightly, and the blood stopped flowing through his digits.

"Ah," Axel stopped only feet away from Blodwyn, and clicked the heels of his boots together. "So you are *the* wizard."

Blodwyn maintained eye contact. He stayed silent.

Mykal cleared his throat, this time so he could draw attention to himself.

Axel looked amused. His eyebrows, though only slightly thicker than his moustache, arched in blatant surprise. "*You* are the wizard who defeated King Hermon during the War?"

Mykal didn't think there was a correct response. Considering they were invited guests in the late king's castle. "I am the wizard you were looking for. My friend and I are here to help the queens as best we can."

"I see." Axel let his lips purse into a pucker. "Thank you, Chamberlain. I will take them from here."

Gembert bowed, backed away, and left the Long Room. He didn't let the doors slam. He closed them gently, until the handle latches engaged.

"This way." Axel was roughly the same height as Mykal. Disheveled clothing did not camouflage bulk and muscle. Black and white made the man's hair resemble grey soot. It looked as though he brushed it only with the fingers of his hand, evidence by a crooked part down the middle, and the rest falling over the ears and just below the back collar. The blood-red rims around his eyelids, however, convinced Mykal the thane must have been working day and night for some kind of resolution.

The young ladies seated at the table were not the same little, chubby girls Mykal had first seen when he, Quill, and his father, Eadric, had been inside the castle searching for the dungeon. At that time, it appeared they'd both been roaming the halls, walking side by side, but in their sleep. It had been eerie then, and seeing them again, now, made him feel a bit apprehensive.

It looked as though they'd shed their baby fat over the last few years.

"Your highnesses." Axel bowed. When he stood up, wisps of hair hung over his left eye. He combed the hair onto the top of his head, and tucked some behind his ear. "This is your wizard."

"You're Mykal, from Grey Ashland?" Queen Sarah's hair was light brown, almost blonde, and hung in loose curls just past her shoulders. She looked a few years younger than the other queen, and not yet a teen. Her skin was pale, but not pasty. High cheekbones were brushed with rouge. Thin eyebrows sat over the most unique eyes Mykal had ever seen; two rings of color encircled black pupils. The first, thickest band, was bright blue resembling a clear summer sky. The second directly around the black orb was gold, and equally as bright as the blue counterpart.

Mykal bowed, as Axel had. He kept his head lowered. "I am."

"And this?" The other queen spoke, Raaheel. Long coal black hair was plaited back, and triple braided. The tops of small ears were reddened, perhaps from the heat of the fire in the hearth behind where they sat. A tiny cleft split the end of her chin. Long, dark eyelashes accented to Mykal the fact that both of her eyes were more normal. They were bright, but brown, and just one color. The only visible jewelry was a necklace with a gold triangular-shaped charm.

The queens wore matching, simple, black iron crowns, and were dressed in sleeved taffeta tunics, the necklines trimmed in ermine fur. And while Raaheel's tunic was a vibrant green reminding Mykal of spring, Sarah's was a deep crimson similar to the cape her father wore during the War. Mykal couldn't help wonder who had raided who's closet.

"This is my friend, Blodwyn." Mykal did his best avoiding Sarah's eyes. They captivated him, but knew she might take the attention as a sign of disrespect.

"Your highnesses." Blodwyn mimicked the ceremonious bow.

"Both are wizards?" Sarah addressed the thane, brow furrowed, jaw set. She pushed back her chair, and stood up, running palms down the front of her tunic. "You've not seen their magic? Of course you haven't."

Raaheel cleared her throat. She didn't hide her suspicion. "Can you demonstrate your ability?"

"Not for my benefit," Sarah said, and chewed the skin on the edge of her thumbnail.

Raaheel slapped the hand away from her sister's mouth.

Sarah shot a look at the other queen, but bit down on her lip rather than address public scolding. "This is the course you want pursued, then pursue it, sister. I believe the fate of our kingdom is better in the hands placed in the hands of our thane. Now, if you'll excuse me. Axel, come with me."

An awkward moment descended on them until the younger queen and the thane left the Long Room. Only after the doors banged closed was there even a hint of relief.

"The queen has been under tremendous stress." Raaheel folded her hands in front of her on the table. Other than stating the obvious, she made no excuses for the behavior, and Mykal wasn't expecting any. Not from royalty. "We do, however, appreciate your travels in weather like this, your desire to help a distant kingdom without obligation to do so."

Mykal bowed slightly, nodding.

"Did you come from across the sea?" Raaheel let an eyebrow arch. A curious suspicion dominated her facial expression. "Doesn't seem like enough time has passed since the scouts were sent in search of you. And I'm not sure how any of them would have crossed the sea. Relations with the Voyagers hasn't improved any, not that they were good before the War, but after I can assure you, they are no better."

"We found Geneva in the north," Mykal said. He noticed Blodwyn remained silent, as if his shadow. It was almost like he wanted to be forgotten. If it played out that way, he could observe unobstructed.

"Geneva?" The Queen tilted her head to the side.

"One of the scouts." Mykal didn't expect a queen—the queens— to remember everyone's name.

"She is the one who found you?"

"That's right, your highness."

"Lovely young lady. Her aunt went missing not long ago, the mother of three children if I'm not mistaken. They're a little older, a bit more self-sufficient, not that losing a parent is any easier just because someone is older. I have not seen the family yet. It is not much of an excuse, but with the weather, and everything going on, Axel has insisted Sarah and I remain inside the castle at all times."

Now Mykal was impressed. The young queen clearly had a pulse on the kingdom. "Has anyone gone missing from inside the castle?"

"I'm afraid so, yes. Two servants. One worked in the kitchen as sort of the baker's apprentice. The other cleaned apartments throughout the castle. And if I am not mistaken, neither had any family." Raaheel's brow furrowed, and then the lines smoothed over. "No. I'm quite certain. Neither of them had family."

"I would like to see the dovecote, and speak with the baron and baroness first, I suppose," Mykal said. "They are still here?"

"They're here. In fact, they said they are not leaving until they find their daughter." Raaheel tried smiling. It wasn't a successful look. Her lips bent toward her chin, and her eye twitched. It was almost as if the muscles in her face fought against any show of contentment. "I would like nothing more than to find all of the missing people, and I certainly hope that calling on you for assistance was the right thing to do. My sister, as you surmised, was against this."

"I will not interfere with your thane."

Raaheel tapped fingers on the table. Mykal couldn't help but stare at the chewed nails as she said, "I want you to do what needs doing to get things done. You're here. It would be best if the two of you could work together. I've given that some thought, though. I believe it will actually be better if you work separately. Share information, of course, but go off in your own directions. Two sets of eyes looking at the exact same problem will most certainly see things differently."

"And we have your permission to roam the castle freely?" Mykal hated asking the question. It was better they have definition, rather than risk insult and embarrassment.

"You do, however, I may just keep Gembert close. He knows the facts of the case almost as well as Axel, Sarah, and myself. More importantly, he'll be able to guide you through the castle with ease, and expertise. Also, I trust him as much as I trust my sister." The queen maintained an even tone of voice while she talked. Each word seemed carefully selected. There was no rush in making her point. "What I ask is that you keep me apprised of anything you discover, and that you don't burden the other queen. Sarah has not been herself lately. I'm a little worried at the moment. Since she is already stressed by your presence, I don't wish to add to her anxiety with you or your partner giving her reports she didn't request. Are we clear?"

"Yes, and thank you, your highness."

CHAPTER 9

"I'm to bring you to the dovecote." Gembert was alone. Mykal wasn't sure where the women were who had been following him earlier. He also wasn't sure what purpose they served. "Unless, you would first like me to show you your rooms. They're in the apartments, and quite comfortable, reserved for foreign dignitaries and such."

Mykal cast a glance toward Blodwyn. As far as he was concerned he was more interested in getting started. The faster he assisted in solving the mystery around the missing Osirians, the faster he could return home. His concern for his mother's health grew. He hadn't liked leaving her back at the Library alone, not while she wasn't well.

It wasn't as if they'd traveled from the ruins to Cordillera's castle, and were tired from the trek. Gembert didn't know this, though. The hospitality was appreciated, however unnecessary. "I think we can start with the dovecotes. Maybe talk with the baron and baroness, and then we can see the quarters. As long as that is acceptable?"

Gembert bowed his head slightly. "Very well."

The castle, despite the fires blazing in the many hearths, was drafty, damp. Thankfully, hanging sigil-bearing banners, and colorful tapestries added layers of diversity to the otherwise slate-gray walls and floors which were drab, depressing.

Gembert led the way. Blodwyn and Mykal followed, side-by-side.

"You've been extremely quiet." Mykal appreciated the tall stained glass windows. The depicted pictures were of dragons, and knights, of forests, and of mountains. Between windows, unlit torches sat in hooks on mounted sconces.

"When I was young I trained for a life that, had I have stayed on the road, our paths might never have crossed." Blodwyn's walk was rhythmic. The end of his staff tapped the stone, then his left foot, and then his right.

"Were you a swellsword?" When the war was still coming, Mykal had made difficult decisions. One centered around his disabled paternal grandfather, Eadric's father. On top of his old age, he'd lost a leg during a battle when he fought for the king of Grey Ashland. This was before Mykal had been born. In an attempt to prevent the war from ever happening, Mykal and his friends set out across the Old Empire. Grandfather remained on the farm. Threatened that the fight might reach their land, Blodwyn called on friends—*friends who had no issue with accepting bags of coin from Blodwyn*—to keep an eye on Grandfather while they were gone. The surly bunch might have looked questionable, but they held up their end of the bargain.

"You could say that."

"What would *you* say?" Mykal found his own rhythm. He concentrated on it. The steady beat the two of them made became almost tranquil.

They reached the end of a hallway, and Gembert checked over his shoulder before starting up a winding staircase. Mykal recalled how high the center and corner towers were when looking at the entire castle from outside in the storm. A climb to the top could prove exhausting.

"Stories for another time." Blodwyn fought a smile.

"You do realize you've been holding that over my head for years now." The stairs were rock, as if carved into the mountain, and the castle built up around it. The soles of Mykal's boots scuffed against each step. They climbed slowly, pacing themselves.

"What have I held over your head?"

"Promises of tales of the past. Dragons, and coins. These cloaks, and a story of your youth, and how you became acquainted with my mother. Shall I continue?" With Blodwyn it was always the same. The mystery is present, and the revelation promised, but he never opened up and shared. Mykal longed for an evening sitting by a fire and hearing about the life he lived before they began training together. Blodwyn had been part of Mykal's life from the day the wizard was born, and after his parents disappeared, Blodwyn and his grandfather raised him. *Why wouldn't I be curious about who he was?*

Blodwyn held up a hand, stopping him. "You have my word."

"I've had it before."

"When we get home, I will tell you all of the stories, answering as many of your questions as I possibly can. How is that?"

"I will believe it, when I hear it." The stairs were never ending. The little bit of talking they did *became* a bit tiring. His breathing became a little ragged, and shallow. There was no denying the start of a burn inside his lungs. The muscles in the backs of his legs tightened. All of his exercise should have better prepared him for the ascent. "Are we getting close?"

"About halfway." Gembert spoke only the two words, but there was no sign of distress in his breathing. Perhaps he was more used to the climb, or talented at masking exhaustion.

When finally, Mykal gave in, and decided collapsing on the stairs was the only option available, Gembert called down. "We're here."

There were a handful of steps left. Thankfully the staff assisted, and was far better than putting hands on cold, damp stone walls. He climbed them slower, his mind already surrendering to the idea of defeat despite the achievement. Huffing, Mykal pushed forward, and was nearly gasping as he reached the doorway.

Stepping outside, there was little relief. Mykal breathed in the air, thankful there were no more stairs, but didn't experience immediate solace. The air was far thinner than he was used to breathing. He sucked air in through his mouth greedily. The temperature was lower. Frigid cold greeted them. It felt ten degrees colder at the top of the tower, compared to when he had stood outside the castle earlier. The wind was obviously angry about having to whip about in the troposphere.

"It takes getting used to." Gembert wasn't sweating, Mykal noted as he dragged his arm across his forehead, and down the sides of his face.

"Hopefully, we won't be up here that long," Mykal said. "How are you, Wyn?"

Blodwyn offered a slight nod, eyes narrowed. Mykal wasn't accustomed to the silence. Blodwyn was usually talkative enough for the both of them. It would take getting used to the idea that, while Mykal was the student in most cases, right now *he* was the one sought after.

"I'm not sure why we're up here." Gembert motioned a hand toward the grey stone dovecote. The round building was another three stories tall. Dormers protruded from the lower half of a cone-shaped roof, facing north, east, south and west. "This is the one place Clairece is not."

Mykal clucked his tongue. "But this was the place of her last known whereabouts. Correct?"

Gembert let his head drop to the side some as he shrugged. "That's true enough."

"How did she know about the place?" Mykal asked.

"Let's get inside. It won't be much warmer, but the wind won't berate us, and we won't have to yell in order to be heard." Gembert pulled open the door.

There wasn't any sort of lock Mykal saw. They walked into the structure, and Mykal, once again, struggled breathing. Although unfamiliar with doves, he'd worked his entire life with livestock. He was as accustomed to the rank odor of manure as he was to the pleasant scent of flowers. The dung inside the dovecote overpowered. Above, dried droppings crusted the crisscross of wood perches from pigeonhole to pigeonhole. The floor below was a carpet of dung, as well. Mykal poked a finger at his nostrils. "Very, ah, penetrating."

"Good word," Blodwyn said.

Mykal showed appreciation with a thin-lipped smile. On the floor beside the door was barrel feeder filled with seeds, and leaning against the wall stood a rake, broom, and shovel. Mykal wasn't sure if the tools were just for show. It didn't seem like they'd ever been used.

"Housed here are seventy-five white doves, give or take. The family has been caring for doves for centuries. Emperor Rye made the idea popular, indicating that only the wealthy raised doves. Why? I'm not sure exactly. We don't eat them. We don't use them as message carriers. All we do is keep them. Here. The doves stay inside this place for their lifetime. They don't get to spread wings and fly as they were meant to. They just sit here." Gembert's displeasure with the birds was blatant. There was disdain in the way he said *here* each time. "Anyway, you asked how the young lady knew of the dovecote? Why the queens told her of about it, just as their father was sure to tell every visitor, as well."

Mykal thought the chamberlain might have said more, but, with some effort, refrained. If he had to guess, keeping the dovecote clean fell under the chamberlain's responsibility. With over seventy housed birds, cleaning even the floor daily would feel like a futile battle. "And did you escort Clairece up here, as you did Blodwyn and myself?"

"I did."

The wind was no longer cause for raised voices, but the soft, drawn-out sound of what could have been birds lamenting echoed like cries inside the dovecote. Wings whistled, as birds flew out of pigeonholes, and back into them. Mykal found his eyes continually glancing up. It seemed inevitable, that sooner or later one of the doves would send droppings onto him. "And how long did she remain here, with the birds?"

Gembert twirled slowly around. "Far longer than she should have, apparently. You see, I brought her up here. I did not stay with her for longer than a few minutes. When it became clear she was in no rush to return to the warmer parts of the castle, I excused myself. I figured up here she was as safe as if she were in the Long Room with the queens."

"It would seem so, and yet, she wasn't." Mykal realized there was nothing out of the ordinary inside the dovecote. The doves fluttered about above, and the mess made was everywhere. "And the last time this was all cleaned?"

"Every morning. I come up here first thing, sometimes before the sun touches the sky. I feed the doves, and then sweep up and shovel away the droppings."

"So this—"

"It's all from today, yes." Gembert placed one arm across his chest. The elbow from the other arm rested on the first, and his thumb rubbed at the bottom of his chin. "For such small animals, I am amazed by the amount of waste produced."

"And after that, after you went back downstairs, did you see Clairece again?"

"No. Never."

"Okay, thank you," Mykal said.

"Beg your pardon? It sounded like you were dismissing me." Gembert's chuckle sounded like the exact opposite of amusement. The furrowed brow only accentuated his discontent.

"That's right. Thank you. Blodwyn and I have work to do," Mykal said.

"I'm not to leave you alone." Dung dropped from above, and plopped onto the ground by Gembert's foot. It was a silent attack that nearly hit the target, Mykal mused.

"Who gave such an order?"

"The queens."

Mykal realized he hated the term. While perhaps necessary under the special circumstances, 'Queens' sounded superfluous, and redundant. "Very well. You can stay, but I am going to ask that you stand back and not interfere in any way."

Gembert's lips moved. No words slipped past his lips. Mykal imagined the snide comments the man was eating as he maintained a hospitable, and para-friendly position with guests of the *queens*. "As you wish."

***

Mykal walked the barrel of feed from by the door to the center of the room, tipping it back and advancing it inches at a time. He snatched up the broom and swept clean the area around the barrel, pushing the pile of dung up against the wall. The broom broke through the crusts, and released a new wave of fresh smells.

Kneeling in front of the barrel, Mykal removed the leather pouch from his belt. He pulled on the drawstrings, and then carefully emptied the contents onto the barrel's lid. "I need a cup, something I can use to mix these into."

"Inside the barrel." Gembert stepped forward and lifted the lid.

"Don't drop those!" Blodwyn's outburst surprised Mykal. He recalled when he met Coil, Blodwyn's childhood friend, the old man had been blind. The lost vision came after an explosion Blodwyn caused. The two had mixed elements without knowledge, and the combination was close to nearly lethal.

Gembert sighed, and Mykal caught the chamberlain rolling his eyes. "I will not drop a thing." Half buried inside the feed was a small bowl. "It's what I use to dish out the seeds."

"It's perfect. May I use it?" Mykal asked for the sake of politeness, only. He retrieved the bowl, and Gembert wordlessly replaced the lid.

Mykal inspected the vials, and set them standing up. He thought on lessons he'd recently had with his mother. He was no chemist. Alchemy fascinated him, however, and he felt confident answers not obviously present were discoverable inside the dovecote.

He poured grains of ground bismuth, a silvery white metal, into the bowl first. "This is one of the sixteen original elements and serves well as a base," Mykal said. Next, he poured in a few drops of balm from Gilead buds. "And the properties involved with this will assist me as I reach out to spirits. It contains a necromantic quality, which I think will prove useful."

"Necromantic?" It was Gembert.

"Necromantic," Mykal said. "Necromancy. It is a way of communicating with the dead."

"The dead." Gembert shuddered.

"You're more than welcome to leave. I've asked you to go already."

"I'm fine," he said. "Continue. Please."

"Lastly," Mykal said, "I'm going to sprinkle these dried centaurea cyanus flakes over the top. The cornflower-like substance was often used to treat issues with sight, and enhance third eye capabilities."

He thought Gembert might pipe up a second time, but the chamberlain held his tongue. Although he'd somehow forgotten the mortar dish, he did have the ceramic pestle, and immediately set to work crushing, and grinding together the three ingredients.

Mykal wished his mother were with them. She understood alchemy far better than he. They practiced potions and spells from books. This was the first time he used this style of magic alone. It wasn't that he had any questions. He was most confident he had the correct combination and suitable for what he intended. The reassurance of having her near just would have worked better at calming the nerves that fired inside him, causing his stomach to fold over on itself, and twist into a tightened knot.

Waving his palms over the bowl, it seemed as if any light inside the dovecote evaporated. White flames ignited the contents, and danced up toward Mykal's hands. The heat rolled across from wrists to fingertips. It took effort not pulling his arms away. Especially after it seemed the fire was traveling inside his arms. Under the skin. Could he be cooking from the inside out? It didn't seem likely. Magic was odd that way, though. There was no telling how something worked, and definitely not the first time it's tried.

The burning sensation spread throughout, rapidly. It felt as if the smoke was clustered together inside his head, his skullcap perhaps the only thing keeping the smoke from escaping his pores, and perhaps, setting his hair on fire.

White smoke billowed up from the small bowl, and around his hands, moving fast and ringing above all of their heads. The smoke filled the room, and gyrated, encircling them as if a twister danced around the room. Gembert ducked out of the way, and Blodwyn waved a hand.

Mykal saw things moving inside the smoke; swimming inside of it.

Eyeless sockets dotted formless, swirling skulls in the beings flying above them. Smokey arms reached, and fingers rolled and unrolled grabbing at air, while open mouths released silent screams.

"Is this supposed to happen?!" Gembert came unglued. He swatted away the spirits as they passed too close to him for comfort, doing his best to protect his head with his hands. "You've awakened demons, wizard! You've doomed us. You've doomed us all!"

One of the floating spirits soared up toward the cone ceiling, and then arched over and down, and returned toward Mykal as if a falcon diving at unsuspecting prey. Only Mykal was not unsuspecting. He was staring up, watching. His legs felt a little like stone. He wasn't sure he could move them if he wanted. As he threw an arm up in defense, about to scream, the spirit entered his body through his mouth, nostrils, and his eyeballs.

He breathed in the spirit.

Screams ricocheted inside his skull

His legs gave way, and he crumpled onto the dung-covered ground.

CHAPTER 10

Mykal climbed the staircase inside the tower. The walls were wet, and damp. A coldness passed through his body. His bones ached. It seemed like he would never feel warm again. Despite the ease of ascent, every step caused pain to flash and flare in his legs, and feet. He couldn't understand why he was going up.

He heard a muffled, but steady, and fast beating of his heart. It pulsed, throbbed inside his ears.

They should be going down, if they were finished inside the dovecote, they should be going down the stairs. The dovecote sat *on top* of the tower, there hadn't been more stairs to climb, had there?

They.

Where was Blodwyn? Gembert?

This was the same *tower, wasn't it?* "Wyn? Blodwyn?"

Mykal heard the sound of his voice, but knew something was different, off. He hadn't spoken out loud. At least he didn't think he had. The words only reverberated around inside his mind, but had not come out of his mouth.

Everything was blurry. The corners of his eyes seemed watery. He remembered when he was pulled into the Isthmian Sea. A fishing accident, was how he wanted the incident remembered. A near-death experience, was in actuality what it had been for sure. Poisonous serpents propelled toward him, while he was entangled in the line. He could not see them clearly, not submerged under the water, and not while he struggled upon reaching the surface and filling his lungs with air, but perhaps that had been for the best. For as clearly as he had seen the monsters trying to eat him, the blur probably preserved a portion of his sanity.

"Wyn!" Yes, it was only inside his head.

He couldn't stop climbing the stairs, though. Nor could he turn his head. All he could do is whatever it was he was doing. And at the moment, that was running up the stairs.

Running.

It didn't make any sense. Mykal felt a little panicked. His muscles didn't respond. He was not in control of his body; his legs, his arms, his head.

He remained as calm as he could, considering. Concentration. Focus. He couldn't let fear get away from him.

There was something he was forgetting. It was there. Close.

And then he reached the top of the staircase, and recognized the door that led outside. He stopped, breathing heavily, and pressed his body against the wood. Pushing the door open slowly, he stepped out of the cold, wet dampness of the tower and into the winter weather.

The howling wind blew gusts of falling, and loose snow around. He didn't feel any different—no colder. He couldn't feel the wind, or the extreme cold. It was almost as if he were still inside the staircase of the tower.

Mykal couldn't wrap his mind around what was happening.

He strained against the muscles in his arms, in his legs. He fought for control of his body. The entire dilemma reminded him of when he was young. Sometimes his dreams got the better of him. They were more like nightmares, actually. One particular dream recurred time and again, with the significant details unchanged. He would think he was awake, standing in the center of a cornfield. Sometimes he was dressed in trousers and a tunic, sometimes in his sleeping gown, and nothing else. The moon would be out, the sky black, and starless. In the distance he heard what sounded like his grandfather screaming in pain. All at once he would begin running, except he wasn't headed toward the sound. He ran in the opposite direction. It didn't matter that he wanted to save his grandfather, that he wanted to turn around. His dream-body responded irrationally, taking him further and further away from the danger, and further from his grandfather. Each time the dream ended before any conclusion was reached. His eyes would pop open wide, and he'd find himself sitting in bed, covered in sweat and panting.

Mykal was always grateful at *that* moment, that it had only been a dream.

He knew he'd never forsake his grandfather. Never.

This, however, was how he felt *now*. It was like he was trapped inside some new dream.

He stood outside the door to the dovecote.

If he could wake himself up, maybe he'd find he was actually in bed. The room for dignitaries prepared by the chamberlain.

He pushed open the door of the dovecote. Again, he noticed something odd, off. It wasn't calculating correctly inside his brain. Too many other things went on, flooding his senses.

The doves were active. Wings fluttered. Songs sung in cooing chirps.

It looked like far more than seventy birds flew around above him.

Above them.

He wasn't alone.

The young woman stood in the center of the room. Her arms were stretched out, as if she expected doves might perch on her limbs. "Aren't they simply marvelous?"

She was marvelous in a bright turquoise cotton dress, under a maroon wool coat. Creamy looking skin, with a tint of red on high-set cheeks, bright blue eyes under thick brown brows, and full lips under a thin, concave nose.

His sudden presence didn't startle her. Not in the least. She *knew* him.

Mykal didn't recognize her, and yet a name passed before him, like smoke from a fire; you could grab for it. It was real. But you couldn't actually touch it, or hold it.

Only if he thought about it, the smoke almost solidified in front of him.

It was white smoke. Brilliant.

And there was fire.

White flames.

Clairece. That was her name. He spoke it: "Clairece!"

No sound came from his mouth.

Clairece suddenly looked terrified. She brought her arms in, across her chest, and backed away.

Don't be scared, Mykal tried. *I'm not here to hurt you. I only want to help.*

She couldn't hear him. His promises futile.

He knew she was about to scream. Her mouth opened wide.

Mykal fought for control of his body, but couldn't stop himself from charging forward. The muscles tensed. His heart rate increased, beating hard. He wouldn't have been surprised if it cracked the back of his ribs, freeing itself from his chest.

That was when he noticed the dagger in his hand.

The blurry vision kept him from seeing details clear enough, but what he now noticed was that *those* weren't his hands.

Before Clairece screamed, Mykal pressed a hand over her mouth with one hand, and slammed her into the wall before the arc of the dagger completed.

And then, Mykal screamed. He heard the sound of his voice. It wasn't just a jumble inside his head. "No!"

***

"No! No!" Mykal was on his back, and saw the doves circling above him. He heard wings flutter. The sound echoed inside his head. Throwing elbows back, he pushed himself up into a sitting position. His hands out in front, ready for fighting, stopped shy of sending bolts at Blodwyn, and Gembert.

"It's okay, Mykal. It's alright." Blodwyn spoke softly. He had a way of calming a situation. The man was good at control. With a subduing touch, he set one hand on Mykal's leg, the other on his arm. "Mykal?"

"Wyn," Mykal said. It was more for affirmation. He could indeed talk. He wiggled his fingers in front of his face. The muscles were under his power. "Help me up."

Gembert reached under an arm. "Slowly," he said.

Mykal groaned. "My head. It feels like someone clubbed me good."

"You went down hard. We couldn't stop you before you hit the back of your head," Blodwyn said. He didn't let go of Mykal, as if afraid he might topple over. "How do you feel? Are you dizzy?"

"I'm okay. I think. We were..." he said. "What were we doing? Where's the girl?"

"You can't remember why we're up here?" Gembert didn't look happy.

Mykal ignored the rolling eyes, and stepped around him. "There," he said.

"What?" Blodwyn stood next to Mykal, looking around carefully as if trying to see whatever it was Mykal was seeing. "There's nothing there. Do you see something I don't?"

Mykal turned around.

There was a barrel in the middle of the room. He pointed at the bowl and pestle. "Those are mine."

"You really don't remember?" Gembert placed hands on hips, and shifted his weight from one leg to the other. "This is unbelievable."

Mykal ignored the chamberlain, and paced around the barrel. "We came up here. I used alchemy for insight into the past."

"You were hoping for clues, or answers." Blodwyn leaned on his staff.

"Clairece," Mykal said.

"I feel like we're going around in circles here. It's getting late. It's cold. Surely you must be getting hungry." Gembert's voice quivered. He sounded more afraid of something, than annoyed.

"She was here. Clairece. I saw her."

"When?" Now Mykal had Gembert's interest. "How did you see her?"

"She's not here now." Mykal went back to the wall where the young woman had been pushed against. "She was attacked. I saw it happen. Most of it, anyway."

"Who did it?" Blodwyn said.

"It's hard to say," Mykal said. He held his hands up in front of his face. He wiggled his fingers. He looked at the palms, the backs of his hands, and the palms again. The other thing about dreams seemed equally as true. Not only did he have little control over what happened while dreaming, but once awake it seemed like the memory of the visions slipped forever into the ethereal. "I—I am trying to remember what I saw. I was there, when it happened."

"You were inside the castle?" Gembert said.

"Not *when* it happened. Just now. I went there, back in time, back to when *something* happened to Clairece." Mykal didn't want any details escaping his memory, what few remained to begin with.

Blodwyn said, "Is she... "

"I don't know. Not for sure. Whoever attacked her, she knew the person," Mykal said, and spun around. "She was here, where the barrel is now. She was alone in here. Alone, until I entered the dovecote."

"So you were here," Gembert said. "What did you do with the Baron's daughter?"

"It was a vision. Please, please, stop talking!" Mykal ground his teeth, jaw set. The man was making him lose his train of thought. "When I walked into the dovecote, she spoke to me. She wasn't frightened. Not at first. She was in awe of the place. It looked like she loved the birds. And then I pulled a dagger."

Gembert gasped, but kept his mouth covered, and didn't speak.

Mykal sighed. He played out the memory of his vision while he spoke: "I pushed the girl up to the wall, and before she could scream..."

Mykal drove an imaginary weapon into an imaginary woman.

"So whoever attacked her, stabbed her?" Blodwyn said.

"Seems likely, but I can't say for sure." Mykal looked down at his boots. "Was there blood in here, Gembert?"

"Blood?" the chamberlain said.

"In here, inside the dovecote?"

"There was no blood."

"None? Not over here, where I'm standing?"

"There wasn't any blood. Not on the ground, not on the walls, not where you're standing, or where I am standing, or where he is standing. There was no blood." Gembert inspected the floor, and walls. "I tell you, not a drop had been spilled inside this dovecote."

Dung was all over Mykal's cloak. It got on him when he collapsed during the spell. He brushed some of it off, flicked his wrist, and flung it onto the floor. "The bird droppings. Did they show any sign of a struggle?"

Gembert laughed, bowed forward, and looked at Blodwyn. Perhaps he expected the older man would appreciate the humor of a such a ludicrous question. "Did the bird droppings show signs of a struggle? I'm not even sure how I could answer a question like that, assuming, of course, that it was a serious question in the first place."

Blodwyn moved fast. He stepped forward, and snatched Gembert by the arm. "See the floor." Blodwyn pointed. "See how this half of the room the dung is fresh, untouched?"

"Untouched?" Gembert said.

Blodwyn shoved Gembert. The man stumbled back. His boots slid. The wall behind him kept the chamberlain from falling onto the ground. Gembert grimaced, eyes furrowed. He might even have snarled. It was all in his bark, and the bark was more a whimper at that. "What's the meaning of this treatment?"

Blodwyn pointed at the floor.

Gembert's lips parted. Mykal saw the understanding in the chamberlain's expression.

"See how the dung is smeared, and flattened, and walked on? That's what we're talking about. That's what the wizard is trying to figure out. When you came into the dovecote after the disappearance of Clairece, and before you cleaned the structure, what did the dung look like?" Blodwyn's face reddened. Mykal thought if Gembert didn't respond correctly, the chamberlain was in real danger of having his nose broken by Blodwyn's knuckles.

"It was smeared. Not unlike it is now. But I have no idea if that means there was struggle or not. The girl was in here on her own for nearly an hour, maybe more. She was all over the place. The dung gets squashed and streaked just the same as if it were walked on," Gembert said.

Blodwyn looked at Mykal. "He's right."

Mykal sat on the barrel, packed his small vials into his leather pouch, and then picked up the bowl of ashes and pestle. He looked at the contents, raked them around with the tip of his finger. The compound created was something new, altogether. He poured the contents into the pouch and drew the strings tight. "I want to speak with the girl's parents, please."

CHAPTER 11

The apartments, located in the top back half of the castle, ran the length of a long hallway filled with tall wood doors. Thankfully, no climbing was involved. Mykal, Blodwyn, and Gembert descended a handful of flights of stairs from the tower. While Mykal's legs felt weak, and barely able to support his weight, he knew come morning his muscles would be tight, sore, and make climbing out of bed a beyond a challenge. There was no sense worrying about morning at this point. Not when a few hours of daylight remained.

At the end of the hall a fire blazed inside a hearth. The heat didn't reach Mykal. He wouldn't mind some warmth. His bones had trapped the cold from standing inside the dovecote. How the birds could survive winters in there amazed him.

"How's your breathing?" Mykal whispered. Blodwyn arched an eyebrow. Mykal patted his chest with fingertips, as he inhaled. "I feel almost lightheaded."

"It's the altitude." Gembert answered without turning around. He walked briskly down the hall. Mykal admired colorful, and unique tapestries on the columns between windows. "It could take days before your breathing feels normal. All of the stairs don't help. You do eventually get used to them, I suppose. I dread them some days. However, if you find you've a headache, we have a curer..."

Gembert stopped walking, and faced them. "Although, I suppose a curer's talents for healing would be wasted on someone like you."

Mykal didn't miss the implication. "Because I am a wizard."

"I suspect you don't even get sick," Gembert said.

Mykal thought of his mother. She looked rough when he left. A cold wouldn't put her out of commission long, but he'd never seen her ill. Coming to Osiris was necessary, no doubt, he just wished he could have stayed and cared for her.

He couldn't recall ever having been sick.

When he'd been poisoned during the serpent attack, Blodwyn, and Galatia helped him recover. That wasn't the same as being sick. There must have been a time when he had a fever, a runny nose, cold sweats. He just couldn't remember suffering through similar symptoms. He'd never caught any of the illnesses.

Was that because he was a wizard?

It couldn't be the reason. His mother was sick. She was a sorceress. It didn't seem like she had anything different than what Grandfather came down with once or twice each winter. Maybe she seemed a little worse.

Gembert stared at Mykal, eyes narrowed as if anxiously anticipating a reply.

"I should be fine," Mykal said, his words sounding guarded. "But if either of us develop symptoms we'll be sure to let you know. Thank you."

"Fair enough. Should the need arise—"

"We'll let you know. In fact, you'll be first."

Gembert smiled, pleased. "And here we are."

Two quick, soft knocks on the door. Gembert then placed his hands together, and let them hang below his waist, passively. His head tilted toward the door, as if he were listening through the wood. He must have heard movement, because he pulled away, and stiffened some. His back straightened, and his chest even puffed out some.

The handle turned, and hinges protested with a groan as the door opened a crack.

"Yes? Oh, Gembert."

The door swung open, then, and inside the threshold a woman stood with one hand on the door, the other on the frame. Her skin was pale, her lips almost ashen. Hair was pulled back away from her face, but in disarray on her head, as if she'd been sleeping for hours. It didn't mask, or properly frame, her beauty. Large blue eyes, high cheekbones, and a thin, delicate looking nose were still, by far, the most prominent features. "Have you found her?"

The woman looked like the child, Clairece. There was no mistaking the resemblance.

"Baroness Henriette," Gembert said, and bowed slightly. "I would like you to meet some friends of the queens."

Although the bow showed his respect, the chamberlain ignored the direct question asked.

Henriette's clasped hands over her bosom. "Richmond is lying down. Please, come in. I'll wake him and let him know we have visitors."

Mykal said, "If it's not a good time—"

"No. It's fine. Like I said, please, come in." She stepped aside.

Mykal told Gembert, "We'd like to talk with them alone."

The request clearly stumped the chamberlain. "I should say not. Absolutely not."

"How freely can the baron and his wife speak to us if the queens' agent is present? Please. Let us have a conversation with these people. I assure you, anything learned I will share with you."

"The queens would not approve." He wanted to stand firm. It was obvious. The rigid stance he was in expressed as much.

"You're not coming in with us. If you don't like it, take it up with your queens. Right now, I'm trying to figure out what happened to their daughter. That child's life is the reason I'm here, and not for any other political aspirations."

Gembert huffed, but when Mykal and Blodwyn entered the apartment, he remained outside, and was not smiling when Mykal gently closed the door in his face.

The staffs tapped on the stone floor and echoed.

The apartment had two other doors. Bedchambers, Mykal imagined. The main room was decorated with polished wood tables, and chairs. On end tables arrangements of baby's breath and colorful weeds stood in blown glass vases.

Mykal looked for, but couldn't find any windows. He didn't think there would be any inside the bedchambers, either. The apartments backed up to the rising flat side of the Rames, unless the view was of the face of steep windward mountains.

"Make yourself comfortable. I won't be but a minute." Henriette didn't wait for any reply. She hurried into a room, closing the door behind her.

"They have a couch in here, a sofa." Mykal pointed at the settle, wondering why more people didn't use cushions padding where one sat. It was an obvious improvement to sitting in comfort. He'd first seen the like when he was on the Isthmian Islands, inside Governor Hobb's private office. She was the ruler of the Voyagers, and maybe, just maybe, once had a fling with Blodwyn. He wasn't positive, it was only speculation, and was on the long list of stories Wyn promised to share one day. Governor Hobbs wasn't like their queen. Everything on the Island was a little more exotic, and surreal than Mykal had seen in the rest of his world. Eventually, he wanted to return. There was much to learn from those people. They'd clearly traveled beyond the Old Empire, and had knowledge more mystical than magic. "It's like a chair, but for two, maybe three people."

"You enjoyed that a little too much." Blodwyn ignored the explanation.

"Enjoyed what?"

"Don't play games with me, Mykal."

"He is not going to shadow our every move. I won't have it."

"What are you so nervous about?"

Mykal sighed, deflating his lungs until his shoulders sagged. They stood close to one another. He loved the friendship they shared. Blodwyn knew him better than he sometimes knew himself. "I don't know what I'm doing. I feel like I'm an imposter pretending to be this insightful know-it-all. And it's a joke, because I'm not. But no one is laughing, because they haven't caught on yet. They will, though, Wyn. They will, and what will I do then?"

"Stop that." Blodwyn looked toward the door Henriette had closed. He clearly didn't want the baron and his baroness hearing the discussion. He continued talking, but lowered his voice. "I see what you're doing. I see exactly what you're doing."

Mykal was careful not to raise his voice, either. The last thing they needed was the baron telling the queen about the two frauds inside the castle. That wouldn't go over well. "How? How can you see what I'm doing if I don't even know what it is I'm doing?"

"You're looking for answers. We're here to help them find out what is happening. Someone, or something, is responsible for the missing people." Blodwyn's spoke calmly. The tone of voice he used soothed.

"I feel like I should be able to just zap something and," he clapped his hands together, "and there's the answer."

"Is that something you can do? Because if it is, you should do it. And we can be gone from this castle, and back home." Blodwyn stood still, eyes open too wide.

Mykal shook his head. He could control the wind, and objects. When he transported them places, it also involved the air, the earth, and nature itself. Lightning was inside him. It was why he brought the pouch with the elements. "No, I. No. That's not something I can do. My magic is different than that. It's more physical."

"I didn't think so, but you see, you haven't given up. Instead you attacked the problem from a different direction." He tapped Mykal's forehead. "This brain inside your skull works, and is more powerful than your magic. I see what you're doing, and I'm impressed. I think Gembert is, as well. Not that the chamberlain's opinion matters much, but he'll be giving reports to the queens. Think of the good that might come from this."

"The good?"

"A forged alliance between the kingdoms."

The idea of there ever being another war gave Mykal nightmares. The things he'd seen haunted his dreams. Most nights the scenes just played out over and over again, which was bad. It became worse when the memories twisted, and knotted, and turned into something even worse, an outcome that could have been. The result was generally the same, regardless. He would wake up, his body covered in a cold sweat, and he would be shaking, sometimes for close to an hour. At that point the night was over, and he would be up for the day.

"I'm not sure what I've done to impress you." Mykal walked over to a vase. He didn't recognize any of the weeds. He wanted desperate to pinch off samples and place them inside his pouch. Alchemy came from the elements, and from nature. The more items he experimented with, the stronger his abilities would become.

Blodwyn sat on the couch. "My goodness, this is wonderful." He patted the cushion on the armrest, and the empty cushion beside him. "We're going to have to craft one or two of these when we get home."

That made Mykal smile; the simple things. "What am I to do, Wyn?"

"When we get to our apartment, I want to know exactly what happened in the dovecote. That was some bizarre stuff back there. Of all the things we've been through, and that we've seen, whatever happened to you shook me up."

"Shook *you* up?"

He waved a hand through the air. "Not here. Not now. When we're alone. For now, ask your questions. I want you to just follow your instincts. It's what I was trying to say a moment ago, I believe between that brain of yours, and your instincts, the answers will present themselves."

The bedchamber door opened. Richmond stepped into the main room. He wore white trousers, and a white vest with eight gold buttons close together. The soft brown jacket nearly reached his knees. Only, it didn't look as though it would keep him warm. It seemed more like a decorative garment, worn strictly for show. Underscored by puffy flesh, bloodshot red eyes looked them over. "Who might you be? Can you tell me, have you any news of my daughter?"

Henriette stepped out of the room. She latched onto her husband's arm, standing behind him, expecting he'd save her life if the strangers inside their room attacked.

"My name is Mykal. This is Blodwyn." When Mykal looked, Blodwyn was already standing, and looking ominous in his cloak, with both hands on his staff. That wasn't going to help the situation. "The queens have brought us here to search for your daughter."

It was partially true, he mused. Finding the one responsible for the unexpectedly growing number of unsolved abductions might have been more accurate, just less comforting.

"And what have you found?"

Mykal preferred *not* telling Clairece's parents about his experience in the dovecote. If it became essential, they would know. Until that point, he saw no reason for scaring them. A rendition of something almost better described as hallucinatory, over what some might want to consider magical, only clouded the line between hope and despair.

"We've only just arrived." Mykal saw the weight his words carried. The man's eyes dropped. He stared at the floor. In that same moment, however, the woman squeezed his arm, and he, struggling, lifted his eyes and looked directly at Mykal. She was his strength, making her a very brave, and courageous person. "The chamberlain has been showing us around. Answering questions. Everyone in the castle is genuinely concerned."

Richmond kept running his hand over the back of Henriette's, while she held onto his arm. They fed each other. The strength was shared between them. They were flailing, failing. He understood that losing their daughter could prove a devastating blow to their union.

"I was hoping you had something that belonged to Clairece, something I could use to help me try and locate her." Mykal didn't know if the queens told the baron and his wife the kind of help they'd enlisted. The way Richmond furrowed his brow, he was suddenly certain they had not.

Henriette, however, said, "Would her hairbrush help you?"

"It might," Mykal said.

"One moment." She excused herself, and went through the second doorway. Returning seconds later, she held a silver hairbrush in her hand. "This had been my mother's. When I was younger, I used it. It was given to Clairece when she was just a child. I remember always worrying she'd lose it. Foolishness, really. It's just a brush. There's nothing important about it. It isn't worth much, other than for sentimental purposes, but Clairece loved it.

Every night she brushed her hair. One hundred strokes on the left, and one hundred on the right, and she always counted out each motion."

"I think that will be perfect."

Henriette picked at loose strands stuck in the bristles. "Let me clean this up first."

Mykal held up a hand. "If you don't mind, leave the hair."

The woman nodded, and offered the brush up.

"I promise I will return it to you as soon as possible," Mykal said.

"It's not the brush we want back." Richmond's lips puckered, and he swallowed. It looked like he was trying to get something sour down his throat, and might not make it without vomiting. "The queens wanted us to return home. They promised they would send word as soon as something of our daughter's disappearance was discovered. I don't fault them for the suggestion. It was thoughtful, we know. As young people, they're doing their best. It's commendable, of course. Very commendable. If they had a child of their own, they'd understand a parent will never rest when something is wrong with their child. I can remember a time when Clairece's fever lasted for several nights. It was the summer she turned four. She cried and cried. And I thought that was the scariest thing. I'd been wrong. It was when she stopped crying that fear overtook me. I'll never get out of my mind the memory of seeing her lethargic in her mother's arms. Her skin was pink, and her eyes unfocused. There is no way we'll leave Osiris until we have. . .some sort of answer. We don't want the brush back. We just want Clairece returned."

CHAPTER 12

Anna woke up, shaking under blankets. Her teeth chattering might have been the sound pulling her out of sleep. Behind her eyeballs a steady, and sharp throbbing started. Closing her eyes only provided a sliver of consolation. Better than the alternative, she kept them closed. The temperature inside the bedchamber was freezing. As much as she did not want to move, she gathered the blankets and sat up in bed. It felt as if everything loose inside her head sloshed around. She waited for the room to stop spinning. When she became aware that it would not, she forced herself up onto unsteady legs. Her shoulders, back and hips ached. She felt sore all over.

With blankets over her shoulders like a giant, heavy cape, she shuffled into the library. It was no wonder she thought she'd freeze to death, at some point the fire had gone out. The small stack of logs needed replenishing. There were enough pieces cut that she wouldn't have to venture outside during the night, at least. Trying to keep the blankets over her shoulders, she stooped forward and stacked wood on the grate inside the hearth.

She aimed fingers and spoke the incantation for fire. Her palms tingled, and it felt like pins and needles pushing through her skin at her fingertips.

Anna sneezed.

The blanket slipped off her shoulders. She reached for it, but was not fast enough. The blanket bunched around her feet.

Her body trembled against the cold.

She tried igniting the fire again. It took tremendous energy, but she spoke the spell with more heart. Her tone of voice was insistent, and commanding.

The tingling returned. Tears welled up along the lower brims of her eyes.

She rubbed her hands up over her nightdress, and tucked her hands under her arms. She hadn't expected the pain. Her magic wasn't working. Although disheartening, her concern centered on the need for heat. On her knees in front of the heart, she struck the flint repeatedly until the kindling under the logs finally caught.

Her fingers closed around the corners of the blanket. Slowly she tugged it up and over her body. The cold was so deep inside her, she feared her bones had turned to ice. Her breath plumed in front of her face each time she exhaled. The hairs inside her nostrils were hard like nails.

Curling into a ball, she laid down on the hard floor as close to the fire as she thought was safe. Slowly flames from the kindling rose and licked at the new logs on the grate. It seemed as if hours passed by before, eventually, the logs blackened, and caught fire.

Wrapped tightly, Anna watched the flames dance.

Her eyelids became heavier. They fluttered a few times, and even though falling asleep suddenly scared her, she couldn't fight the need much longer.

She let her eyelids close.

***

Gembert showed Mykal and Blodwyn their room. It was as equally elegant as the apartment the baron and baroness stayed in.

Gembert provided a needless tour of the room. There were two bedchambers, and the main living area. "If there is anything you should desire, tug on this rope. A servant will arrive outside your door." The braided rope was gold, and red, with gold tassels at the end. "Once is sufficient. If there's anything else? Otherwise, supper will be served in two hours. I will send someone for you when it is time."

He left the apartment, closing the door behind him.

"Think he's mad?" Mykal said.

"Furious."

Mykal didn't want the chamberlain present when talking with Richmond and Henriette. It was essential whatever said wasn't indirectly, or *directly*, influenced by his presence. As it was, they didn't learn much. He wanted to talk with them more. If he could extract more information, or answers from the hair follicles and the brush, he might be able to save them additional pain from his questions.

He supposed over supper there would be an additional opportunity for digging. Someone knew something about the missing people. The images that had played out behind his eyes while inside the dovecote made a few things clear, or clearer, than they had been previously. His head began to ache. "I don't think we're here to make friends," Mykal said.

"That we are not." Blodwyn rested his staff against the wall and shrugged out of his cloak. He rolled his shoulders, and stretched his arms.

"Tired?"

"I wasn't. I hate to admit it, but those stairs took a bit of a toll. Shows how old I'm getting."

Mykal decided Blodwyn had the right idea. He leaned his staff against a wall and removed his cloak as well. "Then I must be old, too. My legs feel like rubber. I never thought after all of the training we've done a single staircase could wipe me out like this."

"Would you think less of me if I retire to the bedchamber for a period?"

Mykal waved his hand around. "No, please. Go and rest. In fact, it's a good idea. The sun will set soon. I doubt we'll have the chance to speak with any other families this night. I'm thinking after dinner we'll do some exploring. The more rested, the better."

"So you'll get some sleep, as well?"

"I may." Mykal turned the brush over in his hands. He thought about what Richmond said. There was no way he could take a mid-day nap knowing the baron was desperate for answers, closure.

"You're staying up, aren't you?"

Mykal's lips pursed together. "I am going to see if there is anything I can extract from this brush, or from Clairece's hair. If I have something right here in my hands, I can't in good conscience, go and lie down at this point. I just can't."

Blodwyn folded his arms. "Then let's see what the brush can tell us."

"I've got this, Wyn. Go. Get some rest. If anything turns up, I'll wake you. You have my word."

"I don't feel right sleeping if you're still working."

"It won't be working. It's more like playing in the dark. I'm not positive what I can learn from these items. It's just something of a hunch I have. Nothing might come from it. You could end up staying awake for nothing," Mykal said.

It was a long moment of silence, and Mykal saw the conflict on Blodwyn's twisted expression.

"Go to sleep, Wyn. I'll wake you. Promise."

"As long as you promise, I suppose I will," Blodwyn said. He gathered up his cloak and staff and stopped at one of the bedchamber doors. "Care which one?"

Mykal laughed. "I was going to pick that room. I'm just kidding. That's fine. The other is mine."

When Blodwyn was in his bedchamber, Mykal walked over to the sofa. He set the brush down next to a bowl of nuts on the small table in front of him. The two outer corners held small yellow candles in tall, thin glass holders. Pointing his finger at the wicks, one at a time, they lit.

He heard laughter. The sound carried in from outside the room. Curious, he went out into the hall. The laughter was an echo of some sort.

At the nearest window he peered out. Below, in the snow, someone was on their back, spreading arms and legs out.

It was one of the queens, but were too far away for Mykal to determine which one.

All while laughing, the child ruler stood, admired the depression in the snow, and then kicked away all signs of the angel she'd made.

Mykal knew with the thick panes of glass there was no way he should be able to hear laughter.

And when she looked up toward the glass, he did the one thing he could: slowly backed away, retreated into his room, shut and secured the apartment door.

He had no idea if she'd seen him, and wasn't sure how she'd known he was watching. Could she have felt his eyes on her? Had it been one of the queens? He couldn't say for certain.

He went back to the table. It was low to the ground, long, and rectangular. Across the room on a table against the wall that held more candles, Mykal emptied out, as neatly as possible, a bowl of potpourri. He started toward the couch, and stopped. He finger-combed through the assortment of potpourri, lifted a hunk of cinnamon stick for closer inspection, set it down, checked out some rose petals, and then decided the materials were too old and dried out. For the most part the mixture had also lost most of its fragrance.

As comfy as the couch was, he removed the pouch from his belt, and knelt on the floor. He set up the small vials of elements and herbs, twisting them so the small labels he'd made faced him. Pulling his hand into his tunic sleeve, Mykal used the clothing's material to swipe clean the bowl before adding any of his ingredients.

Next, Mykal removed as many of the strands of hair from the brush bristles as he could, and set them on one side of the bowl, and left the brush on the opposite side. He had a general idea of elements he'd use for the spell, and began working.

The base was mercury. He let a single, thick silver liquid drip into the bottom of the bowl. It wasn't something that easily blended when mixed. It generally maintained its independent makeup, however, and affixed itself onto everything. The scammony root came from a rare vine. The shavings were an earthy-brown. The energy was best released when fire was introduced to the concoction. Although more medicinal, it contained qualities associated with revenge, and vengeance, which wasn't exactly what Mykal sought, but he wasn't using the root on its own, and understood that mixtures produced an array of effects, in the way combining blue and yellow made green.

The violet petals from the centaurea cynas were packed in tight. Mykal tipped the vial and tapped one out onto his palm. The vibrant purple held his attention for just a moment before tipping his hand and watching the petal drop into the bowl. The opoponax resin, small earthy brownish red pebbles, provided the balance the scammony root required.

Thinking he had the ingredients needed, Mykal sat, with his legs crossed underneath the table and his chest pressed up against it, and using the pestle ground the contents together. He tapped the pestle on the edge of the bowl, knocking free the grains from the bulbous end.

Mykal lightly snapped his fingers over the bowl. It was more of a brushing of skin, than a snap. A small flame caught in the center, and went out. Orange embers smoldered, and a pungent odor wafted into the air accompanied by a thin wisp plume of smoke. Separating a single strand of hair, he twirled the ends around a finger on each hand and tugged. The hair didn't break, the result he hoped for. Strength in the single lock was not essential, but could prove more beneficial overall. He lowered the hair into the bowl.

Picking up the brush, Mykal passed the bristles clockwise over the bowl.

The single drop of mercury scattered into countless miniscule droplets, which all rose to the top of the ingredients, quivering, and before long rolled *counter* clockwise under the brush. Mykal noticed the droplets moved only over the long strand of hair, stripping away the hair's color.

The droplets rose into the air. It was as if the brush bristles and the mercury were magnetized, and drawn toward one another. He felt tremors pass through the handle. It made his forearm vibrate.

The candle flames bent, leaned toward the door, and then stood up straight. The flames extended into the air as if part of an explosion, and then extinguished with a hiss.

The room became darker.

Silver and violet smoke plumed out of the bowl. The colors twisted around each other, rising toward the high ceiling.

Mykal set down the brush, and sat back against the sofa.

He concentrated on the spell, unsure if the connection could be completed, and the contact made.

CHAPTER 13

A smoky mist clouded Mykal's vision. He wasn't sure if it was just a film over his eyeballs. His heart beat faster inside his chest, and his breathing became quick, and shallow. His skin felt clammy; cold, wet. Beads of perspiration dotted his forehead. He swiped his forearm across his brow.

Everything shimmied and swayed. The main room in the apartment made him wonder if he was underwater. He leaned forward onto the table, and pushed up onto his knees. Slowly, he managed getting up to his feet. He held his arms out, like a bird spreading its wings. Wobbling, left and right, he kept his footing. He swayed, but did not fall.

He thought inhaling mercury when the potion briefly burned gave off the aftereffect. It wasn't what he expected. The idea had been a mixture allowing for contact with Clairece's spirit. If she were dead, anyway. And if the young girl was still alive, which he hoped, but doubted, then a lead on where he could find her.

The idea of calling out for Blodwyn crossed his mind. He'd heard it described that too much wine or ale produced similar results. He enjoyed an ale now and again, but never consumed enough to alter his state of mind. The frequent emptying of his bladder was something else altogether. However, Blodwyn needed the rest, and aside from feeling dizzy and hallucinating, Mykal wasn't in any real danger.

"Find me."

The whisper was like a soft breeze that brushed past his ears. Mykal spun around. The sudden movement was too fast. He found himself standing on his heels. He teetered, tottered and fell backward. The couch caught him. Thankfully the furniture didn't crack, or crumble under the dropped weight. Sitting was almost a better position.

Only the wall was behind him.

He held his arms out in front of him, almost as if he were using them for balance, but actually, he pointed them around the room as a guide for his eyes.

"Please. Find me." The voice was female. Close.

Mykal looked at the space beside him on the couch. He expected someone to be sitting there. No one was. He was both relieved, and unnerved. Identifying the speaker was important. Identifying the speaker terrified him.

"Who are you?" He tried. He wasn't sure if he'd spoken the words out loud, or if they were just said inside his mind. Sweat rolled down his temple, toward his eye. He thumbed away the perspiration. "I can hear you, but I can't see you. Who is this?"

By the front door what little light was in the room mixed with the dark. Shadows moved, dancing. A shape formed, solidified.

She stood there in her maroon wool coat, arms by her side, hands pulling at her turquoise dress.

"Clairece." Mykal stood up. The room moved on him, and felt like it was spinning. As best he could, Mykal stepped around the small table in front of him. His knee banged into the corner. Bending forward, he rubbed the knee but did not stop walking. "Clairece. Where are you?"

"Are you here to help me?"

Mykal's eyes burned. They were dry. He didn't want to blink. He feared blinking might cause her to disappear. "I am. I want to find you. Do you know where you are? Where are you?"

"I'm here."

That can't be right. He reached her, and held out a tentative hand.

She reached him, her hand rising slowly.

They touched fingertips. Flesh to flesh.

"Where am I?" she said.

"I'm not sure."

"Where are you?"

Mykal shook his head, but never broke eye contact. "I don't know."

She smiled. It caught him off guard. "That's a silly thing to say."

Mykal let his hand hold hers. She was real. Solid. Standing in front of him. It wasn't a dream, or a side effect from the potion he'd made. "What happened to you? In the dovecote?"

Her smile deflated, brow furrowed. "I don't know what you mean."

"You were taken," Mykal said. Taken was the only word he could think to use. His earlier vision wasn't complete. He'd only seen a few moments captured by time. A part of him assumed the worse, and that whoever had attacked her in the dovecote may have killed her. And yet, here she was now standing in front of him. Alive, and well.

That didn't make sense. None. It couldn't be possible. He hadn't summoned her. That hadn't been the intent of the potion. The spell didn't work that way. Still, she was here.

It wasn't a bad thing. It was good. That was why the queens had called him in the first place. They wanted his help. He didn't think he could help them. He wasn't sure why they'd been so confident. He'd only been at the search for less than a day. Somehow, he'd found her.

That wasn't quite accurate. Found was the wrong word. She'd come to him. Perhaps, she'd answered his call?

He ran his hand up her arm. The smile returned. He liked it better when she smiled.

"You certainly are peculiar," she said, but didn't pull away from his touch.

"Where have you been?"

"Here." She slowly spun around, as if looking at everything in the room.

Mykal's hand never lost contact. His fingertips traced her body as she spun.

He knew she hadn't been in this room. Not for all of this time. Her parents were just down the hall. No one had been inside when Gembert showed them the apartment. Blodwyn would have noticed, and said something.

He would have noticed.

"Who harmed you?"

Again, she frowned, looking away. "I don't want to talk about it."

"Why?"

"It scares me."

"Who scares you?"

"Can't we talk about something else?"

"Who came into the dovecote when you were up there with the birds?"

She shook her head; her eyes were squeezed shut. "I don't want to talk about it."

"I need your help, Clairece. You might be the only one who can help me." He waited for her to stop shaking, and open her eyes. "Don't you want to do that, help me?"

"Of course, I do." She sighed. "What is your name?"

"Mykal."

"I like that name," she said.

This wasn't working. He wasn't getting through. "Clairece, someone is out there hurting people. Taking them. That person needs to be stopped."

Her jaw set. The whites of her eyes clouded over. Her skin, once soft, and creamy looking, yellowed. "Why do you keep bringing up bad things?"

Mykal jumped back.

Her tone of voice deepened.

There was a heat coming off her body.

Somewhere thunder boomed. The temperature in the apartment dropped.

Mykal shivered. He held up both hands, apologetically. "We don't have to talk about that, Clairece. We don't."

The skin lost the jaundice tint, and her eyes were crisp, and blue again. "I think I'm hungry."

Hungry. Supper would be served soon. He was certain Richmond and Henriette would throw a feast. A ball. It didn't seem likely, but their daughter was alive. Returned. The joyous occasion might be celebrated for days. Eventually, when she was calm, and the trauma from her experience subsided some, they could get the answers. Maybe the others that had gone missing were alive as well. One could hope!

Mykal remembered. "There are nuts!"

He went to the table. He wished and retrieved a handful. When he turned around, she was gone. He was alone in the room. The nuts fell out of his hand, and dropped onto the floor.

"Mykal?"

"Clairece?"

"Mykal?"

It wasn't Clairece. It was a man's voice.

His eyelids fluttered.

Blodwyn was in front of him.

Over him.

Above was the ceiling.

He blinked hard once, twice. "Wyn?"

"Are you okay?"

Mykal was on his back, on the floor. His vision was clear. Clearer. It didn't feel like he was under water any longer. "I saw her again."

"Who?"

"Clairece. Only this time, she saw me, too." He sat up with Blodwyn's assistance. "I think she might still be alive."

CHAPTER 14

The long table in the dining hall was set for six at one end. The opposite side was empty; the wood polished, but looked plain and ordinary compared to the white plates, silver forks, spoons and knives, the gold goblets, and folded linens. Each place setting sat on the red velvet tablecloth with gold trim. Two decanters filled with wine, a white and a red, were offset in the center, around the courses hidden under shiny silver bubble lids, and amidst tall candles.

Mykal didn't think he'd be hungry. Once the aroma from the food reached his nose his stomach growled. He placed a hand over his belly, as if calming an excited dog. The magic performed left him feeling a bit queasy, and he knew if he were tested, walking a straight line might prove challenging. However, he thought he could eat.

Richmond and Henriette sat side-by-side, their backs toward one of the near floor-to-ceiling, slender windows. They held hands, clasped together on top of the table. Both offered thin smiles, and Richmond nodded a hello.

Mykal saw the questions in their eyes, the way they made eye contact, but then looked away. He knew it took tremendous restraint not asking. He couldn't imagine the torment kept hidden inside their hearts, and minds. Soon, he hoped he could offer them... something.

Gembert pulled back a chair for Blodwyn. "For you," he said.

"Thank you." Blodwyn sat, and then Gembert pulled back the chair for Mykal.

"Thank you."

"You're welcome. Your host, the Queens, will be joining you shortly."

The hall remained silent. Only the sound of Gembert's footfalls as he walked the length of the hall could be heard. He exited, and gently closed the doors behind him.

The four were not alone.

An armed member of the queens' guard stood in front of each of the twelve stone pillars, which ran the length of the hall, six on either side. They were quiet, unmoving, more like statues than people. They wore dark red tunics, and fitted chainmail under off white quilted vests that bore the Cordillera sigil on the front.

"Supper smells wonderful." Mykal smiled, but ground his teeth, too.

"Yes, it does." Henriette returned the smile, equally as flat, and unnatural.

No one spoke. Blodwyn sat nearly as still as the guards stood.

Mykal's stomach rumbled some more. He wished it to stop. The noise embarrassed him, and he knew his cheeks flushed. Just when it seemed like screaming for the simple release of tension sounded like the best idea, the large double doors at the opposite end of the dining hall opened. The hinges whined as if in objection to having to work.

A guard was at either door, and stepped aside. The queens ceremoniously entered the dining hall. Blodwyn nudged Mykal with his elbow, as he rose.

The others followed suit.

The four dinner guests stood as the queens reached the head of the table.

Queen Raaheel wore her hair down; long, coiled curls bounced like springs with each step taken. The pearl-colored dress was form fitting against a flat belly, and laced at the bodice; pleated sleeves started at wrist, but became puffy around the shoulders.

The younger queen, Sarah, wore a velvet crimson tunic, and silk crimson dress. Her light-colored hair was braided, and pulled away from her face, exposing exquisite eyes. "Please be seated," she said.

The guards pushed in the queens' chairs. The sisters lifted the folded linens, shook them open and placed them in their laps. In unison. It was an odd thing to watch. Mykal followed their lead, setting his linen over his leg.

Raaheel lifted a small bell and gave it a shake.

It rang.

Servants, wearing white aprons, entered the dining hall. For the next several minutes the room was abuzz with activity as the servers prepared dishes for the six of them. Scooping, and spooning, and carving food for each plate.

Sarah separated many of the colorful vegetables out of her meal, grimacing at the tedious work. Raaheel, on the other hand, used her fingers and picked meat off bone; she frequently made *Mmmm* sounds, as if it were the best food she'd ever eaten.

"Blodwyn and I appreciate your hospitality," Mykal said, a fork in his left hand, a knife in the right, and his eyes on the spectacle the queens made.

Queen Sarah looked up from her plate, and as if guilty over having been caught playing with her food, stared at Mykal for a long moment before nodding. "My sister and I also appreciate your services. It was rather an abrupt request we made, and I am sure you were quite busy with your own matters. Word of your great power has spread across the entire old empire, and beyond, we're told."

"You've become something of a legend," Queen Raaheel added, despite a look of scorn from her younger sibling.

If Mykal didn't know better, he'd swear each complimentary word she said was accompanied by the swallowing of chewed glass. "Blodwyn and I are happy to help."

"And have you discovered anything about what has happened to the missing people, or the identity of who might be responsible for the heinous acts committed?" Other than the linen placed in her lap, Queen Sarah showed no sign of interest toward the meal set in front of her. Her elbows were on the table, and her hands folded together in front of her face. She watched Mykal over fingertips, and between knuckles.

Mykal wished he hadn't glanced over at Henriette. Too late.

She also stared at him.

He got the uncanny feeling that supper was more of a prop. It was a shame. The beef smelled perfectly delicious. On top of the now near-constant gurgling coming from the pit of his gut, his mouth was watering. If he didn't swallow some of the pooling saliva, he might drool when he spoke.

"We have nothing to report, yet." It wasn't a lie. Aside from visions, he only had some clues that pointed in a particular direction. It was far too soon for finger pointing. Until he had gathered more information he had no intention of accusing anyone. "There are some things we'd like to follow up on. More questions we'd like to ask."

Queen Sarah rolled her lips into her mouth. She might have been biting down on them, as well. Either way, she looked less than pleased.

"Do you have questions for us?" Queen Raaheel said. This young lady was far more diplomatic. The sisters might not be thrilled a wizard was called to investigate the disappearances over their capable thane, but at least Raaheel knew how to mask the annoyance.

Mykal had the linen bunched inside his hands. It must have been a nervous tick, although he didn't realize he'd been doing it. Absently, and perhaps just out of habit, Mykal dabbed the corners of his mouth, and set the linen down on the table next to a full plate of uneaten food. "Not for either of you, at the moment, your highnesses. But, Baron, Baroness, if you don't mind I do have one or two more questions I'd like to ask?"

The couple looked at each other, and then back at him. "We don't mind," Richmond said. "Please, ask."

"When did you arrive here at the castle?" Mykal wanted to establish some kind of a timeline. He knew the young girl went missing just a few nights ago. While in his first vision he saw through the eyes of an attacker, and in the second was able to communicate with Clairece. He knew that necromancy-related ingredients were included in both mixed potions. He was not willing to accept what that might mean. Not yet.

"We arrived more than a week ago." Richmond still held his wife's hand, but had placed his other hand over the top, and patted softly.

"And you came from where?"

"During the War, King Hermon sent us to live in Eridanus, with hopes of reestablishing the kingdom under Cordillera's reign." The baron nodded respectfully toward the queens. "The castle is still uninhabitable, as are most of the surrounding villages. We're not sure what war the destruction came from—"

"Trolls."

If Mykal didn't know the sound of Blodwyn's voice, he might have wondered who'd spoken the single word. Blodwyn sat still, and silent.

Richmond's next words looked like they might have frozen inside his mouth.

"There are no trolls in the old empire," Queen Sarah said. "Besides, they're not known to be violent beasts."

Blodwyn flinched at the description. He simply nodded, as if rescinding.

"Did you see the trolls attack?" Queen Sarah asked.

They were getting off track, Mykal knew, but the idea of trolls destroying a kingdom, Karyn's kingdom, captured his attention. Karyn came to him before he knew he was a wizard. She claimed she'd dreamed of him, and that it was her duty, and her honor, to protect him. She was a ward to King Nabal in Grey Ashland. Her gift was healing. It was also her demise. Her father sent her to live in Grey Ashland, but before she was old enough to return her homeland was leveled. Blodwyn never mentioned trolls before. Was it that he didn't want Karyn traumatized by more truth?

"I did not."

"Then you can't say for sure, can you?" The queen *humphed.*

"I apologize for my speculation, your highness."

A dismissive wave, and a roll of her eyes, was the young queen's reply. "Please, wizard, won't you continue your line of questioning?"

She sounded bored with it all.

Mykal didn't let that rattle him. "Did you cross the Zenith Mountains?"

Richmond nodded, thoughtfully. "It was quite treacherous. We lost several people in the entourage. Had there of been another way of crossing, we'd surely have taken advantage."

There was another way to get from the west to the east. The Isthmian. People of the old empire weren't likely to attempt the excursion. Dangerous sea serpents swam just below the surface, and Voyagers ruled the sea. Prior to, and during the War, Mykal learned plenty about the Voyagers, and was thankful for the alliance. "How many people were you traveling with?"

"Nearly fifty."

"And how many did you lose before reaching the castle?"

"Fifteen."

That was a lot of death. Mykal understood the baron's desire to pay his respects to the fallen king, and to pledge his loyalty to the new queens. The trip was unavoidable.

"I am sorry for your losses."

"Are you going somewhere with this?" Queen Sarah didn't hide her frustration.

"Sarah!"

"I've a meeting with Axel. Unlike the rest of us, his men are scouring the Rames searching for the missing people, not dining on a fancy meal chit-chatting with guests." The queen stood up. "If you will excuse me. I am sure my sister is more than capable moderating the rest of the discussion. I have a kingdom that needs ruling, and subjects in fear for their safety."

Mykal wondered where the dining on a fancy meal comment might have come from. Not one person had tried a bite.

A guard followed the queen out of the dining hall.

Queen Raaheel's cheeks reddened, and for just a moment she was unable to make eye contact with anyone at the table. She sucked in a deep breath and then quietly exhaled, her hands were folded in her lap. "Please, Sorcerer, continue."

Sorcerer. Mykal thought the title made him sound old. He imagined a sorcerer with a long white beard, and liver-spotted skin; tall and scrawny, with a slight bend at the shoulders. Hunched forward the staff, not for fighting, was used for support to keep from toppling over. "While traveling, did you notice anything out of the ordinary?"

"Like what?" Richmond asked.

"Well, anything. Were you followed?"

Richmond's eyes consulted with his wife's. She shook her head. "No," he answered. "I wasn't aware of anyone following us. And if any of the knights noticed something, they didn't mention it."

"Would they?" Mykal knew the knights would have been loyal to the crown. If this were some elaborate conspiracy... but, no. That didn't make sense. It wasn't that a message couldn't have been sent to Eridanus, where the knights could plot.

"They would. We have worked, and lived side-by-side for the last two years. In that time, I firmly believe we've become friends. I'm sorry, your highness. Their loyalty is for you and your sister, as is ours. The frontier we settled insisted on more than baron and knight, superior and servant."

"No apologies necessary. In fact, it warms my heart knowing bonds were forged. I think my father would have been equally pleased," Queen Raaheel said.

"At any point, on the road, or since you arrived at the castle, can you think of anything that has stood out as odd?" Mykal knew carefully using his words was essential. Broaching delicate subjects about Osiris in front of the queen could easily be misconstrued. Regardless of whether invited, or not, he didn't want his questions considered treasonous and find himself locked away.

Richmond wasn't quick to answer. Again he consulted his wife with just a look. They stared at one another. It was almost like Richmond was looking inside Henriette for any answers, and she inside of him.

Without a sound, Richmond turned his attention back toward Mykal. "Since our arrival, the we've spent days catching up with old friends, and some family. Supper has been spent in the company of the queens, most graciously. And, of course, we've had countless meetings discussing the progress and plans for Eridanus. Once completed it will once again be a magnificent kingdom, only this time under the queens' rule."

Richmond and Queen Raaheel were smiling at one another.

"And Clairece?" Mykal asked.

"What about her?"

"Where was she most of the time?"

Richmond cleared his throat, and tugged at the collar around his neck. "We've family here, both of us. They've not seen each other in some time."

"Was she mostly in the company of your family, baron, or with your wife's?"

Henriette's lips thinned, and her brow furrowed. "What are you insinuating?"

"Nothing, baroness. I don't mean any disrespect. I'm just trying to figure all of this out. I believe retracing everything your daughter did, we'll be able to see what happened."

"See?"

"Figuratively speaking, your highness." Mykal felt thankful he kept the results from the two spells casted from them. They were far too emotional at the moment. Word that he'd seen, and spoken with Clairece would only upset everyone, and create more tension.

"Clairece spent most days with my wife's sister, Elma."

"Your highness?" Mykal was hesitant, but proceeded. "With your permission, I would like to speak with baroness' sister."

"Of course."

"And, the young woman who found us, Geneva? I would like to speak with her family as well. Her Aunt Deidre is also missing. Deidre had three children. Perhaps Geneva can escort us around the villages in Osiris?"

"Gembert would be more than happy to accompany you as you search for answers," the queens said.

"I can tell he is valuable to you. The last thing I want is to burden you with our presence, and occupying all of Gembert's time doesn't seem fair." People were not going to talk freely in front of the queen's chamberlain. The man would prove more of a thorn than an asset in the quest. There was no way of explaining this to Queen Raaheel. Implying anything remotely close would be in poor taste, and bad judgment.

"I insist."

Mykal forced a smile. "Then it's settled. However," he said.

"Yes?"

"I would still appreciate Geneva's assistance, if that is not asking too much," he said.

The request had as much impact on her expression, her poise, as if he'd asked for salt for his uneaten, and now cold meat. "You can have whatever you need, Sorcerer. I want this nightmare resolved. The sooner the better. My sister is absolutely correct. Our people are struggling with too many issues right now. They still mourn the loss of their king, and rightfully so. My father was an amazing man," she said.

Mykal expected the jab would feel like a sharp knife plunged deep into his chest. There was no malice in her words. None he could detect, anyway. Even if she didn't know for sure, rumors alone should have set her on guard against him. After all, the blood from her father's death inadvertently stained his hands.

He decided against responding to her claim, and simply nodded. It wasn't exactly in agreement, but neither would he call her a liar.

Queen Raaheel let her fingers trace the modest crown on her head. Her eyes looked upward, as if she could see the iron. A lackadaisical smile spread across her face. She reminded Mykal of a child playing dress-up. "Two queens confuse the subjects, but slowly, if not surely, they'll come around to accept a dual ruling, and may even one day admit satisfaction of having two views overseeing all matters kingdom related. If you add to those adjustments the fact that several people have gone missing, with nothing but exaggerated scary stories as a means of explanation…"

"I completely understand, your highness." Despite being such a young queen, Mykal could not overlook obvious intelligence. She, and her sister, must have been groomed about the ways of the kingdom since before they were out of the cradle.

"Do you?" Queen Raaheel's bright brown eyes darkened. Perhaps stress caused the shadow, definitely frustration, and fear could be blamed. Her jaw set, she said, "*Can* you?"

CHAPTER 15

"I'm not real comfortable with how the trip is going." Mykal stood in the center of the vestibule, the hearth burning hot behind him. He let his staff rest in the crook of an arm. It was early on the following morning. The sun was not only up, but visible in a blue sky. The storm must have finally passed. It was a blessing. They were headed outside soon. Mykal was set on talking with family members of the people who'd gone missing.

"Why are you talking like that?" Blodwyn, standing beside the wizard, kept both hands on his staff, and as usual, lightly tapped the end on the floor.

"Like what?"

"Out of the side of your mouth."

Mykal couldn't resist an eye roll as he checked over each shoulder. "I was trying to be discreet."

"Discreet?"

"Don't you get the feeling we're never quite alone?"

This time Blodwyn examined the surroundings. He made an exaggerated show of it, leaning forward, bending backward. "There is no one else around. You're whispering so softly I can barely hear you. And we're what, less than a foot apart from each other?"

It was something just beyond Mykal's peripheral vision, a shadow he never saw entirely, but sensed there. Every once in a while, hairs on the back of his neck stood. He'd swear he felt the trace of breath over his skin. The uncanny sense of being watched, eavesdropped on, was genuine, and more than some fragment in his imagination.

He couldn't properly explain it, and just let Blodwyn have his fun. "The queens have an issue with us. Queen Sarah, anyway. I'm not sure what we did wrong, but we've obviously gotten off on the wrong foot. I'm just wondering if there is something I should do to rectify the situation?"

He thought about Clairece. It crossed his mind she was what haunted his eyes, and blew on his neck. Although he'd touched her the other night, he wasn't convinced she'd been real. It seemed more than likely she had been an aberration. He'd not yet confided in Blodwyn the events from the last experience. He wasn't keeping anything from his friend. The idea they were being closely watched was what prevented the discussion from taking place.

"Remember what I told you. Royalty took offense when wizards were called on for assistance. It is like a slap in the face. They take it personally. Kings and queens are accustomed to handling problems on their own. In most cases, they'd prefer a problem didn't exist. Ignoring issues worked for centuries. When an outsider is brought in, however, it solidifies the issue. Makes it real. Others are now watching. They can't pretend everything is alright any longer. They are then forced to address concerns, like it or not." Blodwyn said everything in a barely audible whisper, while talking out of the side of his mouth.

Mykal ignored the taunt, and hid his smile as best he could. "I'm sure you're right."

"Try not to take it personally."

"Hard not to." They were waiting on Gembert. He was off fetching Geneva. She would escort them through the villages, giving Mykal the chance to interview family members. Someone had to have observed something. It didn't seem likely that at least three abductions took place without a witness.

"Any word from your mother?" Blodwyn spoke in a normal tone of voice, and it sounded as if he shouted. The spacious hall was empty, and the hanging tapestries didn't seem to absorb sound they Mykal thought they might have.

Mykal could communicate with his mother inside his mind. It was something she called telepathy. It was a specific kind of magic that not all wizards could perform. "I tried reaching her last night after supper. For some reason, I couldn't get through. I wasn't sure if the winter storm was responsible, or if the mountain range prevented the connection."

Blodwyn set a hand on Mykal's shoulder. "I wouldn't worry. She was either sleeping, or preoccupied. Your mother isn't one to sit idle long."

That was the problem. "I am worried, though. I was also wondering why she hadn't tried reaching me yet. I was starting to think wizards can't get sick. We're not immortal, but knowing that we live such long lives..."

"You are *not* immortal. Sickness strikes everyone, even wizards, I imagine."

Mykal never dreamed of living forever, but at the same time didn't think about his death. He'd only recently reconnected with his mother. She had met Blodwyn when he was a child. Now he looked twice her age. "How come I'm not sick? Or you?"

The sound of footfalls came from behind them. They turned and saw Gembert and Geneva walking toward them.

"Who can say? Try reaching her again. I'll bet last night's storm was the problem."

Gembert kept his hands laced together in front of him, while Geneva's arms swung loosely at her sides. Both of them were dressed for the weather in heavy, long coats. Neither looked thrilled. Mykal was sure the idea of going back out into the cold had something to do with the frowns worn.

"I considered that."

"See," he said. "I highly doubt we're both wrong."

Mykal fell silent.

Blodwyn went back to whispering. "She'll be fine, Mykal. We'll be back home before you know it."

"Thank you, Wyn, but if I can't reach her tonight, I'm going back to the library to check on her." He could transport himself there in seconds, make sure she was doing okay, and return to the castle without anyone realizing he'd left.

It wouldn't matter if anyone knew, regardless. He wasn't a prisoner.

"That's a wonderful idea." Blodwyn was all smiles. "Really, that was a solution I should have thought of. I'm disappointed in myself."

Mykal grinned. "Yes. You should have, *teacher.*"

***

The blue skies and the bright morning sun were a facade, misleading. The wind blew around some of the coldest air Mykal had ever breathed. With his face exposed, he found it difficult catching his breath. They walked against the wind, which didn't help. Loose snow on the ground was whipped into eddies around them. His face felt numb, and by looking at the others, knew his cheeks must be red as ripe tomatoes.

The pass they followed was wide, flat. Almost as if they were on a plain, rather than traversing their way around to the side of a mountain.

"My aunt lives in the village behind the castle." Geneva hugged herself. Plumes of smoke escaped her lips when she talked, and sprayed from her nostrils when she finished speaking. The collar on her coat was raised. She hunkered forward, bracing herself as best she could against the cold. "Lived."

"Don't say that. We don't know what's happened to her yet. And you said she has three children?" Mykal's foot sank in a shallow bank of snow, and it caused him to stumble. He almost fell.

Geneva caught his arm.

"Thank you."

"You're welcome." She smiled. "She has three children, yes. They're around my age."

"And how old are you?"

Something thumped Mykal on the back of the head.

"Ouch!" Mykal rubbed the spot, turning around.

Blodwyn's eyebrows were raised, a silent warning. He pantomimed thwacking him once more with the head of his staff.

Geneva laughed. "It's alright."

"Did I miss something?" Mykal asked.

Gembert had no problem releasing a loud, long sigh. "It is impolite to ask a woman her age."

Mykal looked at Geneva. "Is that so?"

She gave up a tiny shrug. "Like I said, it's alright. I'm ten and eight."

A year older than Mykal? He was kind of surprised, thinking she was at least had him by a decade. It wasn't meant as a cruel thought, but was just based on his perception. He wondered if mountain living took a different kind of toll on the body. Maybe thin air and cold temperatures were averse to aging?

"I look older, I know," she said.

Mykal, again, rubbed the back of his head. He understood the rap received now. "That's not it. I'm ten and seven," he said.

"Are you?" She regarded him closely, but only by staring into his eyes. "I'd not have guessed a day over ten and four. Five, maybe."

He stopped walking.

Blodwyn almost collided into his back.

Geneva laughed, pointing a finger at his nose. "Gotcha!"

She continued on.

Blodwyn leaned in close. "I think she fancies you. But, remind me when we get home that you need some life lessons I'd never thought before to give, *student.*"

Blodwyn and Gembert walked on.

Mykal took just a moment longer behind them.

Geneva fancied him? More importantly he wondered, *Did I really only look ten and four?*

The arrow landed in the snow in front of him.

It was so unexpected, he stood and stared at the fletching with his head cocked slightly to the side. The wind passed through ruffling the trimmed turkey feathers.

It was just a moment of pause, though.
Mykal lunged forward, yelling, "Take cover!"

Chapter 16

"Take cover!" Mykal held his staff horizontally, which made running easier. He knew there weren't many places for hiding.

The arrow came from behind them, and possibly from above. He fought the urge to look back. Once safely out of a line of fire, he'd be in a better position to see what was what. It wasn't himself he was worried about.

Blodwyn pushed Gembert and Geneva in front of him. They made their way toward a crevasse.

More arrows were loosed. They flew fast, and silent, but not true. The wind must have impeded the archer's aim.

Geneva went down.

Mykal thought she'd been struck.

He reached them just as Blodwyn was lifting her back up onto her feet.

The cloaks they wore were made from shredded dragon scales. The plates were not impregnable, but should stop the broad head of most arrows.

Mykal gripped the lapels between the collar and his waist, and spread his arms out wide. He stood over Blodwyn and Geneva, a shield protecting them.

Gembert reached the chasm and wedged himself between the slabs of mountain rock.

Arrows bounced off the cloak.

His head, however, was not fortified, and later he would think about what might have happened if one of the archers sent an arrow through the back of his skull.

He bowed his head as forward as possible as he ran, following behind Blodwyn and Geneva.

Once they were safe, tucked away with Gembert, Mykal spun around.

Anger filled him.

He waved hands back and forth, his arms stretched out in front of him.

Snow encircled him, picking up speed, and buzzing around his head.

The tornado became a part of him, and then he stepped out of the center. He left the storm in front of the crevasse. It would shield the others. No arrow could pass through the chaos he'd created.

Standing in front of the whirlwind, Mykal scanned the range. Someone was out there. Could have been more than just one. With the wind, and sun glare, hiding above them could be easy.

Whoever it was, the attempted ambush was a bad mistake, and now they would pay for the cowardly attack.

As soon as he could find them.

Nothing in the beyond moved.

Mykal scoured every nook and cranny. He didn't see anyone.

He could wait them out.

The cold would get to them. He'd ignore it for as long as it took. Eventually they would make a mistake. He'd spot it.

He'd wait. As long as it took.

It didn't take long. Twenty feet above him, and to the right he caught movement.

He cast his arm out, his hand curled into a fist. A blue light shot from his knuckles. The beam zapped the side of the mountain. Chunks of rock splintered off the face, a large flat section calved. The rock and snow on the range fell away. The slab struck the pass, and toppled forward, shattering as if made of glass.

A man wearing white, holding a bow, stood with his back pressed against the side of the mountain.

Mykal dropped his staff and raised both arms, aiming them at the man. His fingers clutched at thin air, and with a jerk, he flung his arms down, and diagonally. It was as if he had actually gripped the attacker by the shoulders, and pulled the man with the bow off the ledge. Somersaulting through the air, the man landed on his back on the snow. Despite the wind, there was no ignoring the hollow crunch.

Mykal was on him before he had time to catch his breath, kneeling on the guy's chest, he fisted the man's coat at the chest and lifted his head into the air.

That's when he saw it.

Blood spilled from the back of the guy's skull. Red stained the snow, melting it. Steam that smelled like copper rose from the spreading pool.

Mykal saw the jagged rock.

It was an unfortunate death. He'd passed before giving Mykal any answers.

Mykal released the man, and stood up. Waving his hands back and forth, the whirlwind dissipated.

Blodwyn flew out of the crevasse. "Are you okay?"

"He's dead."

Blodwyn stared at the blood, and then looked up at Mykal.

"I'd have killed him. But not before getting answers. He fell on a rock. I suppose you can call it accidental." Mykal watched Geneva retrieve his staff, and walk toward them. Gembert stood by the crevasse. He didn't look convinced the threat was neutralized, his eyes searched all around them.

"Ah, Wizard?" Gembert stood still, jaw dropped open, and the color drained from his face. He pointed up, over Mykal's head.

Mykal knew before looking what he'd find.

He'd been correct.

A wall of warriors dressed in white like the dead man in the snow at his feet lined the ledge. "Geneva, Gembert, get back in the rocks!"

Mykal dropped his arms down at his sides, and then with all of the force he could muster, clapped them together in front of his face with his arms extended. Blue sparks shot off his palms. Heat raced up his arms. Just before a spiraling beam of blue exploded from his fingertips and zapped the mountain, the warriors leapt off the edge. Rocks blew away from the ledge. Steam rose from snow melting. They landed on snow, and rolled safely before jumping back up onto their feet. With bows slung over chest and shoulders, they each held a long, straight-bladed sword.

The magic drained Mykal's energy.

Geneva shouted: "Mykal!"

The warriors didn't waste a moment. They let out a yell—the sound bounced off the sides of the mountain—as they charged.

Mykal spun around. His cloak swirled outward around his legs. Geneva had already launched his staff through the air. Mykal caught it, and continued his turn, arcing the staff around first so that the end of the staff smacked into a sword.

"Run, Geneva! Run!"

The warrior struck at Mykal again, swinging his sword from left to right. Mykal blocked it, and didn't let up. Instead, he used the warrior's momentum to his advantage.

"I'm not leaving you!"

Mykal didn't have time for arguing. He stepped through with his rear foot and pressed down on his staff, pinning the warrior's sword onto the icy ground. "Gembert, get Geneva out of here!"

Mykal's right foot came forward. He placed his leg behind the warrior's so that the top of his thigh was pressed to the bottom of the warrior's, and raised his staff, twisting his torso, and knocking the man off balance, and dropping him onto his back.

Mykal heard Geneva protest. He saw Gembert pulling her away, forcing her toward the crevice. "Wyn?" Mykal held the staff in the middle. In a full chambering motion, slammed the head of the staff, and then the base of the staff into the fallen warrior, who groaned after the first strike, and was silent for the second.

Blodwyn was engaged in a fight, as well. The warriors encircled him. They attacked with swords raised. One warrior thrust a sword toward Blodwyn's gut. Blodwyn swung down with one end of his staff, and followed around with the opposite end which connected with the side of the man's face. He brought the staff down fast on the man's right hand, dislodging the sword from his grip.

The blow knocked the warrior off his feet, *and* knocked him out cold.

Another came from behind, and caught Mykal off guard. It felt like a tree trunk falling across his ribs. Mykal stepped over one of the downed warriors, stumbled, and then dropped. He fell onto his hands and knees.

He wasn't breathing, air felt trapped inside his stomach. Gasping, he struggled for breath.

Sensing another stabbing strike, he rolled over onto his back. He raised his staff in both hands over his chest. The arcing blade clanked against the iron and wood staff. Mykal half expected it would split in two. Thankfully, it held together. Solid.

Air filled his body. It didn't rush back in the way he wished. The process, and the relief, was slow, painful.

There wasn't time for worrying about silly things like breathing.

His life hung in the balance, as did the lives of his friends. The camouflaged warriors wanted blood.

They knew where Mykal and the others were headed, or had been following them.

The warriors must be tied to the disappearances. If Mykal couldn't get back on his feet, it wouldn't matter. He'd never solve the mystery.

He rocked his legs into the air, and kicked out. The bottoms of his boots slammed into the warrior's hips, and stomach, sending him flailing backwards. Mykal twirled his staff back, and over his shoulders, transferring the staff from his right hand, to his left. He spun around, ready to defend himself against more enemies.

Blodwyn spun around with his staff, as well, and struck out with the bottom end, connecting with the flailing man's neck. The propulsion brought the man's feet up so that for a moment, he was nearly horizontal before falling flat onto the snow.

Blodwyn dropped his knees onto the man's back, and threw a punch into the back of his neck.

Mykal stood up. The staff was under an arm, the head pointed out in front of him, and the base behind him. He thrust his left arm forward, palm out, fingers up.

Knowing his energy was nearly spent, his power mostly depleted, Mykal reacted smartly deciding the elements around him would be the easiest defense. His hands moved in circular motions in front of him. A charge tingled in his feet. It rose up his legs.

Behind his eyeballs he saw a flood of colors. Strands of black and bright blue wove around yellows and greens. Wisps of orange and purple twirled at the edge of the back corners of his eyes.

The colors were something new. When another wizard used magic, and he sometimes saw strands of color coming from them. This was different. There weren't any other wizards around. The colors swirled around inside of *him*. It was as if he saw his own magic performing.

Regardless, the bands of color were there, and it was distracting.

Mykal moved snow. Pillars rose into the air. The snow was wet, heavy. He blew his breath toward them, thankful it no longer hurt to do so. The pillars turned into ice, and became nearly transparent. The sun sparkled against the near-glass ice. Prisms passed through, shined like a rainbow spewing from the cylindrical mass.

Stumped by the display, the warriors stopped and stared. The stunned fraction of a second was what Mykal wanted. He pushing against nothing but air, feet away from the pillars. The space between his palms and the pillars became charged. The pillars toppled over, and the warriors dove in an attempt to get out of the way. The pillar came down on the back of a man's legs. He fell forward. His sword flew from his hand. The weight of the ice flattened his thighs. Blood spilled out of his mouth.

Another pillar landed on a different warrior, trapping him underneath, and crushing his legs. He screamed for help, dropped his sword, and punched at the ice with both hands.

There were too many of them.

"Go with the others, Wyn. I'll catch up!"

There was no answer.

Mykal looked over his shoulder, and feared what he might find.

Blodwyn was still on his feet, battling two men. He saw exhaustion in Blodwyn's expression. The man's lips were tightly pursed, his face red, brow furrowed, jaw set. Mykal knew more warriors were coming at him. In order for his friend to escape he needed help. Mykal reached toward the men with both hands. He closed his hands into fists. It was almost like he had grabbed each one by the back of the collar. When he threw his arms to the side, he felt the weight in his forearms. It was nowhere near as heavy as lifting two men, but there was a sensation of mass. The men came up off the ground and passed through the air for about five feet before crashing into the side of the mountain.

"Run, Wyn. Run! Get the other two out of here!"

"No!" Blodwyn shouted. He held the staff with both hands in the center, and slammed one end into the face of a warrior, and then pivoted his weight and punched the opposite end into the throat of a warrior attacking from behind.

A line of warriors with swords drawn started toward them.

"I've got them. I'll catch up. Make sure the others are safe!"

Despite the reluctance evident in Blodwyn's features, he retreated. Mykal couldn't watch long. The warriors were closing in. They demanded his attention. He'd have to assume Blodwyn obeyed the order, and would whisk the others away.

Mykal panted. His breathing became labored once again. He knew the blow he'd taken on the back was going to leave a giant bruise.

With his adrenaline surging, he wasn't aware of the cold, though he saw the plumes burst from between his lips.

The air was thin, too thin. Breathing faster, harder, didn't seem to fill his lungs the way it should have.

Thinking was tough.

He was a wizard, but had no idea what to do next. The elements worked against him. The cold. The air. His energy levels drained. He was almost on empty.

Standing took more effort.

He'd seen a just-born fawn balance better than he could sustain at the moment.

His right arm slid left. Left went right. Legs bent, and bowed, and broke. Men screamed.

Mykal raised an arm in the air. Dropped it down. Then repeated the motions with his other arm. Heads' blew back, bottom jaws shattered. Blood spurt out of noses. Teeth fell out of mouths, and disappeared silently into the snow.

It was lazy magic.

But it was working.

He stepped toward them, some flanked him. He spun around, his arm low, hand sideways.

They went down, one after the other. Hollers echoed. There was no mistaking the pain. The warriors felt it.

Not one was left standing. The bodies were all strewn about.

An arrow whizzed by his head, clipping an earlobe. He winced, and touched a fingertip against the gash. Mykal looked up and saw more men; strange warriors dressed in white, and armed with swords.

He didn't have the strength to fight them all. There was only one option left.

Mykal ran for the crevasse. He imagined a broad head striking his back, piercing not just the cloak, but plunging between his shoulder blades. He almost cringed from the imagined pain. Instead, he quickened his step.

When he reached the sanctuary, he spun around in time to see them jumping down from the ledge and into the snow.

Mykal, leaning his back against the side of the mountain for support, held his hands by his chin. He then pushed them down, and forward.

The ice pillars rolled.

The pass they were on was flat, but there was another ledge. The warriors in white had nowhere else to run. One man attempted jumping over the pillar. He ended up plopping down on top of it. He slid back as the pillar rolled toward over him. The weight crushed his feet. Ankles crunched. The bones in his legs fractured. His screams became gurgles as the blood bubbled inside his mouth he drowned.

Mykal concentrated on snow around the crevasse, aimed hands at the ground, wiggled fingers, and let them stiffen as he raised them into the air.

The wall of snow covered the narrow opening.

He blew onto it, all over the wall.

Just like the pillars, the wall turned to ice.

Mykal knew it wouldn't stop the warriors, but should slow them.

That gave them some kind of head start. There might have been additional passes both above and below. It could mean the lead was merely imaginary, and another small band of warriors waited for them on the other side.

He had let the others run on ahead.

They could be in trouble!

CHAPTER 17

Anna, on her knees in the corner of her bed chamber, rested forearms and hands on the rounded edge of a large, wooden bucket. She'd vomited so much the last few hours nothing was left. Sweating, her hair was matted against her face, and forehead. All at once her stomach heaved. Clear bile rose up from her gut and rekindled the burning sensation from vomiting along the length of her throat. Long strands dangled from her lips. She gasped for air between retching. The muscles in her stomach felt knotted, and sore.

After running a finger along her mouth and scraping mucus into the bucket, she sat with her legs under her and used her hand to brush hair from her eyes. Involuntary tears, and sweat watered her vision.

Chills racked her body, as well as aches and pains. She wasn't sure she had the strength to climb back up into bed. All she wanted was to be under the blankets. It wasn't like she'd be able to sleep. Her illness prevented her from getting any rest, but just the thought of wrapping her body with a blanket gave her the incentive to try. Pushing herself away from the bucket of puke was the easy part.

Crawling, she nearly screamed. She bit back the cry, and chewed on her lower lip. Her bones felt brittle. Old. Radiating pain encircled her wrists, elbows, and shoulders. There was an indescribable throb around her ankles, knees, and throughout hips. When she made it the few feet across the floor, black and white dots floated in front of her eyes. She reached for the edge of the bed with the last of her strength. Clutching onto the blanket, she grew dizzy and dropped. She landed on her arm.

She hadn't passed out, but it was close.

Or maybe she had.

She wasn't sure.

She tugged, dragging the blanket off the bed.

There was no doubt she could get comfortable on the floor, as long as she had the blanket.

She did her best at covering all of her body.

Anna didn't feel any warmer.

She shivered, hugging the blanket tight over her shoulders, shrinking in on herself.

Her eyelids fluttered.

Before they closed she saw it. Under the bed. She remembered putting it there last week. There was no reason for taking it out of the lower vault. It was more safe downstairs with the other relics, and manuscripts.

Seeing it now, she felt that same energy she experienced when she first found the box. The charge from being so close to it returned.

Her body tingled.

How long was it after she found the box that she became sick?

Despite the lack of warmth under the blanket, she hesitated before snaking an arm out. Her fingers grasped at air as they got closer to the box.

She would never forget the sensation of running her palms and fingertips across the elaborate carvings. There was no fear of slivers; the wood was sanded as smooth as skin. Holding the box let a wave of tranquility pass over her, through her.

She never would have set the box down, much less slid it under the bed.

That didn't make any sense at all. None.

Her fingers extended. She could almost touch the box.

Pain ran up and down her arm.

Her fingertips snagged the floor. Her nails scraped as she brought her arm in.

Scratch marks cut into the floor.

She breathed heavy. The exertion was almost too much.

The chills forgotten, she rolled onto her chest. Her cheek pressed against the cold floor. Her eyes, unblinking, locked onto the box. She tried again. Her arm extended as far under the bed as possible. It didn't appear as if she was much closer. Her fingers wiggled helplessly, struggling for a fraction of an inch of reach more.

With her energy spent, her hand dropped. Her palm slapped the floor.

Her fingernails dug in.

New scratch marks.

The nail on her middle finger snapped back, and peeled away from flesh.

Crying, Anna knew she couldn't give up.

She wanted... *no*. She needed the box.

***

Mykal, never having traveled this far east, was taken aback by the view. Beyond the crevasse he'd squeezed through he stopped and simply stared down at the valley in awe. The majestic snow-covered peaks stood like giant sentries, or castle spires.

The sun, shining directly over the village, didn't bring with it much heat, but provided perfect lighting for revealing the scenery below. There was a bright reflective glare from the snow, and rays also bounced off polished tin roofs.

The tops of homes in the sprawling village sat under thin strings of smoke rising from stone chimneys. Faintly he smelled the logs burning. The aroma mostly dissipated in the breeze. The hairs in his nostrils were frozen anyway. He wasn't sure he'd be able to smell something on fire directly beside him, unless the hairs thawed from it. From where he stood, it looked like people milled about in the streets, perhaps selling or trading goods. There wasn't land for growing crops, and only very few trees for wood. Mykal wondered how the queens' subjects survived down there. He couldn't imagine so many people dependent on the royal family for everything.

Mykal's head felt too light on his shoulders. If he moved quickly—like the way it bobbed as he ran from the sword wielding, arrow shooting warriors—he worried it might topple off his neck.

He shivered as a what felt like a finger of ice traced its way up his spine. Between the weakness, pain, and cold, he wasn't sure how far he'd get. Behind him he thought he heard the warriors chipping away at the ice wall he'd set in front of the crevasse. He had no idea the wall's thickness, but hoped it kept the enemy busy a little longer.

His mind reeled. Aside from training with Blodwyn, he'd not engaged in a fight in years. He'd forgotten how difficult... killing was. He'd never grow accustomed to the feeling of taking a life. It didn't matter that these warriors would have slaughtered him, as well as his friends, if given the chance. That didn't change how he felt. Empty. Hollow. He'd stamped out many lives just now. It brought back painful memories. When he'd first learned he was a mage, he'd unleashed bolts of lightning and charred a man to death. The Archer was dangerous, but killing him could have been avoided if he'd had better control of his powers at the time. Battling the warriors just now, there hadn't been a chance to maim. The ambush had been relentless. Defending those with him left little by way of options.

He bent over, and vomited.

Mykal had sent the others ahead. There was no telling how far they'd made it. Even though he hoped they were somewhere far, and safe, he wished they were close and could help him. He wasn't feeling any better. If anything, he might be a little worse.

He'd used a lot of magic. More than he should have, and it wore him out.

Even his eyelids felt heavy.

The pass, more narrow on this side of the crevasse, forced Mykal to walk with his left arm pressed against the side of the mountain. He didn't trust his balance. The idea of fainting scared him. Falling off the side of the mountain was an understandable fear, but equally unnerving was the haunting idea of getting captured, or worse, killed.

Moving slowly, he didn't worry about the footprints he left in the snow. If the warriors made it past, or around the wall of ice he created, he'd never escape. Steady was the key. He didn't have time for stopping. Pushing on was the only certainty.

A sudden shriek pierced Mykal's ears. He looked and saw a blue-black falcon circling overhead. It landed on the rock at his right. The carnivorous bird was as large as a raven, and stocky. The defined legs were barred with grey and blue, and the neck and head were black. Bright yellow, taloned feet clutched at the cold stone, but the falcon shifted its weight back and forth, looking around, and blinking.

The qualities seemed quite human. Mykal considered the bird shifty, and saw him as a representation of an untrustworthy thief.

"I'm just kidding. You're a bird. Just a bird. And here I am telling you that I'm just kidding, like you could hear my thoughts." Mykal clapped a palm against his forehead, leaned forward, and whispered. "You can't, can you? Can you read my thoughts?"

Mykal laughed. His mind was loosening any grip on reality.

He was conversing with a falcon.

And the bird stared at him like it understood. This was crazy. Nonsense.

All at once, the bird launched itself off the rock and into the air.

The hooked beak spread, and three squawks escaped in shrill succession.

Mykal shrunk back, threw up an arm, and shielded his face. He thought the falcon upset, and didn't want his eyeballs plucked from the sockets. "Shoo! Shoo, now. Shoo!"

When he was certain the falcon had flown away, he lowered his arm.

He never stopped walking. The mountain, no longer at his left, abandoned him.

The edge teetered under his feet. His eyes brought the drop in and out of focus. Toward the bottom stood some tall pines, and a scattering of boulders.

Clutching onto the staff with both hands, as though it were a rail for supporting his weight, Mykal pitched forward.

He heard grunts, and whimpers. Something knocked into his nose. His check, directly under his eye was smacked. He saw snow. Rocks. And then stars.

He saw his own knees up close.

The damage to his face more than likely came from those knees. And just as his legs extended, and bent, and his knee rocketed toward his face again, everything went black.

Mykal's eyelids fluttered. He struggled keeping them open. His head throbbed. The last thing he wanted was sleep. It became a fight. He knew he was in a losing battle. There was no giving up. He kept his eyes open for as long as possible.

Large snowflakes fell slow from the sky, as if a feather drifting toward the ground on a breezeless day. His eyes closed.

Darkness. Flutter. Everything looked white, or too bright. The light burned his eyes. There was something else. He wasn't just lying in the snow. His arms were over his head, dragging, as the rest of his body moved in sluggish jerks.

Moved wasn't quite right. His eyes closed.

Darkness. Flutter. The flakes fell. The jerks came from the lower half of his body, his legs. Someone had him by the ankles?

He wasn't walking, he knew. Someone was pulling him; dragging him.

This time Mykal closed his eyes of his own will, and turned his head before opening them. Once opened, he was thankful. It wasn't as bright. He confirmed he was on the ground, in the snow. He felt it now, the cold. It rubbed across his back.

He looked up again, not toward the sky, and the sun, but to see if he could tell who had him by the feet. Instead, all he saw were the large flakes. They fell toward, and landed on, his face, no longer melting on his skin. The warmth was gone from his body. Eventually the flakes would accumulate, he supposed, and he'd be buried alive.

That wouldn't happen though.

He wasn't alone. Surely, the person dragging him wouldn't let the snow cover his nose and mouth. Otherwise, why move him in the first place?

Unless the warriors had him.

The warriors. He was captive, a prisoner.

Darkness. Flutter. He stopped fighting, and resigned keeping his eyes closed.

Whoever had him spoke. The words sounded slurred together. The tone was soft, comforting.

"You are okay now, just relax, just rest."

It was garbled, and concentrating on making sense out of the mess made the wall of brain behind his eyeballs ache.

"You're okay. Hang in there, it will be okay."

It sounded like a man who spoke. The voice was deep, slightly gravelly. It was no one Mykal knew.

It wasn't Blodwyn.

He didn't think it was Gembert, either.

Keeping his eyes closed helped. He was able to think more clearly.

Not clear.

Just more clearly. It made a difference, and the few words he did understand were not threatening.

He no longer believed the warriors had him.

Maybe he wasn't captive. Not a prisoner.

The one question remained. Who dragged him by the feet?

CHAPTER 18

Mykal heard two people arguing.

"I have no idea what you were thinking bringing him here." The woman's voice was high pitched, angry. She wasn't yelling though. At least, he didn't think she was. It was hard to tell for certain since he didn't know who was talking.

"You weren't there, Miriam." A man responded. They attempted keeping their voices down, not to make too much noise. Maybe they didn't want to draw unwanted attention, or they worried about waking him. From the sounds of it, Miriam was already worried Mykal would be unwanted attention enough. He kept his eyes closed. Let them think he was still out of it. It would be safer for them all that way. At least until he got a better sense of what was going on. It didn't seem like they meant him any harm. If anything, he was pretty sure they meant to protect him from the warriors that attacked.

"Does it matter if I wasn't there?" She sounded more scared than angry. Mykal understood fear. They'd been ambushed, and were lucky to have escaped. Hopefully Blodwyn and the others reached safety.

"This boy and his friends fought off a horde of combatants that blended in with the snow, and the mountains. Those warriors were nearly invisible when they attacked. I have never seen anything like it. Well, until this young man and his friend fought back. They used staffs. That staff there, and..."

"You didn't interfere, Daniel? Tell me you didn't interfere?" She sounded desperate, at her rope's end. Mykal imagined Daniel did this kind of thing often, not rescuing people perhaps, but involving himself in business where he didn't necessarily belong.

At the moment, Mykal was thankful for such annoying and uninvited involvement. Otherwise he'd have been left exposed to the elements for who knew how long. Worse, the warriors would eventually make it past the temporary blockade he'd created. If they found his weakened body in the snow... he preferred not thinking about it. He had enough challenges ahead; spending any more time worrying about what could have happened was pointless.

"I'm trying to tell you what happened."

Miriam groaned. Mykal could just imagine her throwing a forearm across her forehead, and spinning away dramatically. "Daniel! What am I going to do with you? What are we going to do about this? We're too old for bringing in strays. And *he's* too old. You call him a boy. This is a man. You've dragged home trouble is what you've done. Trouble."

"He *is* a boy, barely a man." If Mykal was watching the exchange, he believed Daniel's shoulders would have been sagging, droopy.

"He's trouble." Arms must have been folded sternly across her chest. Mykal imagined a sneering scowl. Although he didn't hear one, he supposed a foot stomp to illustrate exclamation wasn't out of the question, either.

"Nothing good would have come from me leaving him lying at the bottom of the ravine." Daniel added some inflection to his words. The authority, however, was hollow enough to echo. If Miriam and Daniel were married, or even brother and sister, then no one was getting fooled by the weak theatrics.

"And what good will come from dragging the boy to our front step?"

They were in the village.

Mykal let his eyes open slightly. He mostly saw his own eyelashes, but worried the slices of light between the strands would send piercing pain into his skull. It didn't. His head felt better. There was no way of knowing how long, or how far this Daniel guy dragged him. Although *thankful*, he was more anxious about finding Blodwyn, and Gembert.

"If I left him out there the cold would have killed him. If I left him, those mercenaries would have found him. They'd have murdered him for sure."

Mykal saw the woman's fists shake. "Look behind you, Daniel. Take a look behind you."

There was a pause.

Daniel must have been looking.

Miriam said, "You think footprints are easy to track? You left a smooth trail as wide as that *boy's* shoulders."

"I'll grab some brush. I can go back and rake it all up. Not even a bloodhound would be able to find us." The man was scared of the woman. His voice exposed him. He couldn't hide the fear if he tried.

Mykal felt a pull on his ankles.

"What are you doing?" Miriam said.

"I was going to bring him in, set him by the fire. The man's frozen half to death."

"That's none of our concern. Certainly not mine."

"Miriam." When someone resorts to begging, they've lost. The upper hand was forfeited, if he'd ever held it... ever.

"Go, hide your trail. It's probably too late already."

"But—"

"Go, and hurry. I'll get him into the house."

"I'm going." It was the first time Mykal heard anything even remotely sounding lively out of the man's mouth.

There were several long moments where Mykal laid on the cold ground. Behind him boots crunched on snow. He listened until there was nothing left to hear.

A falcon screeched.

The wind blew fast, hard, and cold.

Mykal guessed Miriam had lied. She'd told Daniel she'd take care of him. It looked like instead he'd freeze to death.

Boots crunched on snow. "I've got hot tea and soup inside. I'm not dragging you around. Get up and walk, or you can lay there as long as you want. It's your call."

Mykal opened an eye, squinting. The woman looming above him wore her grey hair mostly tucked under a wool hat. She was thin

"You knew I was awake?"

"I figured. Thought I caught you peeking a time or two while I was talking to my husband." She held out her arm.

Mykal took her hand, but worried she wouldn't have the strength to lift him, and he wouldn't have the strength yet to offer much assistance. When she yanked on his arm, however, he was hoisted up onto his feet with minimal effort on his behalf.

"What's the matter? Didn't think I was that strong?"

Sounded like a trick question. Mykal had opened his mouth to reply, but snapped it shut.

Her half smile, combined with a twinkle in her left eye was revealing. "Smart boy. C'mon. Follow me. The soup's not much, but it's fresh. Mostly broth, really. Has some cut up potatoes and carrots. The meat is crow. Hope that suits you."

Mykal dined on crow nearly every night when crossing the Zenith Mountains with his friends just prior to the War. This was back when they were gathering enchanted talismans. The hope then had been to summon wizards who went into hiding. Prior to King Golan Nabal, his grandfather, Grandeer, ruled the Grey Ashland, back when the empire was whole, and the realms were unified under Emperor Henry Rye. Long after the Magic Wars, King Nabal commissioned a lethal team of men known as the Watch. Their sole purpose was to hunt down anyone using magic. Sanctioned by royal decree, they acted as judge, jury, and executioner. The reign of terror lasted for decades. Mykal hoped that since the end of the War, when Nabal witnessed Mykal's power in defeating an evil King Cordillera, Nabal would put an end to the Watch. Unfortunately, the faction still existed, although he believed they were far less... active these days.

Miriam snapped fingers in Mykal's face. "You with me, boy? Don't need you dropping inside my house. You start feeling queasy, take a seat."

"I'm okay."

She had a bowl in one hand, a ladle in the other, and was standing over a black cauldron. The fire underneath the cauldron heated the tiny home. "You sure? Because you went away on me for a minute there."

"Was just thinking." Mykal stood by a small table. "Crow is just fine."

"Okay. Well that's good, because it's all we have." She scooped soup into the bowl, and set it on the table. "Take off the cloak. Sit. The fire will melt some of the cold off your skin, and the soup will thaw your bones."

"I appreciate the hospitality—"

"Hospitality?" Her nose wrinkled. She held up both hands, as if saying *don't thank me.* "My husband is the hospitable one. It's nothing against you, but I'd have left you where I found you."

Mykal held the bowl in one hand, close to his face, and a spoonful of soup ready to eat in front of his mouth, when he snickered.

"You think that's funny? Because it's true. I'd have left you."

"I don't think it's funny. I guess I'm laughing because I believe you."

"That's why you're laughing? Then you have an odd sense of humor." She smiled, and shook her head. "How about a cup of tea?"

The soup was flavorful, despite Miriam's caveat. "This is plenty for me. I won't be staying. I have friends out there. I need to find them."

"Good. That's what I hoped to hear. No offense."

"None taken." Mykal blew on the next spoonful. The broth was hot. He'd burned his tongue on the first taste. "I was real lucky your husband came by when he did. I'll always be grateful. The last thing I want is to draw attention. I don't want to see either of you involved in any trouble on my account."

"You and me both."

While eating, Mykal watched Miriam fill a second bowl with soup. She hesitantly sat at the table across from him.

"Have you been traveling long?"

"This morning."

"Did you come from the castle?"

"We did."

"You're not royalty. Are you a baron, or someone important? I don't recognize you."

"I'm nobody important." Mykal accepted the elderly woman's apprehensions, but trusted her. Until he better understood the situation—where the warriors who attacked them came from and why—the less Miriam knew, the safer it would be for her and her husband.

"It's not what my husband said. But you heard the conversation. Your fighting skills impressed him." Her head listed to one side, and then the other. "This soup would be nice with bread."

"It's fine the way it is. Filling."

"You're just being polite." She made a face where her lips puckered before the next spoonful. After dabbing at the corners of her mouth with the knuckle of a bent finger, she said, "You use that stick to fight?"

Mykal looked behind him, where his staff leaned against the wall. "I do."

"Against swords? I don't see how. Wood is no match against steel."

"A friend had it made special. More than wood in that staff, but I'll admit, it even surprised me today."

"What happened, exactly? Was it bandits, or are these people after you?"

It was a good question. Mykal didn't have the answer.

"Can I ask you something?" She didn't wait. "Are you responsible for the missing women?"

CHAPTER 19

Blodwyn let Gembert take point. They kept Geneva between them.

"Are we being followed?" Gembert struggled walking. Each step taken his leg sank knee-deep in the snow. With his arms raised, he pivoted his body this way and that freeing himself as much as possible before the next step.

"Not as far as I can tell." Blodwyn periodically checked over his shoulder.

The trek wasn't much easier for Geneva even though she followed in Gembert's tracks. She was shorter, and the snow rose halfway up her thighs.

In the mountains, aside from the main path they'd been following, there weren't many options for hiding. However, they took a new route. It led further up the mountain, rather than down toward the valley, and villages.

There was no hiding their tracks. There were too many, and they were too deep. Blodwyn made a cursory wave across the snow behind them with his staff, to no avail. If the warriors wanted to find them, it wouldn't take much effort.

"Why are we climbing the mountain?" Geneva sounded winded. She huffed and puffed. The plumes of breath rose like chimney smoke, and were gone in the wind.

"It might seem safer going into the village, but I think that is the obvious choice. Until we know what's going on, I'd rather be a bit unpredictable. Not to mention, if we get higher we will have a better view. It won't be as easy for anyone to sneak up on us." Blodwyn felt his age in his legs.

His muscles, his bones, ached. The cold, damp weather didn't help any, either.

The fight had taken a lot out of him. If there had been even a handful more warriors, or if the fight had lasted just another ten minutes, they might not have escaped. Even now, he wasn't sure how long he could keep on. His labored breathing had him worried. "We should stop there. By the boulders. It's as good a place as any. Not sure how much further we'd need to climb. I want to get you two as comfortable as possible."

Geneva stopped. "Us two? What about you?"

"I have to go back." Blodwyn had seen Mykal do amazing things. The boy's magic was powerful. If it had been anything different, he never would have left with Gembert and Geneva. The downside to Mykal's power came after. When the energy was spent, Mykal was left drained. The wizard, Galatia, had explained to them that using magic was like exercising muscles. The more you used, the stronger you became, and the stamina increased. However, exerting oneself was dangerous. Pushing it too far could prove detrimental.

In the past, Mykal had come close to killing himself from overuse of magic on more than one occasion.

"I'm not staying here, not without you." She held Blodwyn's attention with her eyes. "I didn't want to leave him. We never should have left!"

Blodwyn looked beyond her at the cluster of boulders. It was a perfect place to hold up. His eyes dropped to the snow. The tracks were ruinous. No one was following them, at least the best he could tell. Not even Mykal. That was a bad sign.

They'd come a long way for nothing. "Okay, then. I guess we turn around. Gembert!"

The man stood crotch deep in snow. He turned his torso. The strain was apparent by the expression on his face. "Yeah?"

"We're going back."

Gembert stared over at the rocks, down at his hidden legs, and then back at Blodwyn. "Of course we are."

Blodwyn wouldn't have conceded as easily if he wasn't confident they were, for the moment, safe. He kept a vigilant watch, just the same. The warriors that attacked were prepared. Their snow-white, and grey uniforms blended perfectly with the surroundings. If a warrior was perched somewhere, unmoving, he might go undetected until it was defensively too late. "Stay behind me."

Geneva didn't argue.

Again, Blodwyn walked in the tracks they'd made. They moved slowly back down the mountain. For once a little luck was on their side. The wind was to their back. Blodwyn immediately noticed the reprieve. Breathing was suddenly easier. He hadn't realized just how responsible the wind had been for stealing some of his breath. With the hood of his cloak raised, his ears finally began warming up. They weren't warm, but now he at least didn't feel a burning sensation on his dangling lobes.

Ahead, Blodwyn saw a man with a tree branch sweep the snow, hiding tracks. Blodwyn held up a hand and, not wanting to alert the stranger, whispered: "Hold up."

Geneva nestled up close beside. "Who's that?"

"I don't know."

"What's he doing?" Gembert stood on the opposite side of Blodwyn. The three of them knelt, looking over the side.

Luckily, it wasn't a beast they spied. It would smell the three of them. Most humans couldn't detect scents that way. Some could, however. "See that spot he's brushing with the leaves and branches? Its body-shaped, best I can tell. He's hiding it."

"Why would he do that?" Gembert asked.

"Who was lying there?" Geneva said.

Blodwyn shook his head, scanning the area for signs of hiding warriors. "I'm not sure. I'm thinking we should find out."

Geneva had taken hold of Blodwyn's sleeve. "You don't think that was Mykal down there?"

It could have been. He wasn't going to assume a thing. It didn't take a psychic to see Geneva's emotional involvement in the situation. At the moment she was manageable. "We're going to find out, but I want you and Gembert to wait here. Am I making myself clear?"

"Perfectly." Gembert held up both hands, as if surrendering. Blodwyn tried hiding the judgment passed.

"Geneva?"

"I'll stay," she said, reluctantly.

"I'm going to need you to let go of me."

Geneva looked at her white-knuckle grip on his arm, and released the hold. "Sorry."

***

The fresh fallen snow was light, fluffy. It didn't crunch underfoot. Blodwyn approached stealthily. There were two ways of attacking the position. One, he could come in fast, hard. Take the man with the tree branch down, and once detained, interrogate him. Or...

Blodwyn stood several feet behind the man with the branch. "Excuse me."

Startled, the man spun around.

Weather and time took a toll on the man's face. The skin was liver spotted, and wrinkled. The grooves across the brow were thick like ruts in dried mud.

There was something familiar. "We're looking for someone."

The man took a step backward.

Blodwyn saw no weapon. It didn't mean the man was armed. "Have we met before?"

"I believe I'd remember meeting the likes of you." Wind pummeled the man in the face. He squinted, protecting his eyes from drying out.

"The likes of me?" Blodwyn did his best at letting the insult slide, for the moment. The voice was familiar, as well. Blodwyn took another step closer, and the man a tentative step back. "As I said, we're looking for someone?"

"I figured you'd be back."

The reply confused Blodwyn some. "And what does that mean?"

"I saw the fight. From above. It was like nothing I'd ever seen before. The boy finished the fight. Magic was what he used. He then collapsed. He's alright, I believe. I brought him to my house. It isn't much of a place, but he's warm. Safe. My wife's protecting him."

170

Blodwyn released a sigh of relief. Some of his worry dissipated. "What's with the branch?"

"I didn't want those other men finding us. The wife wasn't too thrilled I brought the boy home in the first place."

"I can't imagine she was," Blodwyn said, but was very thankful the stranger had been looking out for his friend. A pang of guilt rang inside his chest. "I think they're good and stopped. For the time being, anyway. Snow's falling good. Should work even better at hiding your tracks."

"Still," the man said, sweeping the branch over the snow.

"Why don't you take us to my friend. I'm sure he'll be better by now, and with our thanks we'll be on our way." Finding the man's house would be simple with or without the man's assistance. The tracks were far from camouflaged. The branch sweeping just created an entirely new set of *tracks* was all.

"I can do that."

Blodwyn raised a hand in the air, and waved. "My friends will be joining us."

"The other man, and the young woman? I'm glad everyone is okay."

"Do you know who those warriors were?" Blodwyn asked, leaning most of his weight onto his staff.

"I can't say for certain. I've seen them once, no, twice before. Two separate times. I've looked for sigils, or any kind of identifying marks, but have never spotted any."

"Think they're some kind of militia?"

"Militia?"

"They didn't look like royal knights—not dressed that way, not the way they fought." Blodwyn thought of the

Archers. At one time the band of men served King Nabal. After years of mistreatment, false allegations, and trumped up charges, the group fled the realm and built a city of their own in the treetops of the Cicade Forest. Mykal's uncle was the current leader of the Archers. When they fought enemies it was rarely head-on. Sneak attacks, traps, and blatant bushwhacking was how they dealt with threats. It might not seem proper, but it was effective. There was no denying that.

"To be honest, I don't know who they are. The wife and I think they might be responsible for the abductions going on as of late."

The abductions.

Just as Geneva, and Gembert joined them, Blodwyn said, "Why don't we start to your place. I'm not embarrassed to admit getting out of the cold even for a moment is most alluring to me at this time."

The man tossed the branch far from them, clapped and rubbed his hands together. "I second you on that one."

***

"Did I have anything to do with the missing women?" The sound of boots knocking snow from the soles on the steps outside stopped Mykal before he answered.

Miriam held a finger up to her lips. "Shh."

He reached for his staff, got to his feet and stood behind the woman.

She looked back at him.

He nodded that he was ready. "Stand behind me."

Miriam looked conflicted. Clearly because it was her house she wanted to handle things, but understanding the trouble that could be just outside her door gave her pause.

"Please, stand behind me." Mykal didn't see anywhere else worth hiding; other than behind him, otherwise he'd have suggested she go into another room or under a bed. He would die before letting any harm reach the innocent woman.

The door pushed open.

Mykal thrust his staff forward.

Daniel shrieked, and jumped back as Miriam called out his name.

Before the head of the staff struck Daniel's throat, Mykal stopped the attack, and lowered the weapon. "My apologies."

Mykal heard Blodwyn's voice. "Daniel?"

Mykal couldn't contain the emotion. Those outside entered the house. It was tight, cramped. "Geneva! Gembert!"

Miriam said, "Blodwyn!"

CHAPTER 20

"Blodwyn?" Daniel said.

Mykal, standing beside Geneva and Gembert watched the odd exchange.

Blodwyn offered Miriam a thin-lipped smile. He looked both humbled, and embarrassed.

Miriam clamped her hands onto Blodwyn's arms.

"Wyn?" Mykal said, confused.

"All these years." Miriam studied Blodwyn's face intently.

"After my parents were murdered, I was on the run," Blodwyn said.

"Was in weather a lot like this. Perhaps a wee-bit worse." Daniel held his fingers up illustrating his take on a wee-bit. "Found him passed out in the snow. Just a little lad. Waist high, he was."

"Ironic," Mykal said.

"We took him in for a time." Miriam finally looked away. Her eyes gazing only at the floor. Her cheeks reddened.

"It's okay," Blodwyn whispered. It was almost as if he only wanted Miriam hearing what he'd said.

"It was my call, you know? Daniel wanted to keep you. Said it was the right thing to do. But I was scared, you know. The Watch was a fearful thing. Still are, I imagine."

Murdered? The Watch? Mykal tried following the exchange. The questions pooled inside his brain. He nearly drowned in them. Somehow he kept his mouth shut, which was not an easy feat. He was tired of waiting for Blodwyn to share stories. When they returned from this assignment, they were going to sit down and talk. Mykal wanted to hear everything about his friend's past. Everything.

"I'm not upset. Never was." This time Blodwyn placed his hands on the woman's arms, giving her a gentle squeeze. "Things worked out fine."

She sobbed. Her shoulders shook. "I was wrong to force you out."

He pulled the woman in tight, and hugged her. "I was grateful you took me in. The two of you saved my life."

Geneva grasped Mykal's arm, and chewed on the thumbnail on her other hand as she watched the exchange.

Gembert, despite arms folded, was clearly engaged.

"And your daughter? Is she living here?" Blodwyn said.

Mykal saw Daniel wince, as if he'd burned his hand on a pot.

"She passed. Barely eight years and ten. It was the year the flu ran rampant," she said.

Mykal couldn't recall any outbreaks on the west banks of the Isthmian. He wondered if the virus only plagued the Osiris Realm?

"I'm sorry, very sorry to hear that."

Miriam pulled out of the embrace. She straightened her blouse, with a tug. "There's not much room, but I've plenty of soup. Everyone find a place to sit. Please, sit down. We'll eat."

A pregnant pause followed, and just before it became unbearably awkward Daniel clapped his hands together. "I've a stool and a bench we can fit around the table."

Everyone shuffled about.

Miriam gathered bowls from a cupboard. Mykal and Geneva pulled the table away from the wall. Gembert followed Daniel in search of extra items for sitting on, and Blodwyn stood where he'd been standing and watched Miriam ladle food into bowls.

For nearly an hour, the only conversation revolved around food. The cauldron was scraped clean. Everyone, sitting back, or leaning with elbows on the table, was full. Lanterns provided light as grey clouds hid any last rays of light from a setting sun.

"That was truly wonderful." Geneva held a hand in front of her mouth, the burp was small, but noticed. She blushed, but smiled.

"No shame in that." Daniel burped in response. "It's a compliment to the chef."

Miriam beamed, no sign she'd been insulted by either burp.

"Before the lot of you arrived, Miriam was asking if I was involved with the recent abductions." Mykal arched an eyebrow. The tension from the last few days was gone. There was something about breaking bread in a home that made Mykal somewhat comfortable, but also sad. He missed both his grandfather, and mother. As important as it was to figure out what was going on in this realm, he longed for home. Not just the library. He wanted to plan a return to Grey Ashland, and spend some time with his grandfather.

"Deidre is my aunt. She went missing not long ago. She lives in the valley. Do you know her?" Geneva chewed on her lower lip, and fiddled with the spoon in her bowl.

Miriam stood up. "The name doesn't sound familiar."

"She has three kids. My cousins."

Daniel shook his head, reaching across the table and collected the bowls. "I can't place her, either."

"That's where we were headed, to see her."

"Is that what you're all doing out on the mountain, searching for the missing people?" Miriam took the stack of bowls from her husband.

Mykal stood up. "Let me take care of these, please."

Miriam regarded him for a moment. Silent. Contemplating.

"You fed us all. It is just a small way I can show my thanks." He took the bowls from her. At the counter, he used the water from a bucket to wash everything.

"The queens hired you then, I take it?" Miriam said. "You're from the castle, aren't you?"

Gembert shifted uncomfortably in his chair. "I am."

"Quiet, too. Not surprised. I suppose you'll be giving the queens a full report when you return?"

"I will."

Miriam grunted.

"Do you know anything about what's been going on? The queens have more of a high level of understanding of what's been going on, but not much of the details," Blodwyn said.

"We get word like everyone else, long after the abductions occurred. It isn't often we go into the valley. Two, or three times a month for supplies. Being old, we don't dilly-dally. We get the things we need and come back home." Miriam stood next to Mykal, drying the bowls and utensils as he washed them. "We've no time for scuttlebutt."

Blodwyn said, "Surely you've heard something?"

Mykal caught Miriam cast a sideways glance at her husband. They did know something.

"The boy's a wizard, dear," Daniel said.

Miriam stood statue-still, her eyes locked on Mykal. "He's a what?"

"I'm a wizard, ma'am."

Miriam groaned, set the bowl down on the counter, and cut a way through the room back to the table. She sat down and said, "This just keeps getting worse, and worse."

"Don't fret, Miriam."

"Don't fret? Don't fret? When are you going to stop doing this to me, to us? All our lives you've done this. Every stray you come across, you bring home."

Blodwyn lowered his eyes.

"I don't mean you, Wyn," Miriam said, her hand stretching out across the table.

Blodwyn took it. "I know you don't."

Mykal thought it sound very much like she did mean him, but stayed out of it.

"You can't walk away from people." Daniel showed an austere side Mykal hadn't witnessed before. "It is not in me to walk away. If I can help someone, I'm going to. I feel as if we all have a responsibility to take care of each other. The world doesn't have to be about us and them. If we can just be there for someone else, we can make a difference in that person's life. And then, hopefully, they will learn from our example."

Miriam sucked in a deep breath, and let it out in a long, slow sigh. "I'm just afraid. Every time you help someone else you put us in danger. I worry about you and I first. You're what's most important to me."

"I can't change."

"I don't want you to. I suppose that's part of the reason I fell in love with you in the first place."

"Aww." Geneva cupped a hand over her mouth.

Miriam looked directly at Blodwyn. "I've been scared my whole life."

"I understand fear," he replied.

She turned her attention toward Mykal, without letting go of Blodwyn's hand. "You're him then, aren't you, the famous wizard who fought the war against King Cordillera?"

"I don't know about famous," Mykal said, humbly. "War's an evil thing."

"But sometimes necessary," Blodwyn said.

Daniel nodded. "Go on, Miriam. Tell them what we've seen."

Something banged against the side of the house.

"What was that?" Geneva jumped up from the table. She and Gembert skirted around, and stood beside each other in the center of the room.

Mykal snatched up his cloak. He punched his arms through the sleeves. "Stay inside."

Blodwyn passed him the staff, and grabbed his own.

The top of the small house was filling with smoke.

"Is there another way out of this place?"

Miriam pointed straight ahead. "Just this door."

"Back windows?" Mykal asked.

Daniel nodded. "We've a few. They're not very big."

"Don't need to be. Get to them. Be ready. Don't go out them just yet. There could be someone back there waiting for your attempted escape." Mykal nodded at Blodwyn. "Ready?"

"I am. Are you?"

"Feeling completely rejuvenated." He looked up, but didn't see any flames. "Tin roof?"

"Yes," Daniel said.

"Good deal. Go, get moving." Mykal stood ready to throw open the door.

"Let me go first." Blodwyn shouldered up next to Mykal. "On three."

CHAPTER 21

They counted together. One. Two. Three.

Mykal opened the door. Blodwyn rushed outside. Mykal was directly behind him.

An arrow flew at Mykal's head.

Blodwyn twirled his staff around, batting the arrow away.

Mykal pulled the door closed behind him.

Several arrows pierced the side of the house. Flames rose from the back of the spearheads, and shafts. Towering tongues of fire licked at the wood construction.

"They're hiding." Blodwyn was bent low, ready.

"We need to get the others out."

"It's not safe."

"The fire."

"They could get cut down if they crawl out now," Blodwyn said.

"Cover me." Mykal pointed his staff at the house. The arrows backed out of the frame. The fire fizzled out. "It's in the walls."

"Can you put it out?"

There was no time to reply.

Mykal heard them before he saw them. A flock of fire engulfed arrows lit the sky. Both of them threw up an arm, and crouched behind the protection of their cloaks. A steady rant of *thump-thump-thump* sounded as the broad heads sliced through the outer walls.

Black smoke billowed. Mykal's eyes teared up. "Go around back, get them out."

"We have—"

"Now, Wyn!"

Blodwyn skirted the house, staying as low to the ground as possible.

More arrows launched. The flames sizzled overhead. Embers dropped.

This time Mykal saw where the arrows were coming from.

He deflected most of the arrows away from the house with a wave of his hand, and all of them away from striking Blodwyn, who rounded the corner safely.

Mykal started toward those in hiding. He strode forward.

His eyes flicked left. Right.

The sun was gone. Set. The darkness aided their camouflage.

That wouldn't do. Mykal pulled on the surrounding energy, sucking it in through his palm as his fingers rolled into a fist. He held it inside him, let it quickly fester and rapidly grow. When he unrolled his fingers, each extended open, rays of light shot into five different directions. The pulsed, and the beams expanded, joining together. In a fraction of seconds, a half circle of light lit the sky and everything in front of him.

The hidden warriors were immediately exposed. Several of them threw up arms to shield their eyes from the sudden explosion of light. Mykal aimed his staff and let bolts of blue lightning spew from the head of his staff. The jagged, and twisted spray zapped each of his targets, coiling around them like a hissing pit of snakes.

Arrows were loosed. Razor-sharp broad heads ricocheted off his cloak.

Two warriors came up from behind, a boot crunching on snow that gave the surreptitious attack away.

Mykal dropped the light as he spun around.

This time the sudden blanket of darkness worked to *his* advantage. Mykal thrust his staff forward, stabbing the head into one warrior's gut. The person oomph*ed*, and Mykal pivoted to the side, and twirled the staff up and around his shoulders. In the opposite hand now, he whacked the back of the warrior's knees. Turning yet again, Mykal brought his boot around and crunched the heel against a nose. Bone broke, and despite the darkness, he saw a spray of blood hit the snow. Steam rose, and a coppery smell assaulted Mykal's nostrils.

Mykal cartwheeled over the back of the bent-over warrior. His legs kicked high into the air, and came down on the arm of the second warrior, knocking the sword out of the man's hand. In a fluid motion swiveled around behind the man, and braced the staff across the man's neck, pulling him in tight.

As the man struggled for air, he latched his hands onto Mykal's, trying to pry himself free.

Mykal pulled hard, lifting the man off his feet.

The warrior kicked out in desperation, both legs in the air, and then unexpectedly threw his head back. Hard skull split Mykal's lips. Warm blood filled his mouth. He threw the man forward. The staff swiveled around, and arc downward onto the back of the fallen warrior's neck, flattening him out.

***

Blodwyn reached the back of the house. The place was on fire. He couldn't let that impact his moves. Memories flashed through his mind. He clearly saw his mother...

Blodwyn scanned the darkness beyond for warriors. Daniel hadn't exaggerated. The windows in back were small, and high up. He raised his staff and knocked on the glass.

The window raised. Geneva's head popped out.

"Get everyone out!"

She disappeared back into the house. A moment later feet emerged. Blodwyn set his staff against the house and reached up. He guided Geneva's legs as best he could. She held most of her weight on her forearms and slowly lowered herself to the ground.

Before Blodwyn could call next, he saw another pair of legs emerge.

***

Six warriors encircled Mykal.

He rotated his staff around, and around. The iron and wood cut through the thin air, creating a whistling sound. When the warriors attacked, it was all at once.

Mykal held off on using magic. The little he'd used in the last several minutes impacted his strength. That didn't worry him. His training with Blodwyn was nothing shy of extensive over the years. He could safely rely on the skills learned for defense against the likes of this enemy.

He stepped forward, knee bent, and gyrated the staff around on either side of his thigh. He ignored the vibration of staff on bone, as he fell forward and somersaulted away from an arcing blade. He heard steel clank against rock as he whirled around, his staff sweeping fast and low. Two men tripped, falling hard. One warrior grabbed onto an ankle, drawing his knee to his chest.

***

Blodwyn heard the fire inside. Wood crackled and snapped. "Hurry!" He urged.

Gembert was halfway out of the window. His stomach was pressed on the sill. "How high am I?"

"I've got you, climb down!" Blodwyn stood below the window with his arms raised. "It's only six feet high."

"Hurry," Geneva yelled.

Gembert let go. He just let go.

Blodwyn moved out of the way.

The chamberlain landed on his arse in the snow. "I thought you had me?"

"You jumped," was Blodwyn's explanation. Rather than debate, he focused his attention on the window.

Daniel's head appeared. "It's not that far. A few feet. No. No. Fine. I'll go first."

He wasn't talking to Blodwyn. "Let's go," he said.

"Miriam wants me to go first."

"Fine. Whatever. One of you, let's go!" Blodwyn hated fire. Of everything he encountered in his life, swords and daggers, trolls and sinister kings, fire was what scared him most. From the other window he saw the orange flames. The oxygen was being devoured inside the tiny house, and the thick black smoke had to hinder breathing. There wasn't much time left!

***

The warriors, well-trained with swords, used their weapons similarly to how Mykal commanded his staff. That made the combat more taxing. He deflected blow after blow as best he could. He felt every strike almost as if his palms were burning, and the sensation rattled his arms. The strength behind the attack would overpower him. He needed a way to end the fight as quickly as possible.

Holding the center of the staff with both hands, Mykal swiveled, twirled, and pivoted. They'd lunge, and he'd step back, to the side, or forward to meet the strike. The only benefit was that his staff felt nearly indestructible in his hands. It absorbed the repercussion of so many of the blows. He couldn't imagine how difficult it would have been otherwise.

He let his energy run through his arms. It took away some of the pain, and exhaustion he felt in his muscles. His palms tingled. The staff radiated a brilliant blue. It was as if moonlight spilled from the staff pores. He connected lit iron and wood against steel. The warrior on the receiving end shouted as he flew backward, and landed on his back.

He didn't move. He wasn't getting up. It was one more down, one less person Mykal concerned himself about.

There was a hesitant pause from the few still standing. The awe in the expressions they wore was evident. Mykal knew, unless these warriors were involved with the war, unless they'd fought in Grey Ashland, they probably had never witnessed magic first hand. The wide eyes staring at him confirmed as much.

Unfortunately, the awe was short-lived, little more than a second or two. Their faces hardened, lips pursed, and eyes narrowed, as courage returned. This impressed Mykal. Even fighting for something he believed in he wasn't sure he'd stand against... someone like him, a wizard. They quickly learned the swords they were armed with were nothing but a sword.

Mykal didn't become cocksure. He knew tides changed. Anything could happen at any point. Blodwyn did his best at always preparing Mykal for the unexpected. For that lesson alone, he understood the fight was far from over.

Still, his stamina stuttered. The day had already been long and trying. The reprieve inside the house, the food, and conversation helped, but it seemed as if that was more of a mental healing than a physical. The idea of sleeping, really sleeping—in a bed, under blankets, perhaps beside a hearth with a fire going good—was alluring.

He shook the thoughts out of his head. They were a distraction. The fight demanded all of his attention. He did not want a blade plunged through his chest, or decapitating his head, and he dug deep, and searched himself for more strength.

There were so many trials he'd overcome, fears he'd cast aside, triumphs he'd achieved in the last several years, it didn't seem possible that he was nearing the end of his growth. Blodwyn made sure they always worked on something new each day. It wasn't always about self-defense. Sometimes it revolved around survival. What plants to eat when there was no water, how to build an impressive lean-to using nothing but sand and rocks.

But there were also as many failures endured during the same period of time.

Losses sustained.

These were only negative if you didn't learn from them, grow from the experience, or if you let the end results rip you apart, and tear you down.

Mykal needed balance from both. Success and failure. Calling on his own within, he summoned courage, and strength and energy. The combined were what he was, who he had become. None of it had been easy. There were never any shortcuts he could have taken. He'd grown. There was Blodwyn to thank, but also he gave himself a lot of credit. Just because the tools had been offered, it had always been up to him to use them, to construct who he was into who he wanted to be.

Courage, strength and energy rolled inside him, starting low in his legs. Gurgled, built. The combination mixed and rose inside him. The sensation vibrated as it filled his gut, passed over his chest and then shot out into his arms and up to the top of his head.

He moved faster than he thought possible. Cutting his staff this way and that.

Blades rang out in protest.

The enemy pounced, unthwarted, or perhaps simply unaware.

Mykal rotated left. Right. He raised, and swung, lowered and swept around with the staff.

***

Mykal ran around to the back of the house. His feet slid on wet snow. While his arms waved about overhead, and he nearly clunked himself on the skull with his staff, he did his best to maintain balance. Although he didn't fall, he found himself angled oddly, and thought he'd pulled a muscle in his back.

Heat from the fire met him. The warmth should have been welcome, but was nearly too much despite the cold. He hoped everyone was out of the house. With all of the wood inside, the fire would spread quickly.

"You can't do that!" Blodwyn had Daniel's legs.

Geneva yelled for Mykal. "He wants to go back inside! He's trying to go back into the house!" She waved him over, ushering him to hurry. There was so much that needed taking in. Mykal found himself studying the situation, if only for a moment so he could get his bearings.

"Miriam can't get out," Gembert added.

Daniel looked like he was trying to pull himself back up and into the house through the window. With his hands on the sill, and arms half extended, Daniel squirmed, twisting and kicking for freedom. As unrelenting as Blodwyn seemed, Daniel looked as if he might win. Although climbing back into a house on fire was hardly winning. Prior to, during, and after the war, Mykal had witnessed the power of love.

The chamberlain, so normally poised and dignified, did not wear worry well. He paced, walking toward Mykal, but then turning abruptly around and headed back toward Blodwyn. It was like he planned on helping, but wasn't sure what, or how to go about lending his assistance.

And then it didn't matter.

The second window, the one they *weren't* using as an escape route, exploded with a thunderous boom, and the high-pitched sound of breaking glass. Shards in an array of shapes and sizes cut through the air as deadly as flung daggers. Mykal stepped forward, yanked Geneva inside the protective blanket of his cloak, and shielded them both from harm.

Daniel no longer dangled from the sill. The explosion must have rocked him back *into* the house. Blodwyn was on his back, his arms crisscrossed over his face.

Mykal yelled, "Get back!"

Gembert didn't hesitate now. He grabbed Blodwyn, and dragged him away from the fire and rolling black smoke that was now spat from where the window had been. Geneva rushed forward, and helped Gembert.

Flames rolled out of the window. Heat came at them worse than any winter wind. The hair on Mykal's eyebrows were singed. He couldn't comprehend the fire inside that small house. The smoke alone would have made breathing near impossible. Oxygen, even at this altitude, fed the fire.

The fire roared like an angry beast. Mykal would never forget when the dragon swooped down out of the sky during the War. Flames shot from its mouth, and nostrils. The black sky became lit, and as bright as if the sun crashed into Grey Ashland. When the dragon released a guttural cry, the reverberation shook the battlefield.

Daniel and Miriam did not have a chance. If the smoke hadn't already killed Miriam, the smoke and the fire would now consume both husband and wife. Mykal knew they couldn't get too close to the house. Flames shot out of one window, and it looked as if fire was directly inside the window Daniel had crawled back in through.

Mykal spread his arms wide. His fingers moved slow, bending at the knuckles with a cartilage crack, before straightening. He moved his arms down, hands closer.

Flowing cracks of blue lightning bounced back and forth between his palms. The energy grew, and coursed faster and faster through his entire body.

That same tank of courage, strength and energy gurgled, alive inside him, as if waiting, *wanting,* to be tapped again.

It was a whirlwind flooding every part of his body. His body shook, trembled.

Blodwyn was helped onto his feet.

When Mykal clapped his hands together, pulled them apart, and then stretched his arms out wide again the outer wall of the house blew up.

Wood, and more glass, showered them all.

Darting forward, Mykal and Blodwyn charged the house. They jumped over fire, and into the all-consuming black smoke. It rolled out of the opening and blackened the tin roof.

Mykal only hoped they weren't already too late.

***

Geneva knelt over Miriam. She worked quick, and showed off skills. She tore open clothing where it melted together with, and damaged Miriam's skin. Using snow, and with steady, even hands, Geneva cleaned open wounds as best she could; the snow clumps quickly changed into water—perhaps the hot skin still cooked, even though no long on fire—and washed blackened skin, grime, and gristle away.

The older woman regained consciousness once or twice. For the last several minutes, she's been what Blodwyn called, asleep. Mykal knew there was more to it. Miriam was out of it, not alert. Occasionally, she moaned, or muttered incomprehensibly. Once, she opened her eyes and screamed. The agonizing cry lasted several minutes. Thankfully she passed out again. Her exposed, and charred flesh was blackened, and bloodied. Mykal couldn't comprehend the pain she felt, but was thankful when she passed out. It might have been the only way her body and mind could handle the trauma.

Behind the fire had quieted some. The roar of flames had subsided. Wood still crackled and snapped. Mykal and Blodwyn and scavenged save-able items. There weren't many. The small pile was as hidden as possible by rocks and the few trees in the area.

The fire had burned like a beacon. Mykal knew it drew unwanted attention. Although everything seemed safe now, more warriors might have been dispatched. The still rising black smoke against a dawning sky would lead more enemies directly to them.

Mykal watched as Geneva tore parts of her own tunic into strips, and bandaged the parts of exposed flesh eaten away by fire.

Geneva made direct eye contact with Daniel, and took his hand in both of hers. "You don't want to take these bandages off when they're dry. You'll peel away good skin, and reopen the wounds. Wet the bandage down. Soak it. Do you understand?"

Daniel nodded.

"See these blisters?" Geneva pointed at yellow-colored growths on Miriam's legs, and arms. "You don't pop them, okay? You need to let them break naturally. When they do break, you clean them good. Wash away the pus, and whatever else oozes from it, and then you can cover it with more bandage. Can you remember all of that?"

"I can."

"You soak those bandages good before changing them, okay?"

"Okay. She's alright though? She's going to be okay?" Daniel let his eyes run over his wife's body. His face was smoke covered, and tear streaked. Gembert had rigged a sling for the man's dislocated arm. The material bunched up around the elbow, and was, at the moment, ineffective as an aid.

"You have to change these dressings when they need it, and keep an eye out for infections." Geneva spoke slowly, and calmly.

Mykal listened, knowing they could repeat the directions later. If anything Geneva knew Daniel needed something to occupy his mind. The man was clearly distraught. Geneva's initiative would make a difference in calming the man's mind.

Finally, Mykal walked over and stood next to Blodwyn. The makeshift stretcher the two of them constructed should hold Miriam easily. They'd drag her with them into the valley. Geneva knew a healer among the people. Reluctantly, they'd leave Daniel and Miriam in the woman's care, and check back on them when they returned.

"Their home is destroyed." Blodwyn's arms were flaccid at his sides. His staff leaned against his chest.

Blodwyn shook his head. "Daniel still wants to stay. Place has two charred walls, but they're standing." It hadn't been easy convincing the man going into the valley was best. When Blodwyn explained more warriors would come this way, Daniel finally agreed. "It's not going to be easy nursing his wife back, and while she sleeps, he plans on rebuilding the place."

"I feel partly to blame."

"It's our fault." Blodwyn didn't mince words.

Mykal knew he was correct. It was their fault. There was no way around the truth. "Wyn—"

"We led them right here. The warriors only attacked because we were inside their home." Blodwyn cleared his throat and spit a wad of phlegm into the snow. He wiped his sleeve across his mouth. "When we finish up with why we're here I'm going to help them rebuild."

"I want to help, too." Mykal hesitantly placed a hand on Blodwyn's shoulder. His friend was upset, and agitated. He didn't want to do anything that might add stress. Showing his support, and equal concern was something he wanted expressed. "If that's alright with you."

Blodwyn clapped a hand over Mykal's. "Of course it is. Thank you."

CHAPTER 22

Although the sky slowly morphed from black into a violet purple before finally transforming into a light, sapphire blue, the rising sun was blocked by mountain peaks behind them.

Mykal wore leather straps over his shoulders, and insisted on hauling the stretcher. Geneva held onto Daniel's arm and guided the nearly non-responsive man along the narrow trail. Blodwyn and Gembert followed along, keeping an eye on ridges, and below. When surviving warriors reported back to whomever was in charge, coupled with billowing smoke from the fire, more would be dispatched. After the first attack, Mykal wasn't positive they'd been targeted. Now, he had no clue.

Someone wanted them dead. *Or him.* It was hard not taking it personally.

Mykal couldn't find time for enjoying the view. The visible bustle of morning activity in the valley included the wafting aroma of fresh baking bread, and meat roasting on slow turning spits. There was a steady rhythm of a swooshing axe as it slammed into wood, and the echo of logs splitting, and then falling from a stump into a pile of ready-to-stack firewood. This was actually a comforting beat, reminding Mykal of home on the farm with his grandfather.

He'd still be home if King Nabal hadn't ordered him and his mother to leave the realm.

Nabal was thankful for the magical help he and his mother provided during the War, but couldn't look past the fact they were wizards. At the end of it all, Nabal still harbored discriminatory feelings against sorcery. He indicated his Watch would not be disbanded. If they returned to Grey Ashland, the king would be forced to charge them accordingly. Magic would continue to be outlawed. They were not welcome anywhere on the west side of the Isthmian.

"Mykal?"

Geneva walked beside him. Her arms folded across her chest. Cherry cheeks, and the tip of her nose looked as bright as rose petals, in direct contrast to otherwise pale, white skin.

"I asked how you were holding up?"

"I'm okay."

"I can take a turn." Geneva's jaw set, as if daring him to deny her ability. He saw the silent threat in her eyes.

"I've got a little more in me. When I'm ready, you can take over. I appreciate that."

She nodded, satisfied. "Just say the word."

"How much longer? Seems like the valley is right there, but we keep winding around."

"Can't have a straight path down the mountain. We'd never keep our feet under us." She laughed.

"I understand that. Just feels like we have to walk for nearly an hour to get ten feet closer."

"It is what it is, magic man."

Mykal stopped walking, and lowered the stretcher.

"Want me to take a turn now?" Geneva reached for the leather straps.

"What's wrong?" Blodwyn walked up, and stood beside them. "You see something."

"I can clearly see the valley." Mykal pointed.

Blodwyn pressed his lips tight, brow furrowed. "And?"

"I've never been there, but I can see the place clear enough. Right over there. See the edge of the clearing. I can set us all by the trees. Save us a few hours of walking. Sooner we get there the faster Miriam gets medical attention." Geneva shot him a look. "*Additional* medical attention."

"I don't know if that's a great idea," Blodwyn said. He lightly tugged on the ends of his mustache and beard with his thumb and forefinger.

"You mean like we did last time? When you poofed us to the Cordillera Castle? That was something else, I must admit. Very impressive." Geneva was explaining what had happened to Daniel. The man nodded his head, but the vacant look in his stare made Mykal wonder how much he actually understood.

"What's the problem?" Mykal whispered, hoping only Blodwyn heard. Geneva stared at them, clearly honed in on the private conversation.

"There's six of us," Blodwyn said. Geneva shrugged, disappointed that a number seemed the extent of Blodwyn's explanation for voting down magical transportation.

Mykal didn't need any more. He understood. Part of him wanted nothing more than to adamantly deny any need for concern. The last few days he'd used a lot of magic, and had dabbled in new forms of magic. The alchemy shouldn't have been nearly as taxing, but it took a toll. The recent fights with the warriors felt almost deadly afterward; he'd even collapsed. It didn't help that for the better part of the night, and the first few hours of morning he'd been carefully maneuvering his way down the mountain dragging Miriam on a stretcher. His body was physically worn, and his mind was off-kilter. "I'll be alright."

"It's a risk." Blodwyn tilted his head slightly to the right before his body turned and he faced the valley. It was as if he now intently studied the distance from where they were to where they wanted to be.

"It's not about me. You said it yourself. We brought that trouble to their doorstep. This couple would be fine, their home still standing if it wasn't for me." Mykal ground his teeth, and narrowed his eyes. He wasn't angry with Blodwyn.

"Us," Blodwyn countered. "We brought trouble to their doorstep."

Mykal said, "I just want to get her help."

Geneva cleared her throat.

"More help," Mykal added.

"Trust me. I get that. But the best way you can help them, protect them, is by staying healthy. Look up there." Blodwyn pointed at the smoke still rising against the blue sky. "Whoever is after us has made two attempts. They've come close each time to taking us out. If I were a betting man, I'd put every last coin I have that the attacks aren't over."

"You don't think they're going to stop?"

Blodwyn shook his head. "Why? Do you?"

"They'll be back."

"Exactly. I don't know who they are, or where they come from, but I can tell you this: they're well-trained."

Mykal wondered if Blodwyn was feeling out maneuvered against the warriors? His friend held his own, and wielded his staff with a master precision. "We keep walking. I'll rebuild my energy. When the third attack comes, we'll be ready."

Blodwyn's half smile was uplifting. "I'll take Miriam from here."

Geneva, who still held onto the stretcher straps, set them over her shoulder. "It's my turn."

Mykal saw Gembert silently watch the entire exchange and raised an eyebrow in question. The chamberlain merely shrugged. "Okay. Let's get going."

***

Before noon they reached the valley. The aroma of baking breads and cooking meats when on the trail down the mountain was nothing compared with standing amidst the bakery and open fires. Mykal's mouth watered, but there wasn't time for eating. "Daniel, where is the healer located?"

Daniel looked ten years older than he had the night before. Grey stubble coated his cheeks and chin, and underneath his face was gaunt, but skin sagged around the sides of his mouth, and his eyes were underscored by dark flesh.

"We need to find the healer, Daniel." Geneva spoke softly, in great contrast to Mykal's tone of voice.

"I'll show you." It was the first words the man had spoken all day. It was a start. It might even be considered a good sign. Mykal wanted the healer to check out both of them. Daniel might not have been burned during the fire, but his mind was clouded over from the trauma.

"Can you take them, Gembert," Mykal said. "And stay with them?"

"I can."

"Aren't we going with them?" Geneva seemed unwilling to relinquish the leather straps.

"We're not." Mykal picked his staff up. It had hitched a ride alongside Miriam on the stretcher. It felt good in his hands. Oddly, there was a certain separation anxiety that overcame him when they were separated. That couldn't be a healthy feeling. At some point he would ask Blodwyn if he ever felt similarly. "I don't really think it's safe for anyone in this town the longer I'm around. Blodwyn and I are going to stay here, by the trees. Geneva, I want you to go to your aunt's place, and bring back something of hers for me to work with."

"I have no idea what that means." Geneva stared at Blodwyn with an expression that asked, *do* you *know what this one's talking about?*

"A hairbrush? A nightgown? I just need you to bring me something of hers that she uses regularly." Mykal sometimes forgot more meaningful explanation was necessary. Inside his mind he'd been working through this scenario. He imagined using Deidre's brush and his alchemy to see what happened to the missing woman, much like he had in the dovecote for Clairece.

"A nightgown?" Geneva did not hide her surprise. "What are you going to do with my aunt's nightgown. No. You know what? I don't need to know. You two are going to wait here?"

Blodwyn stepped in. "We'll be here, as long as it's safe."

"And if you're not?"

It was a good question. "We'll find you."

"What about my niece and nephews? They're going to have questions. Suppose they may be even a bit more put off if I come in and rummage through my aunt's drawers."

"Keep them out of it for now. If it looks like we need to speak with them, we will. But let's worry about that only if it becomes necessary," Blodwyn said.

"I agree." Mykal placed a hand on Geneva's shoulder, and looked her in the eyes. "I want you to be safe. I believe the warriors are after me, or Blodwyn and I. I can't be certain though."

"They could be after me?"

"I don't think so."

"But you don't know."

Mykal shook his head. Now, the idea of sending her off on her own didn't sound as promising. There were too many variables. It seemed impossible to prepare against everything, and right now Mykal felt as if they couldn't prepare for anything. "I don't."

"Don't worry about me. I'll snatch up a nightgown for you. And I'll be safe about it."

Mykal didn't want the warriors following after her. He didn't want danger delivered to the house where three kids lived, currently motherless. "You be careful."

Blodwyn said, "Daniel, can you show Gembert where the healer is?"

"I can."

"You stay with the healer, Gembert, too. We'll be by when we have a better idea of what's going on. Clear? Gembert?" Blodwyn produced a pouch from a pocket in his cloak. Mykal recognized the pouch from their earlier travels. It was another one of Blodwyn's mysteries steeped in a past Mykal knew little about. "There are enough gold coins here to care for the entire village if a plague hit. You assess this healer. If they seem worthy, pay them well for their services. Give them all of the coins if you believe it necessary. I just want to make sure Miriam is properly cared for."

Gembert nodded for several seconds, tucked away the pouch of gold, and then kept looking over his shoulder toward the town inside the valley. "Understood."

Blodwyn and Mykal stood between trees, each leaning on their staff. They remained silent as the four ambled away. Gembert pulled the stretcher. Being tall, and lanky, he was having a much tougher go of it than Geneva had.

"I have a bad feeling about this, about separating," Mykal said. The sensation twisted inside his stomach.

"It's safer this way. For them."

"The warriors are after us?" Mykal asked.

"It's you they're after." Blodwyn sighed. "I can't be positive, but I thought I recognized one of the men who attacked us the first time. This might be a rogue outfit, but they've got a leader in high places."

"Who do you think it was?" Mykal said.

"I have my ideas." Blodwyn told him.

CHAPTER 23

Queen Sarah wore practical clothing. The royal garments restricted movement, and made the young ruler feel somewhat claustrophobic, and ancient. She preferred black trousers with leggings, and a white tunic. She doubted her father would have approved. Since he was dead, and she was queen—one of the queens, anyway—it didn't matter. By the window she held a small doll in each hand. She bounced them along, changing her voice as each spoke.

"Your highness, you are doing a most wonderful job ruling the kingdom."

"That is kind of you to say. I appreciate—"

A knock at the door startled her. She turned and whipped the dolls across the room, into a corner. "Enter!"

Axel pushed the door open.

"Have a seat," she said, and then paced the length of the Long Room in a casual manner, but made sure the dolls were lost in shadows as she made her way around and around the table. Seated on the east side was Axel, his hands folded together in front of him. She didn't comment about the cuts and bruises visible on his face.

"I did as you said, your highness." Axel's face was marred with bruises, and stitched up cuts. His swollen lower lip was purple. His thumbs dueled, absently. "They followed the trail along the Rames, apparently headed for the valley, as you suspected."

"I'm not happy about them taking the investigation outside of the keep. Clearly, we could have summoned anyone they wished to interrogate." Queen Sarah rolled up her sleeves to just below the elbow, and pulled out a chair across from her thane. She dropped into the chair and brought up her legs so the heels of her shoes shared the lip of the chair. She wrapped her arms around her legs, and rested her chin on her knees.

"Best guess is they are headed to see Geneva's family. Perhaps to talk with Deidre's children. The kids are older, nearly full grown. They may have details we've not yet acquired. That's best guess," Axel said.

The news unsettled Sarah. She almost acted out. It would have been a tantrum, she knew. She'd thrown them often as a child. Heck, her mother had practically encouraged them, claiming it was an effective way of getting what one wanted. The fact the wizard was on the way with his little entourage to ask questions of the missing woman's kids, and they hadn't thought to do so first was what upset her. The fact Axel hadn't thought to do it... She bit down on the flesh inside her cheeks. She was the queen now. One of them, anyway. She didn't need tantrums to get what she wanted.

She didn't need to yell. Instead, while there were just a few moments of silence in the room, she stared directly at her thane until she was quite certain he sensed her displeasure, and had grown uncomfortable.

Then she smiled. It was thin, weak, but it was a smile nonetheless. "When Gembert gets back, I want to see him. First thing."

"Of course, your highness." Axel sat rigid in the chair, as if made from stone. He opened his mouth, but then closed it before uttering a word.

"You were going to say something?"

"Actually, I was going to say it looked like you might be about to say something. I didn't want to speak out of turn asking what was on your mind." It was clear from the way he didn't make eye contact he understood the extent of her displeasure with him. That was good. A good thing. Axel then gave a slight nod of the head. "I'm sure if it was something you wanted to share with me you would have. Excuse me, your highness."

Sarah waved a dismissive hand. "Nothing to excuse, Axel. I *was* about to say something. So, if anything, that was very astute. What concerns me is the young wizard. I understand my subjects desire answers. The abductions have everyone on edge. There's no faith in Raaheel and me. I know what they say. We're kids. Too young to rule this kingdom. I'm more confident in you and your team. In fact, you have no idea how much I'm pulling for you to solve the offenses first. It's for selfish reasons, I know. However, if *my* thane can figure out who's behind the crimes it will most assuredly restore a level of faith, and respect in the crowns."

Axel stood up. He pressed his hands together in front of him, and bowed. "I have no doubt, your highness. Now that I've brought you up to date on what I do know, I'd like to get back to work. Unless, that is, you have other matters you'd like to discuss?"

Sarah appreciated the slices of light cutting through the tall, thin windows. "Please. I don't want to keep you. Thank you for the update. If you learn of anything else…"

"I'll be sure to let you know at once."

Sarah smiled. "Thank you."

Axel started toward the door. His boots clapped on the floor.

"Axel? Have you seen my sister recently?"

The thane stopped walking. He turned around, a thoughtful expression contorted his facial features. He spoke slowly. "Not since yesterday morning, I'm afraid. Would you like me to find her for you?"

Sarah hadn't seen Raaheel either. Last time they'd spoken was when the wizard was with them. An abrupt departure was probably rude, but she wasn't concerned. She was a queen, and didn't have time for holding hands with the sorcerer. Raaheel was truly the one who pressed the issue, advising it best to send for his help. Let her do the coddling. "No, no, that won't be necessary. I was just curious."

"If that is all?"

"It is, Axel. Thank you."

When he was gone from the Long Room, Sarah stood beside the center window. She gazed out at her kingdom. It stretched further than she could see, and on a clear day— such as today—she could see quite far. Having a castle in the sky gave better perspective than living anywhere else, she supposed.

Sometimes it was difficult getting past the illusion of security that came from the castle. While other kings had waged war against the Osiris Realm, none had ever marched against the keep. It would be foolish. Those living in the valley were far more vulnerable, but even still every king has protected the whole of the realm.

She would have to check records because she could not recall when the last war on their land occurred. Fifty years ago? A hundred? Two hundred?

Enemies were smart enough not to start a war they couldn't win.

After many failed attempts, apparently, the attacks stopped altogether. It didn't mean war didn't happen. It did. One just ended two years ago. Her father died fighting in it, and at the hands of the wizard now freely wandering around the Osiris.

But the point was the subjects had grown accustomed to feeling safe.

Until now, until the abductions started.

She'd been informed a wave of fear spread throughout the Rames.

Fear without answers, without explanation, would cause panic.

She and Raaheel did not need a panic on their hands. It was partly why the two had—eventually—agreed to call on the wizard for assistance. Truthfully, the summons had been little more than a gesture meant to pacify the people.

The wizard was so legendary; she'd been apt to doubt his existence.

Never had she dreamed one of those sent in search of him would, or could, actually find him.

The wizard's presence complicated matters. It turned the abductions into something of a game. Her thane against a wizard. Who would solve the disappearances first?

Axel had better.

She didn't want to say that to him, but she was certain he understood the situation well enough. He was a smart, clever man. Putting a puzzle together was one of his skills. When the pieces needing assembling were large and obvious, even a child could figure out what's what.

Games.

She rolled her hands into such tightly clenched fists her fingernails dug into her palms, drawing blood.

***

Anna carried box, blank parchment, quill, and a small bottle of black into toward the table in the center of the room.

She thought about what she might write most of the night. Several times she thought she had the words perfectly aligned in her head. When she mustered the strength to get out of bed, the words floated out of her mind, as if pollen blowing around on a summer breeze. Poof. Gone.

It happened more than once. Quite possibly she'd been up and down all night.

The one thing she needed most was sleep. Rest. Realistically, sleep wasn't going to make much difference. Not really. She didn't want it because she thought it might make her feel better. She wanted to sleep because she was tired.

So tired.

When eventually she fell asleep, she woke up less refreshed than when she'd originally gone to bed. If it wasn't for the slivers of sunlight inside her makeshift bedchamber, she'd never have believed it was morning. Her head, and the rest of her body, would have her presume it was the middle of the night.

Getting out of bed, she recalled there was something important that needed doing. She stood, swaying slightly, and closed her eyes. That didn't help with the dizziness, or wave of nausea that overtook her, but for just a brief moment she thought she could almost recall what it was she wanted to get done.

Almost.

It was the parchment, quill and ink by the bedchamber door that sparked the memory. She'd gathered the supplies, and the box from under her bed, and made her way downstairs.

Now that she was downstairs, and had everything with her, she wasn't sure if she was just going upstairs, or down.

She stopped halfway between the table and the entrance, and did a once-around. "Oh, dear." She gazed down at the box in the crook of her arm. The parchment. The quill. The ceramic jar of ink. "Oh, dear."

"Mother?"

Startled, Anna jumped back. She looked up. No one was above her. The voice didn't exactly come from above her, though. Not exactly. She rushed forward and set the items down on the table.

Something about that felt... right.

She remembered not sleeping. There had been ideas she needed recorded. No. It was more than ideas.

A message.

She needed to write out a message.

That was why she'd come down here in the first place. The box needed to go back where it belonged. She would do that first, while the idea was fresh in her mind. After, she could worry about what letter she was going to write, and who the letter was for.

"Mother?"

Startled, she pushed away from the table. With eyes wide, she looked up toward the ceiling. There was no one up there.

The voice was familiar. Haunting?

She turned around. The door out of the lower level was halfway across the room. Was someone at the top of the stairs calling her name?

What is my name?

She knew it this morning. *Probably. I never do think of myself by name. It's no wonder I can't recall it now.*

She saw a box on the table. A corner sat on top of an edge of parchment. A long, soft looking feather quill pen was dipped into a ceramic inkwell.

This is why I'm down here, she thought, *to bring the box upstairs with me. The box is such an odd thing. I must have seen it earlier. I'm really not feeling well. It must be late. I can put the box beside my bed, and get a good night's sleep. In the morning, I'll take a closer look.*

Anna carefully lifted the box in both hands. She held it up near her face, and smiled. "This truly is an unusual artifact." Anna clucked her tongue as she pulled at edges, confusion set in when the lid didn't open.

***

"I'm really getting worried, Wyn." Mykal squatted with his back against a tree.

"No luck reaching your mother?"

Mykal shook his head. She had been pretty sick when they left her. He should have known better. At the time the idea of an adventure was kind of exciting. If he was being honest, anything would have been better than staying another day at the library with nothing but lessons to look forward to. Putting his own boredom over his mother's well-being, though, that was a new low. "I tried several times. I'm not getting anything back from her. Not as much as a whisper."

"She could be asleep. It's not like you could enter her dreams and wake her," Blodwyn said. He leaned against the tree directly across from Mykal, but now leaned forward and whispered, "Can you?"

Mykal got to his feet. He brushed snow away from his cloak, shaking his head. "I don't know. Haven't tried anything like that before. It's really the first time we've been apart in two years. We haven't needed to communicate like this since the War."

"I know you're anxious about her—"

"We need to get things wrapped up here. I'm ready to go home." Mykal walked out of the trees, and stood almost in defiance staring at the not-so-distant thoroughfare running through the main part of the valley. "Where is Geneva?"

CHAPTER 24

Mykal did his best at ignoring the pangs of hunger that rolled inside his belly. The constant aroma of cooking meat and baked breads reached them. Hovered. The temptation grew, but Mykal fought the desire. Heading into the valley for a meal was a bad idea. He didn't bother running it by Blodwyn. His friend would have agreed. The people were already in danger just by them staging so closely to the town.

One plus, which barely made up for the mounting negatives about the trek, was the temperature. The wind was steady, but not brutal. The sun continued shining, although heat from the rays barely penetrated the near-frozen landscape. It could be worse. It could always be worse. Thankfully it wasn't snowing, or sleeting. They were dry, and for the most part, warm.

Blodwyn sat, back to a tree, and used a small knife to whittle bark off a branch. It was an absent task, clearly something to bide the time. He slowly worked the end into a point, and when finished, tossed the stick behind him. He dropped his arms onto his raised knees, and sighed. "Feel like we're wasting time. There's no telling how long we have until more warriors come for us. I don't like just sitting here, waiting."

"You and me, both." Mykal had his thumbs hooked in the waistband of his trousers. He stood, slouched, a leg up, boot against a trunk, and stared up through bare branches at blue sky, and swiftly moving puffs of clouds. Above a raven soared, circling them. It had been there for some time, as if watching the strangers hiding in the trees. "You think we should go after her?"

"Go where? Do you know where this Deidre lives exactly? Or should we just knock on doors until we find them? The young lady has proved herself time and again. We'll wait."

Mykal breathed in a through his nostrils, and clapped a hand over his stomach.

"There'll be time to eat."

"I know." Mykal once again searched the sky for the raven. He wasn't sure why he was so drawn to such birds. Something about them always fascinated him. Their size, compared to the more common sparrow, for one. There was something else, too. He couldn't put a finger on it, though.

"Here she comes." Blodwyn got to his feet.

Geneva walked at a casual pace, head down. She knew how *not* to draw attention. Once she reached the edge of town, however, and made her way toward the tree-line, she'd be noticed. There'd be no way around that. A woman, alone, headed out of town?

Eyes followed her.

Mykal shouldered up to the closest tree, despite knowing his dark green cloak masked his presence.

Geneva must have felt others watching her. She quickened her step. Small tendrils of breath rose as high as her forehead before dissipating.

Time moved slow, at least it felt that way. Mykal took in Geneva as she walked toward them. Even with her head down, Mykal noticed the little things. The straight part of her black hair. Long eyelashes, that earlier had trapped snowflakes. The slant of her nose, with the tip nearly as red as a tomato. She ground her teeth against the cold, her lips as purple as fresh bruises. Slender fingers tugged at the edges of the cape, as if in despair that spring would not arrive any time soon.

She was several years older than him, and he was fairly certain any sentiment he felt wasn't equally shared.

"I'm sorry that took so long." Geneva's hands were bright pink. She cupped them in front of her face, blew into them, and then vigorously rubbed her palms together. "My niece and nephews are distraught. I wasn't ready for it. I suppose I am too. More than I let on. I busied myself with finding the two of you. It kept my mind off of what happened. I hadn't forgotten, but it helped me not remember so much. Not them though. Those poor kids have been sitting home, waiting. What else can they do?"

"We're doing everything we can." Mykal knew his response fell flat. There was no telling where the investigation would lead. What's uncovered might not bring about positive results. He tried showing optimism, but they all knew how unpredictable the situation had become. Sticking with an honest, truthful answer was the best he could offer. "One way or another, we're going to find out what happened."

With lips pressed tightly together, she nodded as if she understood the direness of their circumstances better than he had let on. "I have some of my Aunt Deidre's things. Although, I'm not sure exactly how they'll help, but I hope it's good enough. I brought you a blouse of hers."

"That should work just fine." Mykal held the blouse by the shoulders, before folding it over his arm.

"That's a good thing. My niece, Sierra gave me an odd-ways look about when she caught me stuffing it down my... you get the point."

***

Mykal wanted away from prying eyes. It wasn't as if they were inside a forest. There were some trees. Some rocks. Still, he moved as far from the town as possible. They found a large boulder, and knelt around a smaller, flatter rock. It seemed like a perfect table for working on, too. So at least there was that.

Un-cinching the pouch on his belt, Mykal set up the alchemy contents.

"What are these?" Geneva squatted by the rock, pointing at the small vials.

"Let's let him work now." Blodwyn stood directly behind her, reaching toward her shoulder.

"It's okay. She's fine watching." Mykal knelt in the snow. The air was cold, and crisp. He breathed in and out through his nose. It felt invigorating. He enjoyed the alchemy aspect of magic, although it offered little by way of control. Perhaps it was the surprise element that excited him, despite the ghostly apparitions experienced inside the Cordillera castle. That was something he'd have to discuss with his mother when he returned home. The experiments they attempted never reached the level of intensity he'd witnessed over the last several days.

Using the rock as his mortar, Mykal carefully looked over the minerals.

"You know what all of these are?" Geneva asked.

Mykal said, "I do."

"And what do you do with them?"

"When they are mixed together they do different kinds of magic." It was a terrible explanation. Mykal had never been asked to define alchemy.

Geneva's eyes opened wide. "So I can mix some of this with some of that, and do magic?"

"Not exactly," Mykal said.

Blodwyn, resigned, found a place and knelt beside Mykal and Geneva.

"Then how does it work?"

"Generally, alchemy was used, or is used, for discovery. Finding new elixirs and things like that."

"Healing elixirs?"

"That, and as a means of creating new things."

"New things?" She let her face pucker, and brow furrow.

"Like, if you mixed water and dirt, what do you get?"

"Dirty!" She laughed.

"Mud. If you mix water and dirt you get mud. But people might not know this unless an alchemist discovered the combination in a lab."

"Or if it rained," she said.

Mykal allowed half a smile on the left side of his mouth. It didn't linger long, and soon his face went back to something more somber, and tired. "That was a simple example, I know. I was just trying to make the explanation understandable."

"What? Because you think I'm stupid or something? Because I'm not a famous wizard like you I don't understand anything more complicated than mud?"

Mykal's eyes caught Blodwyn's stare. "That is not, that was not, I did not mean anything by that. That was exactly how my mother first explained alchemy to me when she started teaching me."

Geneva said, "And you know what they do?"

She no longer seemed insulted. The anger left her face as quickly as it had overtaken her features. The transition came and went as fast as a finger-snap.

Mykal said, "For the most part."

"For the most part?" Geneva said. "You mean you just can mix them all but not know what to expect, what the outcome might be?"

"Each element, herb, oil, has a base to it. Properties associated with it. I've been studying the origins. Memorizing, actually. Sometimes it makes sense. Like, if you combine blue and red it makes..."

Mykal wanted Geneva to answer, so as not to insinuate anything, but instead she stared intently, as if waiting for the answer.

"...purple," he said.

She shook her head, her jaw set. "What does that mean? Red and blue make purple?"

"I hate to interrupt the lesson and everything," Blodwyn said, "but we've got a time is of the essence thing happening here. When that sun sets, who knows how cold it will get. Could even be another blizzard brewing. I don't want to speak out of turn, but maybe we should move this along?"

Mykal closed his eyelids before rolling his eyes, even though he knew his friend was absolutely correct. "Point made," he said.

"You're going to explain that purple comment later," Geneva said.

Mykal chose a vile, and removed the stopper. "I will. I promise."

Geneva pointed. "And what's that?"

He removed a small pebble of silver and set it onto the flat rock. "This is zinc. It is considered beneficial to pregnant women, and then equally important for restoring strength after the baby's born. It is useful in magic because of its electrochemical reaction, or electrical current."

Mykal ground the pebble into a fine dust with the pestle, while eyeing the small bags of herbs. He decided one, and removed some small, dried leaves. They crumbled between his fingers, and he sprinkled the flakes over the zinc.

"What was that?" Geneva asked.

"Pennyroyal. Otherwise known as *dweorge dwosle.*"

"Dwe-what?"

"Dweorge dwosel. Translated it means, dwarf destroyer."

"You plan on killing some dwarfs?"

Even Blodwyn chuckled at that exchange.

"No," Mykal said. I don't plan on killing any dwarfs. It's just a translation."

"Smells minty."

"We're using pennyroyal because it was sometimes used as an abortifacient, and since we are dealing with missing, possibly dead women, the pennyroyal and the zinc seem like a potential combination that might spark answers." Mykal worked the pestle again, grinding the two ingredients together.

"Abortifacient?"

"People who don't want a child to be born, kill the life inside them before delivery," Blodwyn said.

"Why would someone do such a thing?" Geneva sounded upset, her tone of voice raised more than an octave, and she placed a hand over her chest as if breath was suddenly trapped in her lungs.

Mykal said, "We're also going to add a drop of hyssop oil. It offsets the adverse implications of pennyroyal, and has been known to actually warn off death."

"So why use such opposite items, don't they then cancel each other out?" Geneva said.

"Yes, and no." He let two drops drip over the ground powder on his makeshift mortar. "Both the pennyroyal and the zinc are still included in the mix. You can't erase the effects completely, unless you remove them. However, the oil will blend the ingredients more completely, unifying them. This way the dominance of one is leveled when compared to the dominance of the other. Does that make sense?"

"None."

Mykal pursed his lips. Blodwyn rolled a finger around and around. "On with it," he said.

Quickly, Mykal used the pestle again, and turned the ingredients into goo. "Might want to sit back." The last few times he'd combined alchemy with his magic, the results had been intriguing, but unexpected. The powerful visions rocked him. He didn't want anyone getting hurt. He draped the blouse over the rock, over the gob that was the mixture he'd created, and then he waved a hand over the blouse.

He let power build up inside his body, and the heat from it spill out of the palm of his hand. Brilliant blue bolts raced around his hand. Hissed, and snapped. The hairs on his arm stood on end. Through the cyan glow, Mykal noticed Geneva's amazed expression. She kept turning toward Blodwyn, either making sure he saw what she was seeing, or to ensure he wasn't missing the display.

Blodwyn watched, as well, but hid any revealing expression from Mykal.

Mykal heard something above him. A buzz.

He looked up and saw vibrant butterflies with iridescent blue wings falling from the overhead tree branches. The fluttering was as loud as a swarm of summer flies. There were hundreds of them.

It looked like they were trying, but couldn't fly away.

He sensed their fear, panic. Did butterflies have hearts inside the thorax?

It was as if they were drawn toward the blouse, or more appropriately, that the blouse pulled them toward relentlessly toward *it*. The butterflies manipulated a path around Mykal's hand one by one, before dropping onto the gooey blob he'd created. Immediately, each butterfly burst into a flame, and then disintegrated into black ash and a small puff of smoke.

He heard a scream from each butterfly as it died.

As more butterflies fell onto the blouse, the size of the fire grew. The blouse material didn't catch, it didn't burn. The rising smoke became black. He smelled nothing but the charred remains of the butterflies.

The white snow on the ground was covered with the remains of iridescent blue butterflies. They weren't all dead.

Thousands of wings flapped, beating an impression into the snow.

The ground was alive with the butterflies.

He had no idea why there were so many butterflies, or what it meant.

A shadow started toward them from the north. An outline. It could be a woman. Each step she took the butterflies flew away before getting squashed into the snow.

The closer she got, the clearer he saw her.

He thought it might have been the same ghost he saw in the castle.

Clairece.

This apparition was blue.

Wings, all over her, fluttered.

She was nothing more than thousands of butterflies. "Please help me."

The voice came from flapping wings. A loud whisper. A soft scream. The breath of the words brushed by his ears.

That was what Clairece wanted.

Help.

"I am trying to find out what happened."

Butterfly arms rose, and butterfly hands touched middle fingers, and thumbs creating a triangle space between them. "There isn't much time. The danger extends to you."

"To me?" Mykal wasn't shocked, but was looking for clarification. There was no doubt he'd been in danger from the moment they left the castle with Geneva and Gembert.

"Help me. Help us."

"Where do I look?"

"Help yourself."

She stood over him. Because she was parchment thin, when wings flap he saw through her, and out the other side.

Her eyes were the colorful pattern designs on the back of butterfly wings.

"Where do I look for answers?" Mykal asked. "Is Clairece alive still? Deidre? Do you know them? Are they okay?"

The butterfly woman didn't turn around. However, the individual butterflies did. And then she started walking away.

"Please! I want to help you; I just need something to point me in the right direction."

The butterflies shifted all around. In a spin they transformed for just the briefest moment into a sunburst of yellow, orange, red and black, and in a flurry of flapping, changed back into a glowing iridescent blue.

Arms rose. Hands met. The triangle appeared once again. "You should run."

Run? "From who? To where?"

Fluttering. Turning. She walked back toward where she first materialized.

She left him with nothing but a warning.

A strong wind blew. The gust passed through the thin line of trees. The butterflies rose off the ground, and whirled about. Climbed higher and higher, some flew this way and that. The very air surrounding Mykal was filled with nothing but blue butterflies.

The sinister sound of a swarm was replaced with an almost calming beat. Tranquil. The cries from their deaths were replaced by song. There were no lyrics. The music was odd, percussion, but uplifting, and encouraging.

Mykal watched the mass exodus in awe, and then stood staring upward, spinning around and around; some of the butterflies perched on bare tree limbs, while others landed along the trunks, and some just continued ascending.

They resembled a spinning cluster. And then they were gone.

Mykal felt a sudden emptiness from having lost sight of them all. He couldn't find even one left on a branch, or on a tree trunk.

Gone.

They'd all simply vanished, or flown away.

CHAPTER 25

Mykal saw towering treetops pointing at a blue sky. The bright of it all made him close his eyes. He squeezed them shut.

"He's awake!" He recognized the sound of Geneva's voice.

"Mykal?" Blodwyn.

Their faces suddenly blocked his view. He reached up a hand. His fingertip touched Blodwyn's nose. Blodwyn pulled back. "How are you feeling?"

"Am I lying down?"

"You are." Blodwyn held fingers in front of Mykal's face. "How many?"

"Five."

Blodwyn shook his head. "It's two."

"Two up, three folded down."

"Help get him up." Blodwyn didn't appear to be in the mood for jokes. "How's your head?"

"Feels like my brain's swimming around inside my skull." Mykal was aware of a steady throb. Squinting eased some of the pain. Everything sounded very loud, as if every noise exploded inside his ears. "Am I standing?"

"Not really." Geneva grunted. "We're holding you." She was tucked under his left arm. She held onto his shoulder, and chest. Mykal didn't think she could support his weight on her own, until he realized his right arm was limp at his side.

"What happened?"

Blodwyn said, "You ignited the blouse on fire—"

"I kind of promised Sierra I'd return the blouse when I was done with it. She really wanted an explanation on why I was taking it in the first place. Like I said. Wasn't easy stealing clothing from their missing mother. But when I promised I'd bring it back..."

"Geneva," Blodwyn said. "Please."

"Sorry."

"What happened to all of the butterflies?" Mykal let his eyes ease open. His lashes skewed the light from blasting his eyeballs full on.

"Butterflies?" Geneva asked.

"You fell back, Mykal. Hit your head on a rock." Blodwyn stood in front of him. He held up a finger. "I want you to follow my finger with your eyes. Try not moving your head at all. Okay?"

"Got it."

Blodwyn moved a finger past Mykal's eyes, "Keep your head straight."

"I am."

"Let's try it again." Blodwyn passed his finger by Mykal's nose in the opposite direction. "Just follow my finger with your eyes. Keep your head still."

"I am."

"You're not," Geneva piped in. "Your entire head is turning."

"I would love to bicker this back and forth, but I'm about to throw up. I suggest you stand aside." It was all the warning he could muster.

Geneva jumped back.

"Is he going to be alright?"

Blodwyn clucked his tongue. "Basically, he took a pretty serious knock on the head. I'm thinking maybe we should get him to the healer. Can you take us to where Gembert went with Daniel and his wife?"

Mykal, bent over and dry heaving, reached back with an arm. "I'm fine. I just need a minute."

"You're not fine," Geneva said. "He's not fine. Tell him, Wyn."

"You're not fine."

"See?" she said.

Mykal set his hands on his knees. He breathed in slow, deep breaths. When he felt certain he was all done being sick he stood up straight. He wiped his lower lip clean with the back of his thumb. "Neither of you saw the butterflies? Blue butterflies?"

"Where was it? Maybe we overlooked it?" Blodwyn said, turning left, and then right.

"There were thousands. Tens of thousands. They were everywhere." Mykal saw the look exchanged between Geneva and Blodwyn. It was an easy to read expression on their faces. They thought he'd gone mad. At least he assumed they'd blame the crazy on the thumping of his head. "I think we're endangering the people here. We should start back to the castle."

"Did you learn anything from the blouse?" Geneva asked.

Mykal shook his head. That had been a mistake. It felt like his eyes might drop out of the sockets from the motion. He touched his temples with fingertips to keep the entire world from spinning in front of him. "Nothing."

He couldn't tell if what he'd experienced was from magic, or from knocking himself out on a rock. Had he a vision of a butterfly person asking for help and trying to warn him, or was it little more than an episode brought on by the concussion?

The entire segment was so surreal, he couldn't differentiate. If anything, the more he thought about it now, the muddier it all became. The vision had been completely dream-like, so that didn't lend any assistance in differentiating between the two.

"If you didn't learn anything, then why do you think we're endangering the villagers?" Blodwyn asked.

"The previous attacks," Mykal said.

"You don't sound sure of yourself. Was there something more? Something else you saw?" Blodwyn arched an eyebrow.

Mykal recounted for them the details of what happened. "She said to run."

"The butterfly lady?" Geneva asked, and Mykal nodded. "Run where?"

"That's what I asked."

"And did she answer?" Blodwyn smoothed the long hairs hanging that grew from his chin.

"She disappeared."

"I see."

Mykal sighed. "So now what?"

"Now we have to interpret what it means. I think you're right, though. The longer we stay here the more danger the villagers are in. We'll gather up Gembert. Daniel and his wife are with the healer. They should be relatively safe. No one is after them," Blodwyn said. "We should leave, and we shouldn't be quiet about it."

"What does that mean?" Geneva questioned.

"The more people that see us leave the valley, the better. Should those warriors show up here, a number of people will be able to testify we've left," Blodwyn explained. "This way they're honest about what they know, and no one gets hurt."

"That makes the most sense." Mykal asked, "And the butterflies?"

Blodwyn shook his head thoughtfully. "I have no idea what they mean. I suppose it might be something only you can answer."

"I don't know what they mean, either."

"Maybe not right now, but that could change." Blodwyn turned around. "There might be something we missed. A sign? I don't know. We're aware of it now, so we'll just have to keep our eyes open."

"Where are you going?" Mykal asked.

"To fetch Daniel. You two wait here. We'll be leaving posthaste!"

***

The sun set. Replacing the blue sky was a star-speckled black one. The half-moon sat diagonally tilted amidst the vastness above. The temperature dropped, changing from a crisp, cold day into a far more chilling and frigid night. Gembert the Chamberlain didn't look as reserved. His short cropped hair was about all that remained of his dignified look. The gold trim on his red robe was muddied, and there were small tears in the velvet fabric. The thin mustache over his upper lip was surrounded by an entire face badly in need of an evening shave.

"The healer pulled me aside while Daniel tended to his wife." Gembert spoke as they walked the path up the backside of the mountain. "He didn't come right out and say it, but it doesn't sound promising for Miriam."

Mykal thought Blodwyn winced at the words. "I'm sure the healer will do everything they can to care for her. Wyn's paid well for those services."

"I gave them all of the coins." Gembert sounded timid, as if he feared a scolding might be delivered. "I hope that was all right?"

Blodwyn nodded. "That's fine. It's what they were for. I just wish the outlook sounded more promising."

Mykal had seen Miriam's condition after the fire, knew when awake she'd again be in great pain. He wondered if death after so much damage might not be best? If Karyn were still alive, Miriam would be fine. "I can try healing her."

Blodwyn continued walking.

"Wyn? Did you hear me?"

His friend stopped and turned around. He tapped the end of his staff into the snow, as if it helped while he searched for words. The creases across his forehead were deeper than Mykal remembered.

"I believe if you tried healing Miriam, she would live. Her pain would vanish. She's near death. I'm not telling any of you anything we all don't already know. I'm afraid if you step in with magic and save her life, irreparable harm will come to you. This mission we're on, it's an important one, but not at the risk of losing my friend." With that, he turned away and continued walking.

Mykal didn't think he'd die if he saved Miriam. It would deplete his strength, and yes, overdoing it could result in his death, but he was a much stronger sorcerer than he had been two years ago, even two months ago. It didn't feel right not trying, and knowing he was far more capable than the healer.

If only he and his mother had covered elixirs in alchemy training. He was sure he'd have the skills to concoct a potion worthy of taking away the woman's pain and suffering at the very least.

He wasn't giving up on the idea of helping her.

The only reason he wasn't trying now was because he feared the longer they stayed in the village, the more likely it could turn ugly when the warriors arrived. And they would show up. He was certain of that.

CHAPTER 26

Although the doorway to the dungeon appeared sealed off, and after making sure no one was around, she depressed a brick in the wall and it unlocked. Slipping through, and closing the door behind, she made her way down the dark spiraling stone stairs. Tracing her hand along damp, cold walls she carefully descended into the black.

Black iron bowls sat on either side of the widening mouth at the bottom of the stairs. Red burning coals glowed bright in contrast of the surrounding walls of nothing but darkness.

She removed an unlit torch from a sconce and touched the cloth wrapped end to the embers. Igniting, a large orange flame came alive. She walked the room, touching the end of her torch to the others still hung in sconces on the walls.

The dungeon was alive with moving shadows.

The cells were crudely carved into the mountain, and secured with iron bars. The ceilings were low, sharp, and jagged, as were the side walls, and floor.

The odor of mold she could handle. The pungent smell of feces and urine turned her stomach. Those were not scents she'd ever get used to, and why should she?

Most of the king's torture equipment remained. The table in the center of the chamber was untouched. On pegs on the walls were an array of devices that looked imposing, and threatening, and dangerous without even knowing for sure how they operated.

She thought ghosts existed.

Sometimes she would swear she heard them whisper.

Countless people died in the dungeon. Not just at the hand of King Hermon Cordillera, but also at the whim of his father, King Elroy, and all the kings before them. The room was designed for inflicting pain. Physical, emotional, and psychological. The temperature was frigid. Mold covered the rock. The walls leaked in the summer months, and iced in the winter.

Unless the dungeon master was unleashing pain and punishment on a poor soul, the chamber was plunged in an almost eternal pitch black darkness.

And then there were the ghosts.

But she wasn't afraid of the spirits. In fact, it soothed her knowing they were gathered around. It meant she had picked the best place to continue her personal studies.

The only way she could achieve all the goals she set was with the help of those lingering between worlds.

She didn't understand, *yet*, how ghosts existed, only that she knew they did. They were prevalent in the dungeon. Some scared her, their anger almost... visible. Death baffled her. She knew long, long ago people attempted to explain death, and after-lives. It was long before Emperor Rye that such beliefs were outlawed, and any search for answers into what happened to a person after death could be seen as dangerous and punishable by torture, up to and including execution.

What she studied in the dungeon was forbidden, and not just because in a way she was exploring what happened after death, but because she also sought out gaining power through magic.

She knew once she secured immortality, knees would bend before her.

Heads would bow, and every knee not just in the Osiris Realm, but across the old empire would bend. She would succeed where her father failed. She would not only rule as the sole queen, but eventually as the new empress of the lands and sea!

The thought gave her chills, and she chuckled. The high-pitched sound echoed, bouncing off the cell walls.

And the whispers circled around her. She could not ascertain what was said. There were too many voices. Not all whispered. Some just cried. There were screams, too. Agonizing screams.

Someone sniffled.

It wasn't a ghost, though. It came from one of the cells. The center one, perhaps.

"Water." The voice sounded frail, weak.

That wasn't surprising.

No one knew anyone was down here, but her, and most of the time she completely forgot to bring provisions.

Ignoring the plea, she shined the light from her torch by the bars, and then set it in a sconce on the wall between two cells. She clanked a tin cup between iron bars.

The woman, covered in grime and bruises, scurried away. Bare feet, knees, and hands shuffled through the straw strewn about, but otherwise generally used as bedding.

"Don't you want your water?" It was a heartless trick, and while she had nothing against the prisoner personally, it was difficult not thinking of her as anything less than a specimen.

The notion water might be available caught the woman's attention, and she scampered toward the bars. Her head was bowed, hair covered all of her face. She held out a hand. "Please. Water?"

The pathetic display made her stomach roll. It was that or seeing the growing pile of excrement in the back corner. "Your hand." It was not an uncommon request. They knew what she wanted. She was down enough for more.

For a moment the woman remained motionless, sitting on haunches, huddled in on herself, and silent. She didn't ask a third time for water. Perhaps she understood the truth: there was no water.

"Your hand!"

The woman lifted an arm, and let hesitantly gravitate toward the bars.

She reached through the bars and snatched the woman's wrist. "I don't have time for this!"

She drew a dagger across flesh. The sharp blade easily sliced into the woman's skin. Blood spilled from the straight line splitting open her forearm.

Lifting the woman's wrist in the air, the blood rolled down the forearm, and dripped from the elbow into a tin cup.

When the cup was filled, she released the woman's arm.

The woman drew her arm in, and cradled it against her chest. Fresh tears streaked dried dirt down her cheeks.

"Don't cry. I'll be back. You'll have water, and food." She meant what she said. The other two were dead. This one, the youngest of the three abducted, was the most effervescent. The difference was evident in the blood. There was a freshness, an undeniable stimulation she experienced when drinking it. She couldn't let this one die, too.

Not yet.

Not until she was certain she'd reached her objective.

Immortality was obtainable.

And she was close, perhaps closer than anyone else had ever been before.

As she whirled away from the cell, and started back toward the stairs, she chuckled some more, and just like before, the chuckling echoed throughout the chamber, only it sounded much more like a cackle than a laugh.

***

The Cordillera keep rose into the sky with the matching and passing the highest peaks of the Rames Mountains with clouds, oftentimes, below the various rising spires. The one specific tower she didn't think anyone was aware of was where she went most often. It was where the king had kept his sorceress, Ida, locked away. The room carried an enchantment placed over it by King Cordillera. He was not a natural-born wizard, but had become a self-taught magician, mastering spells little more impressive than party tricks.

The sorceress stocked the shelves and any available space with an array of herbs, oils, and elements. Each was precisely labeled. In the center of the room was an iron pit for fire, and two moderate sized cauldrons.

Cordillera was vocal about his dreams and aspirations of acquiring magic. He began an elaborate collection of ancient books and manuscripts on the art. His search for more, and more was not exhaustive, but impressive nonetheless. At the end, he'd discovered a secret—a way to siphon the power and energy of wizards into his own life-force. In the end, it didn't fare well for him, but it was because he went about it wrong.

All wrong.

Somehow he'd lost touch with reality in his drive, and let desire overpower mind and reasoning. He bit off far more than he could chew; tried running before he learned to walk. Ultimately, his ambition was his downfall.

He fell hard, went down in flames, or so she was told.

Thankfully, when the War ended there was no siege. The Osiris Realm was left alone to heal from wounds. Thousands of lives were lost in battles on land, and on sea. For months those in the kingdom feared the king of Grey Ashland would cross the Isthmian and attempt occupying their land.

It never happened.

The War was never about kingdom versus kingdom. It was about King Hermon Cordillera versus the wizard.

Mykal.

Somehow, the boy had defeated the man, the crown.

Somehow that boy was still alive, and the king was dead, and gone.

Her hand trembled. The thick blood sloshed around inside the tin cup. There wasn't enough that it might spill. Still, she set it down, just in case. It was valuable, and she didn't wish risking the loss of even a drop.

Despite large lit lanterns, moonbeams entered through the one iron barred window. She set the book of spells on the ledge and pulled on the silk marker holding her place between pages. Glancing over the text, she realized she almost had the incantation committed to memory. She didn't dare try reciting the words without the book. A missed word, or infliction, could drastically change or void the spell entirely.

She removed her necklace, and dipped the triangular charm into the cup. The gold chain dangled over the side. The triangle was solid silver, and a conduit for the transfer of energy. She peppered the blood with herbs outlined in the recipe. Reaching for the cup, she passed a hand over the rim as the beginning of the ritual demanded.

And when the incantation was complete, she lifted the cup with both hands.

She could smell the coppery liquid, and salivated.

She was hungry.

So hungry. She knew exactly what she was doing; knew exactly what the continued diet would bring about. The hunger might never go away, the thirst, or the need— the desire—to hunt. It didn't matter, though.

She drank, and in a gulp, drained the tin cup of the contents. Gasping, her tongue licked any trace off her lips, and off of her charm before running her finger around inside the cup. Hungrily, she sucked the remaining blood off her finger, and smacked her lips together when it was done.

She was far from satisfied.

She was famished.

It was far too dangerous stalking new prey. Once Mykal and his old friend left the mountains, she could return to the hunt with more vigor. For the time being, it was best if she rationed the blood. The nightly cups quenched her thirst, but teased her soul, and only stimulated her hunger.

That was what she told herself.

She repeated the idea over and over, trying to convince herself of the best course.

And yet, in the dungeon cell, more blood waited.

She thought she could smell it.

Most certainly what she sensed came from the cup in front of her, and from her own breath as she breathed.

It didn't the change fact, that Clairece was hers for the taking!

CHAPTER 27

Mykal debated transporting them from the mountain trail back to the castle. Blodwyn, as usual, argued against it, insisting he save his energy for when truly needed. Unfortunately, with the night came dropping temperatures. His energy, along with the heat inside his body, escaped the longer they stayed outdoors.

No one complained. Everyone was cold. Mykal heard teeth chattering. Could have been his own.

Mykal heard his own labored breathing inside his head. Exposed skin felt as if it were on fire. His cheeks and ears burned. Snow spotted the face of the mountain, sticking to the rocks. The wind howled like an angry beast.

The wind was, in fact, a relentless enemy. It raced down the mountain and slammed into their faces. If it weren't too dangerous to do so, they'd walk backwards. As it was, they hugged the side of the mountain. Visibility was limited to less than a foot or two. A misstep could be detrimental. If tumbling off the side didn't kill the person, it would make a rescue just a tad bit treacherous.

The four of them stayed close together. Blodwyn led them. Geneva kept a hand on the back of his cloak. Hopefully Gembert was keeping up, although he was less concerned about the chamberlain.

When at last they finally reached the castle, Mykal nearly cheered. He wasn't sure he had the strength. It was ironic because, while his legs were weak and rubbery, and he'd stumbled more than once leaving him off balance, they also felt like two solid blocks of ice. Heavy. Nearly impossible to lift.

No, instead of cheering he exhaled releasing a long, loud, and thankful sigh. Truth was, he'd been steps away from ignoring Blodwyn's plea and using magic.

***

Mykal never suspected feeling half as excited as he did now that he was back inside the Cordillera castle. The fire burned hot in the hearth in the main foyer. The crackle of flames eating away at logs was a most welcome sound. The little heat coming from the fire gave the illusion of pure sanctuary. He shook off the cold as much as possible, brushing snow off his shoulders, and shaking it out of his hair.

Blodwyn rested his staff in the crook of an arm, and spent several moments curling and flexing his fingers. He cupped his hands, blew into them, and then vigorously rubbed his palms together.

"Can we stand by the fire? Just for a minute or two?" Geneva looked up at Mykal, begging with her eyes. "I can't feel my face."

"You don't need my permission." Mykal wasn't sure why she asked his consent. "Please, warm yourself."

Gembert stood still feet in front of the closed door, wearing a somber expression, his eyes downcast, his hands laced behind his back.

"What about you, chamberlain? Aren't you freezing?" Mykal gauged the man for a reaction, waiting, watching.

"I have been away from the castle far too long. I am most certain the queens will want a debriefing. Unfortunately, I have much to report." Gembert then turned his head slightly away. "I am not sure how she'll react to events that unfolded on our investigation. If it suits you, I will be going."

The chamberlain did not seem at all anxious about seeing the queens.

Again, Mykal wasn't sure why everyone sought his approbation. "We'll be fine."

"I'll assume the queens will want a word with you, as well."

"I assume so. If you'll be so kind as to explain. We are tired from the journey. It's late. A change of clothing and a warm bed are at the top of our priority list at the moment. Surely, she'll understand."

"I should hope so."

His demeanor had changed, a one-eighty in personality from the man that had been on the road with them earlier. It was a shame, really.

Without another word, Gembert started away.

"Our next step, Wyn?" Mykal wanted guidance. Although he kept mostly silent, Mykal valued Blodwyn's insight. Age, and experience were tools he'd yet to acquire.

"I believe what you relayed to the chamberlain is ideal. I know getting out of these cold, wet clothes is first and foremost on my mind. My thighs feel raw, and in desperate need of thawing." He smiled.

"Geneva," Mykal said. "We're going to retire for the evening."

"Very well," she said.

"Unless you are busy tomorrow, I plan to speak with Elma, the baroness' sister. I'd like you present."

"Me?" She pointed at her chest.

"I believe Wyn and I might frighten her. A friendly face could diffuse any tension."

She smiled, and nodded. "I'll will be here. First light."

Mykal arched an eyebrow. "That early?"

"Noon?"

"First light is fine," he said, grinning. The snow in his hair was melting. Cold water rolled on his scalp, and both down his forehead, and the back of his neck. A shiver raced up his spine. His shoulders shook. "Thank you for your help today."

"But we didn't learn anything." She sounded disappointed, upset.

"Actually, we did. A lot. We're closer to the end than you might realize. There are a few more things I want cleared up tomorrow, and I believe we'll have this mystery solved."

Her eyes opened wider. "Then I shall see you both in the morning!"

Mykal watched Geneva reluctantly back away from the fire. She held out her hands, palms up, with each step savoring every last bit of heat before turning around and leaving the foyer.

"I'll make a deal with you, young mage." Blodwyn stood with fists on his hips, and a crooked smile. There was a curious gleam in his eyes.

"I'm listening."

"I won't tease you about your feelings for the lady," he said. "If..."

"Still listening."

"If you don't tell a soul you've helped me out of my boots."

Mykal held out his hand. Blodwyn eyed him suspiciously.

"We have a deal, then?"

Mykal said, "We do. Deal."

They shook on it.

CHAPTER 28

Mykal and Blodwyn stopped in the hallway leading toward their apartment. Standing by their door was the thane. He wore a bright white tunic and vest. His hand rested on the hilt on his sword. His facial expression changed when he noticed them, turning more stern, and serious, and he stood at attention.

"The Queen Sarah requests an audience with you." Axel's jaw set, as his eyes blatantly roamed over them. It was done callously, without hiding his open inspection.

Mykal's lips thinned, and he knew his cheeks puffed. "It's late. We're wet, and still cold. Though we were only gone a few days, we're tired." Axel didn't move a muscle; didn't even blink. It was why they were asked here, Mykal realized. They needed his help. He could sleep later, or tomorrow, or the next day. He bowed his head slightly, conceding. "But give us a moment so we can at least change into something dry, and more presentable. We can meet you in the Long Room I presume?"

"I'll wait and provide a proper escort."

"Of course you will." Mykal said.

Blodwyn and Mykal stopped at the door, and only then did Axel move, stepping aside.

"It appears our door was left open." Blodwyn commented in a tone of voice just loud enough for the thane to overhear. The intent behind the statement clearly conveyed.

However, Axel did not take the bait. "I shall wait in the hall while you change."

Mykal tore into the burlap bag for dry clothing, tossing pants and a tunic toward Blodwyn, and dropping his onto the sofa in front of him. "I am not liking this. Not any of it."

"We need to stay focused. The ends may be fraying." Blodwyn removed his cloak, and peeled off his tunic, using it to further dry his hair, before discarding it onto the floor.

"I've noticed. I still want to speak with Elma, she may be the final piece I need. If she confirms what we talked about, then we will at least have some answers."

"The who. Yes. But not the why. And that's what troubles me." Blodwyn's voice was muffled, as he pulled the fresh tunic over his head, and poked arms through the sleeves. He quickly laced the front, and tied it off in a long, dangling bow.

"There is a bottom to this mess. We're close. Very close."

Mykal had been working the puzzle over in his mind. The small clues he'd picked up on meant little on their own. He still couldn't see an entire picture. He felt confident the border pieces were aligned, and what was left were the few remaining wedges that needed to be fit into place.

They stepped out of the room, closing the door.

"Are you ready?" Axel said.

Mykal said, "We are."

They followed Axel back down the hallway. He led them to the Long Room. Inside Queen Sarah sat with her elbows on the table, her chin propped on fists. Her thin crown was in front of her, almost as if it had been discarded.

"Please," she said. "Be seated."

Puffy eyes made it seem as if she hadn't slept in days. Maybe she hadn't.

"Are you alright, your highness?" Mykal asked.

The queen forced a smile. Mykal needn't remind himself that the child was merely eleven years old. Joint ruling couldn't eliminate the stress that came from running a realm, especially when the shared responsibility was with a teenager.

"Spent endless hours the last several days holding court. The bickering between the people is never-ending. My head is throbbing, and my eyes just want to close." She stopped talking, closed her eyes, and let the smile broaden. She waved a dismissive hand, and looked at her visitors. "Please, please, excuse me."

"The wizard and his companion have just returned from visiting the valley." Axel stood at attention.

"At-ease, at-ease."

Axel relaxed, clasping his hands together behind his back. Mykal thought the thane still looked rigid. It must have something to do with the steel personality, or lack thereof.

"And what did you learn on this... excursion?" The queen had transformed. She no longer exhibited any signs of exhaustion. She locked eyes with Mykal.

He couldn't look away, enthralled by the two different colors in her eyes. "We learned more than expected. At the same time, we've come up with additional questions."

The queen shook her head. Her hair passed in front of her face from the motion. She used both hands to tuck lengths behind her ears. "Is that a wizard-thing?"

"What, your highness?"

"Riddles. Because if that's something you wizards do, I don't have the time or the patience for it." Her pale white skin reddened her cheeks. She gritted her teeth.

"I apologize."

Again, she waved a dismissive hand. "Spare me the apology, and just tell me what happened."

The door to the Long Room opened.

Queen Raaheel entered.

Attention shifted.

Mykal watched Queen Sarah's reaction. The young girl looked disheveled, and worn out. The junior royal lady did not look at all pleased to see her sibling. If anything, she looked annoyed, and wasn't trying, or wasn't trying too hard, to hide her emotions.

"I didn't know there was a gathering. Did I miss a formal invite?" Queen Raaheel sauntered into the room, a book clutched against her chest.

Queen Sarah stood up. Her chair legs scraped on the floor. "The wizard is back from the valley, and was just about to give us a report of any progress made on the investigation."

"Us?" Raaheel smirked. "Again, was there a formal invite I missed, because I was not aware of this meeting. Sharing the throne, I should suspect a debriefing of this magnitude would require we both be in attendance. Am I wrong?"

Sarah sat back down. "I didn't know where you were."

"Did you look?" It came out as a sneer.

"You're here now, sister. Would you care to join us?"

Raaheel waited for Axel to pull out the chair next to Sarah. She sat, and set the book down on the table. "As a matter of fact, I would."

An awkward silence fell over them. Sarah's jaw set, she finally nodded toward Mykal. "Can you please continue?"

"What did I miss?" Raaheel asked. She tapped a finger on the book. It inadvertently drew Mykal's attention, throwing his confidence off balance.

"A riddle." Sarah laced her hands around her crown. Her knuckles white.

"I don't understand," Raaheel said.

"Neither did I, which is why you've missed nothing, and our wizard was about to explain himself."

Mykal didn't care for the bickering. It was unbecoming, perhaps because they were royalty. Although he never knew how long they'd be on this matter, he felt like he'd already dedicated too much time. His mother was sick. Unresponsive. He had far more pressing matters he wanted to attend to, and they just didn't get it. Mykal said, "On our way toward the valley, we were attacked—"

Raaheel pressed a palm against her chest. "Attacked?"

Sarah, looking equally shocked, said, "What happened?"

"It was a band of well-trained warriors who wore camouflaged clothing matching the snow and mountains." Mykal retold the list of events to the best of his ability. Part of him wanted to leave Blodwyn's friends out of the rendition. There was a good chance someone would report back to the queens about the fire. Others might send word that the woman was in critical condition with a curer. If he left out those bits of information and the queens knew, or somehow found out about it, his reputation soiled. He decidedly kept some of the magic performed out of the tale.

It was the first time he'd been called on to advise.

He wasn't sure if he wanted it to be his last.

And that was the thing. He *wasn't* sure.

Sarah leaned back in her chair. "Thane?"

Axel stepped closer to the table, moved his hands and cupped them in front of his torso. "This is the first I've heard of a foreign force on our soil. Not sure if there is a rebel awakening in the valley? It doesn't seem likely. What the wizard is describing sounds like a highly-trained militia. The families don't have the time, or the ability. I will have a scout snoop around. See if there is something we can come up with."

"Anything you learn, regardless of how insignificant you think it is, I want to know," Sarah said.

"We want to know," Raaheel corrected.

Queen Sarah eyed Mykal, ignoring her sibling's outburst. "Is that all?"

Is that all. It came off insulting. Mykal cringed. He hoped the queens couldn't tell. He caught Axel's eye. The thane saw his muscles tighten, and arched an eyebrow. "I'm sorry?" Perhaps he had misunderstood her question.

"Did you leave anything out? Is that the end of the story?"

"I've told you everything."

"And the butterflies?" Queen Sarah asked.

"What about them? I'm not sure what you mean."

She slammed a hand onto the table. "Are you playing games? There isn't time for games. We have three people missing. Three young ladies. My kingdom—"

"*Our* kingdom." Raaheel spat.

"Not now, Raaheel!" Venom came with the words. "What is the significance of the butterflies?"

Mykal shook his head. "I haven't a clue. I was hoping when I told all of you it would make more sense."

Under the table, Blodwyn set a hand on Mykal's leg. It was more than likely meant to calm him, a silent way of telling him it was time for regaining composure.

"If you can think of anything else, anything at all, I want to know immediately." Sarah spoke in an even tone of voice. Her eyes were cold. The blue around the black pupil was like ice. The gold band around the blue was on fire.

"We want to know." Raaheel wrung her hands together.

They were being excused.

The thane cocked his head toward the door.

Blodwyn stood up first, and pulled back on Mykal's chair. "Thank you, your highnesses," he said.

Mykal mirrored the sentiment.

CHAPTER 29

In the apartment, Blodwyn draped Mykal's wet clothing over the back of a chair. "Did you really just leave your things balled up on the floor?"

"We were in a hurry." He sat on the sofa, legs bent, feet propped on the edge of the small table. Resting elbows on his knees, Mykal let thumbs massage his temples. "Did you see the book Raaheel had with her?"

Blodwyn sat in a chair, not with wet clothing on the back, and twisted it around so he faced Mykal. "I noticed she had a book, yes."

"She kept tapping on the cover. It was hard *not* noticing. I couldn't figure out if she wanted me to see the book, or if she was trying to make so light of having the book with her, I wouldn't notice."

"And why would a queen care whether you take notice of her reading habits, or not?"

Mykal dropped his legs, feet on the floor, and leaned forward. "I could be over reading it, no pun intended."

"And yet, relevant." Blodwyn smirked, but the smile did not mask the dark, dark skin under his eyes.

"I recognize the book from our library."

"You've read it?" Blodwyn asked.

Shaking his head, Mykal said. "I've seen it. Shelved. Or, maybe my mother was flipping through it. Something. I just know I recognize it."

"So it is a book on magic." It wasn't a question. "That is most interesting."

"Most troubling, if you ask me." The queens' father messed with magic. His head swelled. He wanted more, and more power. His delusion was once an all-powerful mage he'd conquer the realms in the Old Empire, and then the combined kingdoms as a new, and untouchable emperor.

He'd come close.

That was what had been so scary. The crazy ruler had almost pulled off something no one else thought possible.

It came to an end with the War, where King Hermon Cordillera was defeated.

It made an ironic kind of sense that his daughters might also dabble in magic.

King Golan Nabal, from the Grey Ashland Kingdom, ran the Watch. This elite group of highly-trained knights roamed the lands in search of anyone using magic. They then acted as judge, jury, and executioner. Few who encountered the Watch survived.

Mykal had no intention of judging Cordillera's daughters.

However, it did raise issues. Should magic be regulated? Had there ever been some sort of counsel keeping wizards in line? Mykal couldn't pretend to know the answer. Perhaps there were books, or scrolls, maybe minutes from sessions documented in ledgers stored somewhere within the ancient library. He would discuss the topic with his mother when he returned home.

"Do you think them playing with magic has anything to do with the missing women?" Blodwyn asked.

Mykal pursed his lips, as he nodded. "I don't see how it can't have something to do with the missing women. I think it would explain all the paranormal activity I've been experiencing. It's them, or some form of them, reaching out to me for help. Not the other way around. In fact, the few times I've tried connecting, I think I've seen only what they want me to see." Mykal stood up, and chewed on a fingernail.

"Stop. That's a bad habit. And dirty."

Mykal lowered his hand away from his face. "Wyn, I can't be sure any of the women are alive."

"Is that what you sense?"

"No. Not really." There was something, though. The butterflies bothered him. How could they be significant? Were they significant? It might be too soon to tell. "Based on what we discussed in the valley, I just wonder if Sarah is using magic, as well?"

"Can't you tell? Isn't there a way you can know?"

There was a way. When a wizard used magic, his mind saw wisps of color coming from them. It happened often before, and during the War, back when he'd first discovered his abilities, his identity. "Only when they are using magic, and if I am looking for the usage at the time. I think. I just wish I knew more about the book Raaheel was reading. It might just be bedtime stories for all I know."

"You need to forget their ages. Don't get hung up on that. These are powerful young ladies."

"I understand." It was hard to overlook, though. He'd try. "Tomorrow, we'll talk with Elma, Henriette's sister. Hopefully the final pieces of the puzzle will fall into place."

"If they do, our job won't be easy."

If Blodwyn's suspicions were correct, solving the crime around missing women could trigger another war. A civil one, this time, but a war nonetheless.

"Let's get some sleep. My mind is a jumble of thoughts. Nothing's making sense at the moment, and I can barely keep my eyes open."

"I couldn't agree more. Perhaps, after a solid rest, things will appear more clearly."

"That's the plan."

CHAPTER 30

Gembert arrived at the apartment with breakfast. The two women who had been with him on the first day they'd met wheeled in a cart and set the food out on the short table by the sofa.

"Won't you join us, chamberlain?" Blodwyn offered.

Gembert waved off the invitation. "Thank you, but no thank you. I'll return in an hour. Have you a plan in mind for this morning?"

"Actually, we were hoping to speak with Elma."

"Of course. She is staying in the room next to her sister and brother-in-law," Gembert said. He stood stiff, arms at his side. His skin was red, splotchy, burnt from the time exposed in the icy cold conditions.

Mykal and Blodwyn sat on the sofa side by side, picking at the fruit, cheese and nuts.

"If there's anything else?"

"We won't need an hour," Mykal said. He crunched into an apple. "And we're anxious to begin this morning."

"Very well. I can wait outside, if you'd like."

There were things Mykal wanted to discuss with Gembert, but it could wait until after the meeting with Elma. "We won't be long."

He bowed, it was slight; mostly a nod of his head, really. He ushered the women out of the room first, followed, and then closed the door behind them.

"I'm actually ready," Blodwyn said, tossing almonds into his mouth.

"I am, too. I didn't want him thinking we didn't appreciate the hospitality," Mykal said, waving a hand over the abundance of food.

"How much did they expect us to eat?"

They laughed.

***

Elma opened the door. Mykal thought they were at the wrong apartment. It was uncanny how much the woman in front of him looked like her sister, Henriette. They shared pale skin, as if neither ever saw sunlight. Elma wore long in hair in thick braids, and shared similar large blue eyes, defined cheekbones, and a small nose. "Please," she said, and stood aside. "Come in."

Mykal wore his cloak. Blodwyn insisted it was their uniform. They should never venture anywhere without their staffs, and wearing their cloaks. His was heavy, still holding melted snow in the fabric. It was cold on his shoulders, and made the bones in his spine, and up his neck ache. "Thank you."

"Have you any news about my niece?"

Elma was younger than Henriette, by several years. He couldn't pinpoint an age, but neither did he think it important. It was more or less just something he'd observed. "Unfortunately, no."

The tears fell. She made no attempt at wiping them away. She did raise a hand near her mouth as if it might help stop her lips from quivering. "I'm going out of my mind. I have no idea what to do. I just keep pacing around in this room. I'm too wired to sleep. I mean, how can I rest knowing my niece is out there somewhere? I can't stop my mind from having horrible, horrible thoughts. Closing my eyes tight doesn't stop them from coming. Nothing does."

Mykal placed a hand on her arm. She looked unstable, as if her legs might give out. Her hands shook. "Why don't we sit down?"

Except for the pattern of cloth material, the sofa in Elma's apartment was identical to the one in Mykal's and in Richmond and Henriette's rooms, as were the small tables in front of them.

On the table was a glass encased shadow box made of shellacked wood.

Mykal saw what was inside and cast a glance over at Blodwyn. "This is lovely. Can you tell me about it?"

Elma sat down. "My Clairece loves anything that flies. It's why she was so excited to see the dovecote. To be honest, she wasn't at all interested in coming to Osiris. Leaving her friends and home, to travel didn't excite her much." She smiled, as if she'd spoken treasonous words. "No offense, chamberlain."

"None taken," Gembert assured her.

"It's just heading up into the mountains during winter wouldn't appeal to many young women. Boys may be different, I suppose. I wouldn't know. I don't have any children of my own. My husband died during the War. We wanted kids. Talked about starting a family. Just never had the chance," she explained. "I'm blabbing, forgive me."

"There's no need," Blodwyn said. It was perhaps the softest tone of voice Mykal had ever heard the man use. It sounded quite comforting, calming.

Mykal held the box in his hand. "And this? Where did it come from?"

"Yes. Again, I'm sorry. This is Clairece's. She rarely goes anywhere without. Richmond made the box for her; her father."

"He does very nice work," Mykal said. Behind the glass pinned to a square swatch of tanned leather. Pinned by the wings were several rows with an array of butterflies, no two the same. In the center was a bright blue butterfly, trimmed and detailed in black. "She collects these?"

Elma nodded, her hands folded together in front of her chin. "She loves butterflies, birds, anything with wings."

Blodwyn caught Mykal's eye, nodding his head. The butterflies. The connection was an in-the-face kind of obvious. Mykal Just wasn't sure he comprehended the significance. Part of him feared Clairece was dead, and her ghost, or a spirit had been reaching out to him during his incantations. He hoped there was a... happier explanation. At the moment, he just couldn't think of one.

"In fact," Elma continued, "I was admiring your dragonfly brooch. It's something I know my niece would simply love." (I know 'brooch' doesn't look right, but it is. Trust me.)

Mykal's hand reflexively touched the opal brooch affixed to the outside of his cloak. "This was given to me. It's very special." Karyn had given it to him. He missed her. Oftentimes he wondered if roles were reversed would he have been courageous enough to sacrifice his life for hers.

He liked to believe he would have done the same.

"It is very beautiful," Elma said. "And like I was saying, the way Richmond persuaded his daughter into wanting to come to Osiris, because she was going either way it was just easier on everyone if she was optimistic about the trip, was by telling her about the magnificent dovecote the queens kept at the top of the tallest tower at the castle."

"Do you recall anything unusual about the day Clairece went missing?" Mykal could think of no other way to ask the next series of questions.

"Unusual?" Elma stared upward, lips puckered. "This is my first time at the castle. It would be very hard for me to say one way or the other what is considered unusual."

Mykal hoped for a better answer, a more compelling reply; anything that would point in one direction over the other. "Think back. Can you remember anything *you* thought seemed unusual? Like, maybe it just had you wondering why, or what, or raised red flags in your mind?"

Elma tilted her head just a bit to one side. She breathed in a deep breath through her nose, and after a long, slow exhale continued. "Gembert, maybe you can better answer this question. You were the one who accompanied Clairece to the dovecote..."

Mykal and Blodwyn spun around and faced the chamberlain. They wore mirrored expressions. Their eyes were opened wide, and jaws dropped.

"Nothing unusual comes to mind." Gembert was good. He played it off well. If it weren't for the half shuffle step backwards Mykal would have applauded. The performance was that close to perfect.

"I want to thank you for your time." Mykal took Elma's hand. He held it in his own for just a moment.

"That's the only questions you have for me?" She seemed surprised. "I want to help in any way I can."

"You have," Blodwyn said. "And, again, we thank you."

"Chamberlain? We're done here." Mykal heard the sharp tone of his own voice, and almost cringed. He couldn't imagine what Gembert felt. If he was smart, he'd feel scared.

Mykal did his best to wait until they were down the hall, and as far away as possible from Elma's apartment before he stopped walking.

He knew he gripped his staff too tight, and worried his hand might cramp. It was taking all of his control not to pummel the chamberlain. There were spells he thought about casting that would have Gembert begging for mercy. He kept his temper in check, however. The fate of this man was not his to decide.

Something stirred in Mykal's gut; an unease that made him constrict his abs. If Gembert was the culprit... "Take us to the queens. Now."

CHAPTER 31

Mykal was somewhat surprised Queen Sarah didn't hear them approaching. She stood in the main foyer in front of the polished wood table holding the iron bust of her father. The likeness was close, but nothing uncanny. Mykal was more impressed by the amazing tapestry hanging on the wall behind the monumental display.

The white cloth in the queen's left hand dabbed at tears cried.

Mykal allowed the young girl a moment more with the thoughts of her father. He felt guiltier about witnessing the private moment, than about interrupting it. He didn't think the queen would appreciate knowing he'd observed her in a vulnerable state. Mykal cleared his throat.

Queen Sarah lowered her head, and with a quick swipe cleaned away any remnants of tears, sniffled, and tugged on the midriff part of her dress as she stood up straight. Head high, she turned around.

Gembert spoke up. "We apologize for disturbing you, your highness."

Queen Sarah forced a smile: lips pressed tight, eyes wrinkled. She wrung her hands together. "Just tell me you have some answers. Tell me you've learned something new. I'm not sure I can handle more bad news at this point."

Mykal looked over the foyer. They were alone. That didn't mean they would be speaking in private. "I think we should go somewhere and talk."

Without a response, Queen Sarah walked from the foyer, and down the hall. The others followed. She led them, not surprisingly, toward the Long Room. With both hands, and without pause, she threw open the doors. The hinges let out small cries of protest. The heavy wood creaked some, as well.

Because of where the sun sat in the morning sky only dim slices of light angled into the room. Without hesitation, Gembert went about the task of igniting mounted oil lanterns. Shadows came to life dancing in time with bouncing flames on the end of wicks.

Mykal saw his breath plume out in front of his face.

Queen Sarah didn't bother with her seat at the head of the table, as usual. Instead she stood by the foot and crossed arms across her chest. "This had better be good."

Blodwyn closed the doors, and then stood by them as if a sentry on post.

"You might want to sit down." Mykal regretted suggesting she sit the moment the words were out of his mouth, and too late to retract. And he was correct in feeling regret. The queen cocked her head to the left, and stared at him as if she'd found a disobedient animal inside her home. "Or stand. The point is, I don't think this is going to be easy to hear."

He wanted the blow softened, even though inside his innards boiled in anger.

Queen Sarah made no show of moving, other than exhibiting signs of impatience as she drummed fingers on her arm, and Gembert wasn't going anywhere.

"All this time we've been here—your chamberlain has never once mentioned that he was the one who took the baron's daughter up to the dovecote." Mykal gave pause, letting the accusation sink in. He fully expected Gembert to deny everything.

Queen Sarah shook her head. "And?"

Mykal caught Gembert staring at him, almost a bemused expression on his face.

The queen didn't wait. "He was also the one that brought the two of you up to the dovecote. You've climbed those stairs. The tower isn't easy to find. Did you think Clairece wandered up there on her own?"

Mykal hoped his eyebrows didn't raise too high above his eyeballs in surprise. "My point is—"

"Yes. What is your point? Please get to it."

"He was the last one to see her before she was taken." Mykal laid it out, nice and simple. The queen wasn't completely aware of the vision he'd seen when working the incantation in the dovecote.

"Are you suggesting he had something to do with her disappearance?"

Mykal, in a most clumsy fashion, folded his arms. His staff between a bent elbow, knocked into the side of his head. "That's correct."

"And what did he have to say for himself when you accused him?" The queen looked anything but pleased. It was the exact opposite reaction Mykal expected. "I'm assuming, of course, you have a confession?"

"Well, I haven't discussed it with him. As soon as I learned this, I demanded he bring us to see you." Mykal could not recall a time he'd ever felt so foolish. There may have been something from his childhood, something truly embarrassing, but if there was at the moment the memory escaped him.

Queen Sarah shifted her weight around. "Gembert, did you take Clairece to the dovecote?"

"I did."

"Did you stay with her the entire time she was up there with the birds?"

"I did not."

"And why didn't you stay with her the entire time she was in the dovecote?"

"You had asked me to bring her to see the birds, but to immediately return because you wanted—"

Queen Sarah held up a hand, silencing her chamberlain. However, she never broke direct eye contact with the wizard. "Is there anything else?"

"May I?" Mykal said.

"Be my guest."

Mykal said, "You see, when I was in the dovecote I saw the abduction through the eyes of the abductor."

Queen Sarah arched an eyebrow, possibly intrigued. "Go on."

"The one thing I noticed was that Clairece was comfortable with whomever was inside the giant bird cage with her. There wasn't any sign of fear, or anxiety. In fact, quite the opposite. It was almost like she hoped they were sharing the joy of the experience with her." Mykal paced, taking small steps, and deliberately used his staff as if a walking stick. "Two things you said, Gembert, struck me as odd."

Gembert sighed, as if bored with the interrogation. He didn't provide the obligatory question, stealing some wind out of Mykal's sail.

"Inside the dovecote, I told you I saw blood. Do you remember how you responded?" This time Mykal didn't wait for Gembert. The question was now purely rhetoric. "You said, 'There wasn't any blood. Not on the ground, not on the walls, not where you're standing, or where I am standing.'" Mykal stopped walking, two to two with Gembert. "You said, 'I tell you, not a drop had been spilled inside the dovecote.'"

Gembert rolled his eyes, letting them stop on the queen for a brief moment, before turning reverting his attention. "I remember saying that, yes."

"Why were you so insistent that there wasn't any blood inside the dovecote? I saw blood during the incantation. How do you explain that?"

"The spell didn't work properly?"

It sounded like such a sarcastic reply, and yet, Mykal couldn't refute the possibility Gembert was correct.

"Also, when I went back up to search for the child, I didn't find any blood inside the dovecote. I did, however, see drops outside leading toward the tower door," Gembert said. "As you yourself just quoted, I said, 'I tell you not a drop had been spilled inside the dovecote.' You never asked me to explain that comment at the time. I didn't think anything of it."

Mykal's confidence was diminishing. "When we returned from the valley, you said something about how you weren't sure how she would react to everything that took place during our journey. You said she. Not they." He recalled Gembert's exact wording. He was not prone to quote the man a second time.

"It's not much of a secret," Gembert said. His head lowered some. "While Queen Raaheel is fair, and loving and compassionate, I am more partial toward Queen Sarah. I am more than likely to seek her out first. She knows this, and yet I've never spoken that truth out loud before. I mean no disrespect toward the crown."

"No offense has been taken, Gembert, and we'll not mention it again."

"Never, your highness."

Mykal had nothing. They'd been in the Osiris Realm for days and he was no closer to solving the abductions. Perhaps centuries ago the wizards were better skilled at assisting people with issues. His inept abilities seemed only good for dragging a shroud of embarrassment over him like thick blanket.

"I think it best if you and your old friend leave the realm. Return home. Or go anywhere you please outside of our borders."

The queen was eleven, and wiser than Mykal ever hoped to be.

"You have my deepest apologies. My intent was not to waste your time, but to help. All I wanted to do was help." He hated admitting defeat. Returning home without having solved the crimes felt horrible. The hand placed over his belly did nothing to stop the flips and flops of his stomach.

"Well, while you were busy helping, we've had yet another abduction."

It felt as if someone had sucker punched Mykal in the gut. His breath was trapped in his lungs. The level of his failure intensified. "When?"

"A few hours ago. It was that woman you traveled with. A shame." Queen Sarah shook her head.

"Wait." Mykal needed a second before the impact of what the queen said registered. "Who was taken? Not Geneva?"

"Geneva. Yes. That was her name."

CHAPTER 32

"A servant saw someone snatch Geneva from behind. Wrapped an arm around her waist, and covered her mouth, stifling her screams," Queen Sarah said. She made it sound matter-of-fact, keeping any sign of emotion out of her words.

"Your Highness, I beg you, let us stay longer. I can't just leave—"

"I've ordered you to leave!"

"I didn't mean I won't leave. I understand your order. I just meant, I don't want to go without helping."

"You haven't helped at all since you've arrived. All you've done is tie up my chamberlain's time, taking him away from duties and chores that others have had to bear the brunt of while he was gallivanting around the realm with the likes of you!" The queen was full of fire. Not even five feet tall, she exhibited bite enough to match her bark. Gallivanting was a harsh description. It made the entire investigation sound light and fluffy, and not at all dangerous. Had she forgotten about the camouflaged militia attacks?

Mykal took steps backward, and away from the riled-up queen. "I just want to help."

"And what would make your helping now any different than it has been the last few days?"

"Let me speak with the witness. Since it just happened, the trail is fresh. We'll have a better chance of tracking down the abductor!"

"Axel is already in pursuit. The snow is treacherous at times, but is also revealing." The queen shook her head.

"My sister won't understand any of this. It's bad enough she didn't want you here in the first place. If she finds out I was wrong in having everyone search for you just for... well, *this*, I will never live it down. She'll use all of this against me. I don't have a right to ask this of you, but I would prefer to keep the entire conversation just between us."

Mykal didn't think he could have been wrong about anything else, but he'd been wrong again. "Wait. Queen Raaheel didn't want my services?"

Sarah laughed. "It's bad enough I sought a wizard's advice to help us solve the abductions, but the mage responsible for our father's death? No, *Mykal*, she did not want you here. We argued over the topic for days. But, I finally won out. And now look what's become of the investigation." She shook her head, biting down on her lip.

Raaheel had been the most hospitable one of the two. Sarah always avoided them, was curt, and rather rude.

"You look confused," the queen pointed out.

"It just seemed like you were the one that didn't want us here. Your sister was the one always meeting with us, keeping us informed of things." There wasn't really a question in what he said. He just started voicing his thoughts.

"You're some powerful wizard, right? I've a kingdom to run. Court to hold. I was spreading myself too thin. Raaheel loves the crown, the clothing, the respect, just not the responsibility that goes along with it." Sarah pressed her lips tightly together. "I am not going to speak ill of my sister."

She didn't have to say another word. Mykal thought he understood. "I've a question."

"Might as well ask it." Sarah looked very tired. She didn't share the same bags under her eyes that Blodwyn wore, but when she stifled a yawn, Mykal was sympathetic. He had continually reminded himself of the ages of the queens, but not about the constant responsibility facing them.

"How long has your sister been dabbling in magic?"

"Raaheel?" Queen Sarah looked past Mykal, toward Blodwyn. Perhaps she wanted to gage whether the wizard was joking or not. When her eyes locked on Mykal, her jaw set, and she rolled her shoulders forward. "That is a serious accusation you are leveling against the crown."

Mykal was caught off guard. He didn't realize King Nabal's narrow-minded ways reached across the Isthmian still. There must come a day when mages of all strengths could freely roam the old empire without fear of persecution. "I wasn't leveling anything against the crown. It wasn't an accusation," was what Mykal said. "She is studying magic. The book she had earlier—"

"What about it?"

"The same one is in the library where I live." He wasn't sure if Geneva reported where she'd found them when she was sent out. He wasn't comfortable with many knowing they resided in the ancient library ruins. Some things were better kept secret. The safety of Blodwyn and his mother was what he was most concerned about. They didn't need trouble knowing their address.

"And you think my sister is practicing witchcraft?"

"I can't say for sure, but why else would she read a book like that?" Maybe Mykal and Blodwyn hadn't been completely wrong with the assessment. Instead of Sarah and Gembert being behind the abductions, the warrior attacks... It made sense, actually. It was Raaheel who had kept her finger on the pulse of their activity.

"It was how our father started," Queen Sarah said.

Mykal battled against King Hermon, *The Mountain King*. The king had become a powerful sorcerer. Mykal did not know much more about the man, though. The fact that he now worked for the dead king's daughters was more than a bit ironic.

"My uncle died when they were both young. My grandfather blamed the death on my father, labeling him a witch, when all my father wanted to do was find a way to help my uncle. My grandfather humiliated and punished my father for years. Embarrassing him whenever there was an opportunity." Queen Sarah's fingers fidgeted. With almost vacant eyes she stared out the window. "He continued his study of magic. In fact, because of the way his father treated him, his interest in magic only increased. By the time I was old enough to remember things... He kept a sorcerer as his advisor in one of the towers."

Mykal had questions. There were so many things he still wanted to know, things he wished he knew. The mystery behind the Mountain King kept him awake many nights. Answers behind the mad man's drive for power, rise to power, might bring some sort of closure to the matter. Too many people died during the War. Before it, as well. Although they'd ultimately stopped a tyrant, he wished he and his friends could have been faster and stopped the king before the war ever started.

He felt, and might always feel, responsible for the War and the deaths.

"We didn't interact with her much, the witch," Queen Sarah said. There wasn't a negative connotation inflicted on the way she said witch, but there was no love in the statement, either. "The few times I did encounter her, I was scared. I remember that. Look at me. Look at my hands. They're shaking. She'd be hidden away inside this black cloak, hood up, and all I could hear was her breathing. But I could always tell she was staring at me. Couldn't see her eyes, but I knew. When we were in a room together, she was watching me. Which I thought was bad enough, until one day, this one time, I saw her with the hood down. I wish I hadn't. There can be no unseeing such horrors. I had nightmares for so long after that. It's true that sometimes, I still do. Some nights I wake covered in a cold sweat. And while the essence of the dream has escaped my memory her face is still there, just looming in the corners of my chamber, a bodiless face floating in the shadows."

The queen's entire body shuddered. She turned away from the window as if there was no heat coming from the light, or there was no way of warming her bones, regardless. "She had this bald head with stray clumps of white hair." The queen looked as if she were reliving the memory. Her shoulders were hunched forward, and she stared at her palms like she had clumps of the mage's hair in her hands. "And her skin was a dead-grey, spotted. Her jowls sagged, loose on her bones. But, what was worse—*what haunted me most*—was when I finally saw her eyes, the ones that stared at me. Black, lifeless eyes. She had these thick, knotted sockets, and the blackest, beadiest eyes. I don't even know of an animal with eyes like that. Only thing that could have eyes that black is something that is purely evil."

Mykal watched the queen shiver, and then hug herself, either for comfort, or warmth. He couldn't help wondering how the queen would assess him once he'd left their realm? He didn't suspect her memories would be fond, but did he make her skin crawl in a similar fashion. "Where was this tower where your father kept the sorceress?"

Queen Sarah tugged at the puffy material of her gown at the shoulders. She lowered the dress down her body. Mykal was too shocked to turn away.

Underneath, the queen wore black trousers, and a loose white tunic. She bunched the dress up in her arms and placed it on the table, and then removed and set her crown on top of the heap. "That is the thing I like least about being queen. The way I'm supposed to dress. I may write a decree saying I can wear anything I am comfortable in."

Mykal smiled, and shook his head, appreciating very much the lighter side of the queen.

"The tower. It all comes back to that one room," she said, as she strode toward Blodwyn, who yanked open the Long Room door. "Follow me!"

***

More stairs. So many stairs. Mykal concentrated on his breathing. One step at a time.

Watching Queen Sarah run up them, didn't make him feel much better. All the time he and Blodwyn spent training. Day in and day out. Was it for nothing? He felt out of shape, and was tired of having everything blamed on the altitude.

"I just want to say," Blodwyn said, not the least bit winded. He was ahead of Mykal. He talked, looking back over a shoulder. "You handled yourself very well."

"Really?" Mykal lost count of the stairs climbed. They were past one hundred, and the number was climbing. Literally. "I did not think that went well. Not at all."

Blodwyn winced. "It didn't start the best. The point is, you remained calm."

"How could we have been so wrong?" It made sense *now*, but of course it would. Why wouldn't it? The answers were placed in front of him, served on a royal platter. If anything he suspected Blodwyn of dishing out a compliment just to keep his confidence from shattering. The cracks were there, webbing outward. Nothing's been shattered. Yet.

"The thing about it is, we can't know it all until we've figured it out. Sometimes all you can do is work with suppositions, go with hunches, and see what's what." Blodwyn turned around.

The queen was no longer just ahead of them. She might have made it to the top already. Gembert stayed behind. He would keep an eye out for Axel, and Queen Raaheel, but not follow or confront them.

Mykal felt guilty about accusing Gembert. The man had been loyal when they trekked into the valley.

Above, Mykal heard the distinct sound of hinges moaning.

That was the best sound he'd heard in a while. It meant they were close to the top. He had had it with stairs.

The room where the sorcerer was kept long ago was filled with dust, first. Underneath it all were wood shelves lined with small, labeled jars. Iron bars secured the one window. Beyond, Mykal saw the sea.

"Someone's been up here." Blodwyn noted the lack of dust on the table.

"Raaheel?" Sarah didn't sound sure of herself. The air of mistrust spewed in the one word spoken. It wasn't the first time Mykal noticed it, but this was the most distinct. There was a disconnect between the sisters.

Was there some unseen unrest in the kingdom? Perhaps a secret, and silent battle over the crown? It made sense. Having one king control the laws, the people, the land was daunting, he imagined. Two sharing control couldn't be easy, and siblings besides? It was nearly incomprehensible, really.

Rather than dig deeper, and revealing bitter, buried animosity, Mykal browsed the chamber. The collection of small glass vials, and ceramic bottles with cork stops was impressive. Many of the same herbs, and oils, minerals, and elements matched what he and his mother had at home. She also had tongs, beakers, unlit burners under glass flasks, and tubes connecting many things together.

At the dust-free table, Mykal closed his eyes and placed his palms on the wood, but then pulled back a hand, and winced.

"What is it?" Blodwyn stepped forward, a defensive grip on his staff, and his eyes darting around the room. He did not mask how uncomfortable the chamber at the top of the tower made him feel.

"It's okay." Mykal bit at his palm. Spat. "Splinter."

Blodwyn sighed, and relaxed his stance, and loosened the grip on his staff.

Trying again, this time Mykal set his hands down on the table, and then closed his eyes. It eliminated the surprise of unexpected pain from touching unfinished wood. For an advisor of the king, the sorceress' lab was not particularly special. There was nothing elaborate about it. Except the burners. He liked those. He was used to crushing together ingredients. How were the properties altered under different degrees of heat? This would be something he and his mother could explore when he returned.

Mykal shook his head. His thoughts wandered. Focusing was essential. If Raaheel had been in this room recently, he hoped he'd be able to sense her. Find a trial. He looked for anything that might lead him closer to finding Geneva.

Although they had no proof the older queen was behind the abduction, something about the way the puzzle pieces finally fit together felt right. The fact Raaheel used this room at all suggested there was far more than met the eye. She was a sly one. Sneaky, and perhaps, sinister.

"Mykal?" Blodwyn pulled him out of his thoughts. "Anything?"

It hit him like a bolt of lightning.

Mykal fell backward, stumbling. His legs wobbled.

Queen Sarah grabbed onto his arm. "Mage?"

Mykal placed an arm over his chest, a hand over his heart. "There's blood on the table. Butterfly blood."

Blodwyn arched an eyebrow.

"Butterfly blood?" Queen Sarah's tone was harsh, doubtful. She clearly possessed an icy side, cynical, and had no problem wearing it like a smile.

Blodwyn bent at the knees. His nose was inches from the wood. His fingertips traced the tabletop. A bubble of dark red fluid affixed itself onto his skin. He stood up and rubbed the thick liquid between forefinger and thumb, and then smelled it. "It's blood, alright. A smear, barely noticeable. How much blood could a butterfly's little body hold?"

"It isn't actually blood from a butterfly. It's Clairece. She is the butterfly." Mykal took Blodwyn's wrist. He moved the hand closer to his own face and inspected the blood on his fingers. "This is her blood."

"It's fresh," Blodwyn said. "Several hours old, but no more than that."

It was a good sign. The baron's daughter might be alive after all.

"The question is why her blood is in here?" Queen Sarah stood poised with fists on her hips, and her head cocked to one side. "Why is anyone's blood in here?"

For the most part, it was in fact a solid question. Mykal didn't think he was the only one suspecting magic afoot. However, he racked his brain in an attempt at determining what kind of magic was performed. Raaheel was up to something, but how did it involve Clairece, Clairece's blood, and what did it have to do with the other missing women?

Raaheel was up to something. He just didn't know what, until he saw something by the window. It was on the stone ledge. A small cup. He picked it up, turned it over in his hands. He smelled the inside, and then ran a finger around the rim. As Blodwyn had done, he rubbed his fingers together before lifting them up to his nose.

The queen was drinking the blood.

"We have to find your sister," Mykal said. "Would she have gone with Axel looking for Geneva?"

Blodwyn, who had been watching him closely, cleared his throat. "That is assuming Axel is actually out looking for the woman."

"What do you mean?" Sarah asked.

"Think about it. If, for whatever reason, Raaheel needs these women in order to perform whatever rituals she's performing, then Geneva is not really missing, is she? And neither is Clairece, or the others." Blodwyn tapped the end of his staff on stone. "The thane is as much at fault as your sister, with all due respect. If that is the case, then he is not out looking for anyone. He may be, in fact, the one responsible for the abductions."

"The warriors we faced along the route to the valley?" Mykal said aloud.

"A rogue military headed by Raaheel, at Axel's command," Blodwyn added.

"They knew where we were headed, where we would be." Mykal closed his hand into a fist, as if he'd suddenly caught a fly.

Sarah shook her head. "I knew where you'd be, as well."

"Did you have us ambushed?" Blodwyn asked, eyes locked on the young queen.

"I most certainly did not!"

Blodwyn said, "Raaheel is behind this."

If the missing women were alive, where would Raaheel hide them? Where was Geneva being kept?

Somewhere in the...

"We have to go to the dungeon," Mykal yelled.

"It's been sealed off," Queen Sarah said. "It's one of the first things we did as queens after having the carnage cleaned away."

Sealed off. "There must be another way in," Mykal said.

"If there is, I am not aware," she said.

The chamberlain. "If anyone would know of an alternate way into the dungeon, Gembert would!"

CHAPTER 33

Going down stairs was easier than climbing up them. When your legs felt weak, however, it wasn't much easier. Once again, the queen took the lead, showing off her youthful energy as she bounded down the stairs. Her arms were out, her hands traced the walls.

Mykal did his best at keeping up.

He heard Blodwyn shuffling along not far behind him.

They were close. He felt it inside. It stirred behind his chest. *Anticipation.*

Breathing in quick, shallow breaths, Mykal tried not getting ahead of himself. There was always the chance they were wrong, misguided, and now concentrating all of their effort on one target. If that proved the case, then they were then wasting time. Geneva's life might hung in the balance. He didn't have time to kill.

He didn't think they were wrong.

Raaheel was behind everything. The sister queen wanted the crown for herself. He wasn't sure how magic fit into the equation, but it did. Somehow she was planning on, or already, conjuring up spells to keep the crown for herself.

Raaheel wanted to be the sole ruler.

Was Sarah also in danger?

Or was it the presumed failure of Mykal and Blodwyn that would cause Sarah such public shame for relying on a wizard to solve a realm matter, she'd be forced to forfeit her position on the Cordillera thrown? Political plotting was ruthless. A revolting game invented and mastered by kings, and queens.

Mykal knew he'd just fit another piece into the puzzle. The picture was nearly complete. He thought he knew how some of this might play out. In a way it encouraged him.

When they reached the bottom of the stairs, they found Gembert sitting on the stone floor, his back to the wall.

"What are you doing here?" Queen Sarah seethed.

Gembert got up onto his feet. The weight from the events of the last few weeks creased his brow. "The knights know where I am. If anyone learned of anything they'd come find me. No one has come looking for me since. I just wanted to be by your side, is all."

Before the queen could chastise the chamberlain, Mykal stepped between them. "The dungeon's been sealed."

"That's correct."

"But there must be another way in," Mykal said.

Gembert's eyes flicked toward the queen. "There is not."

"You will not get into trouble. If you know of another way into the dungeon, you must share that information with us now." Mykal was insistent.

Gembert appeared apprehensive, as if he might be holding his breath in lieu of providing an honest answer.

"Gembert," Queen Sarah said. Her tone was deep, strong. It clearly stated, without saying, even if there was going to be a punishment for lying before about all of the entrances having been sealed, he'd better come clean now.

"There is quite possibly still one way into the dungeon, a way that was overlooked when the other access routes were closed off." Gembert sounded suddenly timid, and shy. He clearly feared reprimand.

Sarah spun him around by the shoulder. "We'll discuss this later. Right now, take us to that way in!"

As they followed behind the chamberlain, and the queen, Blodwyn whispered: "She's drinking the blood?"

"That's my assumption."

Blodwyn clucked his tongue. "That's a bad sign."

"You know what that means?" Mykal found Blodwyn's fountain of knowledge bottomless. While he recognized the book cover the queen studied from, he had no idea the contents between the pages. That left him feeling inept.

"Keep up!" Queen Sarah called over her shoulder.

***

"We've got to get in from underneath." Gembert was by a back door in the castle.

Outside, Mykal saw the wind whipping about. He couldn't tell if it was snowing, or if the wind carried loose grains with its fury. Regardless, it looked cold. He was growing to detest winter. When spring, and eventually summer arrived, he would remember never to complain about the heat.

They followed Gembert outside.

The sun fought hard against growing grey clouds. Rays sliced through here and there, the only signs verifying it was daytime.

Gembert pointed.

There were deep tracks in the snow.

Several sets.

Encouraged, Mykal responded, "There's not a moment to waste!"

He didn't like the idea of Raaheel alone with Geneva. There was no telling what the queen had in store. Drinking the blood of her victims could only be a part of the ritual. Blodwyn clearly had some ideas about the whys behind it. There couldn't be a good explanation behind the consumption. Misuse of magic, as the Mountain King, and his sorceress demonstrated, was the best, albeit vaguest, answer. What was the end-goal?

The wind howled. It blew fast, hard. The cold stung exposed flesh. Mykal's breath caught in his lungs. Breathing was difficult. He lowered his head, covering his mouth and nose as best as he could. Despite the tracks, the snow was still deep. Trudging along was difficult. Every muscle in his legs ached. The stair climbing had done him in long ago. He hoped Blodwyn fared better. He'd grown increasingly worried about his friend's health.

Just ahead there was a fissure in the face of the mountain. It didn't look wide enough for a large dog to fit through, however, Mykal changed his mind once they reached the crack. Perhaps a large dog could fit through the crevasse. He pointed. "Through there?"

Gembert nodded.

Mykal held his breath. His heart beat fast. It didn't matter how cold out it was, beads of sweat peppered his forehead, and under his arms.

Tight spaces made him apprehensive. Claustrophobia got the best of him time and again. Often he'd tell himself his fear of tight spaces was nothing more than an imaginary disability. He'd convince himself of it, in fact. That is until he found himself next faced with an actual challenge.

Like a tight fissure in rocks.

He didn't want to go through.

"There's a downward slope. It's tight, but safe," Gembert said, pressing himself sideways between the narrow cleft.

"Straight shot?" Mykal managed asking.

"Mostly. At one point, when it seems like you can't go any further, you need to get down on your belly. There is a short tunnel. Once you crawl through there, you're home free," Gembert said, and disappeared into the side of the mountain.

A short tunnel. Crawl through. Mykal gasped.

"You okay?" Blodwyn clapped a hand onto his back.

"Wonderful. Just wonderful. You? How are you?" Blodwyn knew about his friend's phobia. He'd often explained the best way to battle against the fear is by confronting the phobia.

"Breathe slowly. In. Out. In. Out. We can do this." Blodwyn's tone of voice soothed, but didn't completely defeat Mykal's anxiety.

Queen Sarah pushed into the rift. Her head, right arm, and right leg were all that remained. "Is he alright?"

"Strategizing," Blodwyn hollered.

Whether she was convinced, or annoyed wasn't clear. The queen continued into the mountain and was gone.

"I want you to go first," Blodwyn said.

"No. You. I'll follow," Mykal promised.

"It's not that I don't trust you," Blodwyn said, and pushed him gently forward. "But I don't. I'll be right behind you. We're going to get through this together. And then there is always the bright side."

"Bright side?"

"We will blast a way out of the dungeon and into the castle if we have to," he encouraged.

He could have used magic and blasted their way into the dungeon, had he thought about it. Conserving energy was the main concern. He wasn't sure what waited for them in the Cordillera dungeon. If Raaheel had become some kind of a wizard, if she were anything like her father, it could turn into quite the battle of power. He needed all of his mental strength at the ready.

Fitting between the cracks in the mountain was truly the only reasonable way into the dungeon.

Geneva might be inside. She could be in grave danger. The other missing women could still be alive. "You'll be right behind me?" Mykal asked.

Blodwyn said, "Directly."

Mykal exhaled three quick breaths, and then sucked in a lungful.

Blodwyn slapped the back of his head. "You're not going underwater, boy. Breathe. In. Out. In. Out."

"Right. Right." In. Out. In. Out.

The mountain felt like giant blocks of ice. He fit himself between the halves and sidestepped out of the snow and into the mountain.

It was tight. Not nearly as tight as he feared. There was a little room to maneuver. Although some light filtered inside, for the most part the passage was dark. He could walk normally. The sides of the mountain expanded away from him with each step. It was almost as if they were inside the opening of a cave. "This isn't so bad," he said, before walking directly into rock.

He palmed the stone, feeling around.

"Down on your stomach," Blodwyn said from behind.

The short tunnel. The idea of the entire mountain pressing down on his back choked off his air. Were the walls closing in on him?

"Mykal?" Blodwyn barked, pulling him away from mounting panic.

"I'm okay." He'd made it this far. He could keep up his courage. Nothing would stop him now. Mykal knelt, and found the small mouth by his feet. "Not really a tunnel, as much as it is a slope, an opening."

Sighing, Mykal laid on his belly, and then pulled himself through the opening. He couldn't imagine Queen Raaheel and Alex taking this route to the dungeon, especially dragging along prisoners.

Had anyone bothered checking the door inside the castle?

Mykal hated when he had thoughts after the fact.

It should have been the first thing asked. Even if he didn't use magic, perhaps they could have knocked away whatever barrier had been installed.

"All the better. You first," Blodwyn said.

CHAPTER 34

Queen Sarah and Gembert held lit torches.

The casted shadows flickered on the uneven rock walls. The odor of mildew, urine and feces was overpowering, which Mykal took as an excellent sign.

"This way," Gembert said.

"One moment," Mykal said. At this point, he didn't need a guide. The pungent and acrid smells would have led him directly through a maze of hallways, and unmarked passages. "Your highness, I would like you to stay between Wyn and I."

"This is my castle."

"And I have reason to suspect Raaheel means you harm," Mykal said.

"You've been wrong about every assessment so far," she retorted. It was a lucky thing her words weren't connected to venomous fangs. He'd have been infected long ago by the bite she inflicted.

"I've been off, but not exactly wrong."

She opened her mouth, most certainly about to debate his statement, but closed it.

"Raaheel is after the crown. She let you call on us for help, confident we'd fail solving the mystery of the missing women. I believe she was then going to hold that over your head. She'd use it and rally your people against you," Mykal said.

"She wouldn't dream of such an underhanded move."

"I think she would. I also believe she didn't expect us to make any progress on the matter. When we showed signs of advancing, she became unnerved and reacted in a harsh manner.

It's why she had the warriors attack us in the valley. It was a perfect opportunity to hinder, if not put an end to the investigation." Mykal knew he needed to tip his hand. If Queen Sarah wasn't on board with them, it might prove wasted efforts. Her continued support was essential. There were no telling what dangers lie ahead. They needed to face them together.

"So what are you saying?" she asked.

"I want you between us. For your own protection. If something goes down when we reach the dungeon, it's important that you stay safe. Those people out there need a queen they can trust. I believe you have nothing but their best interest in mind," Mykal said.

The queen didn't look as if she appreciated orders coming from a wizard, but she nodded in agreement, just the same. "Okay. I will put my safety in your hands."

"Gembert," Mykal said, "lead the way."

Mykal held his staff at an angle, and in both hands. The staff was his first line of defense against any attack. He felt almost at one with the specially-crafted weapon.

They took twists, turns, stayed close to one another, and then Gembert stopped. "The dungeon is two lefts away."

Mykal caught the tremble in Gembert's voice.

"I'll take it from here." Mykal readied his mind. A story Blodwyn shared with him during training came to mind. It had to do with a special breed of geese. They nested on mountain peaks. It kept eggs safe from predators. However, after the geese hatched, the babies needed food. The parents soared to the ground where the food was. It was four hundred feet below the nest. The parents would then call out to the goslings, encouraging them to follow. At two days old, and unable to fly, the goslings would then leap from the nest and free fall down the face of the mountain. Many did not survive the plunge. Blodwyn said he'd witnessed the event on one occasion, and would never forget the sight. He'd watched as the parent geese hurried along, the surviving goslings followed, and the dead forgotten.

That was how Mykal felt now, like a flailing gosling. Even Gembert stepped back relinquishing the lead. Going forward almost made little sense. The unexpected was anything and everything in front of him. There was no preparing for that.

Geneva.

Clairece.

"Wait here." He found it somewhat troubling these words came from him. He didn't wait and analyze it.

"Take a torch," Gembert offered.

All he could imagine were spiders lying in wait. Those eight-legged monsters loved dark, damp places. "I'm good. If they don't know we're down here by now, the firelight will only tip them off."

Mykal started forward, and kept his back as close to the damp wall as possible.

Two lefts.

All he heard, at first, was the sound of his own breathing. It took tremendous control not hyperventilating. Blodwyn would be so proud. Although, he hadn't made it to the dungeon yet, so there was still plenty of time to let his friend down.

He saw light.

He worried, at first, he'd gone around in a circle, that he was now behind the others and when he rounded the corner would come face to face with Blodwyn, Gembert and the queen. The odors were stronger than before. So strong he struggled not getting sick. Bile rose in his throat. Somehow he managed swallowing it down.

They weren't alone in the bowels under the castle.

Someone whimpered.

Mykal counted back from three inside his mind. After one, he rounded the corner, staff ready to strike.

His eyes quickly adjusted to the light. He breathed out of his mouth, but even then the pungent fetor of feces assaulted his nostrils. His eyes teared.

There was a woman inside the caged cell. She was balled up, and tucked back in a corner. Another stood, hands clutching the bars.

Geneva.

"Stay still!" Mykal walked the dungeon, ready for an attack. It seemed as if they were alone.

The dungeon brought back horrific memories. He could still envision Galatia shackled on the table. The Mountain King had tortured her for information on summoning the other wizards. She'd died from the injuries sustained.

On the floor, not far from where Galatia had been restrained, Mykal had found the body of his grandfather. The great sorcerer had been ambushed when he arrived. It had been his mother's father. Telling her about the loss had not been easy.

He'd been too late to rescue them.

That failure will always haunt him.

Always.

Not this time. Geneva was alive.

"Stand back."

Geneva rushed over and laid her body protectively over the woman curled into a fetal position. "Am I safe here?"

"Yes. Stay right there. Cover your head." He held his staff out, perpendicular, in front of him, hands close together. He knew what he wanted to have happen. Unlike his mother, he didn't need incantations for working his magic. His mind called up actions, and the magic obeyed. It was because he was a natural wizard, unlike his mother, or even his grandfather.

He moved his hands apart, and the iron bars bent. By the time his arms were spread wide, the bars had burst out from the stone. Rocks, and rock dust sprayed forward.

Quickly, Mykal checked the dungeon again, to ensure the deafening sound of crumbling rock didn't bring unwanted attention.

He heard footsteps running toward him.

Blodwyn rounded the corner first.

Mykal exhaled. "In there."

Blodwyn ran toward the women, Mykal right behind him.

Geneva said, "She's still alive. Barely. That is Clairece." She shivered. Her lips were chapped. She leaned her weight on Mykal for support.

"And the others?" Blodwyn asked.

"I don't know about any others," Mykal said.

Geneva pointed, and then Mykal turned about to follow in the that direction. "That's my aunt. Like the others, she was dead already when I was locked away in here."

Bodies were mostly covered with strands of straw. Arms. Legs. Deidre was off to the side. She was flat on her back. The remaining straw was thinly placed over her body like a shroud.

The skin was nearly as white as the snow outside.

Geneva cried. Her shoulders shook. "It was the only thing I could do. They were lying here and there. Clairece was too weak to move them. It's one of the most horrible things I've ever experienced. I couldn't get their eyes to stay closed. The women just stared at me. They wouldn't look away."

Mykal pulled Geneva in tight, an arm around her. "You did the right thing."

Blodwyn tossed Mykal his staff, and then scooped the young woman into his arms.

They stepped out of the cell.

The queen stood still, arms limp at her sides, as she cried. Tears streaked her face. Gembert stood silent, a comforting hand on her shoulder. "The baron and his wife, what will I tell them?"

"You can tell them that their daughter is alive." Mykal handed Gembert Blodwyn's staff, and then brushed hair out of the young woman's face.

"My sister is responsible for this."

Mykal didn't know if it was a question, or an accusation, or, quite possibly, a surrendering admission.

Clairece's skin was milky white. "She's lost a lot of blood."

Geneva lowered her eyes. "Raaheel has slowly drained them. She steals their blood, mine, too."

It was confirmation their theory had been correct. Mykal was still baffled by the action, though. "Drinking the blood. Why? Does strength transfer from one host to the other?"

"She is siphoning their life-source, stealing their youth," Blodwyn said. "I imagine drinking the blood, coupled with the magic inside the book she was carrying around makes the transformation complete. She is searching for a way to be youthful forever. Immortal. There is a name for those who drink blood, *haematophagy.*"

Mykal didn't know the word, but understood the meaning of immortal. As a wizard, he would live for centuries, maybe a millennium, but death would come, it would claim his life sooner or later.

Blodwyn continued, "The creatures that do this, drinking another's blood, are known as vampires."

"Vampires?"

"An ancient evil, as old as time. Rest assured, there are consequences for their actions," Blodwyn added.

"And maybe we can discuss those consequences elsewhere. I think right now we should get out of here," Mykal said. "This girl needs food, some water."

"How are we going to get her through the passageway?" Gembert was looking back in the direction they'd come.

"We won't. Everyone get close."

"Close?" Queen Sarah asked.

"You're going to love this, your highness," Gembert said, unable to contain his wide-stretched grin.

Geneva shook her head. "I can't leave my aunt, or the others. Not here. Not in this place!"

"There's no time. We'll come back. They won't be left here alone for much longer," Blodwyn said.

"Take hold," Mykal instructed.

"There are six of us, Mykal. Is this such a good idea?" Blodwyn, always the concerned one.

"I've been storing my energy for a long time now. I've got this." There were limited options. He had no idea what had been used for barricading the main doorway. It could take twice as long trying that route as an exit. There wasn't time enough to waste.

"Come close. Grab on." They took hold of each other.

Mykal let the swirling smoke surround them, ignoring how wide Sarah's eyes grew. She looked terrified. He closed his own eyes, and concentrated on the transport.

He could hear the smoke gain speed as it spun faster and faster around them.

He heard feet shuffle closer.

And then they were gone.

Mykal placed them in the front castle vestibule. They avoided the cold completely. As the twirling smoke dissipated, Sarah was giggling.

She caught herself, and stifled the laugh. "That was... truly amazing."

"Thank you, your highness."

"That *was* truly amazing." The voice came from behind them. Everyone turned to look.

Queen Raaheel wasn't alone. Encircling them were warriors dressed similarly to the ones who had attacked

Mykal and the others on the way down to the valley. Arrows were nocked, and bow strings pulled taut.

A simple command from the elder queen and they'd all be dead.

CHAPTER 35

Queen Raaheel and her warriors had them surrounded. Blodwyn set Clairece down on the floor, and not gently. He snatched his staff out of Gembert's hands. He stood with his left leg forward, right back, and knees slightly bent. The staff was angled in front of him, gripped loosely in both hands at the center.

Pushing back with his arm, Mykal tucked Geneva behind him. He mimicked Blodwyn's stance. Gripped, and re-gripped his staff. His heart pounded inside his chest. Transporting the six out of the dungeon and into the castle front foyer drained his energy more than expected. He'd worked on this move time and again with Blodwyn. It was not one he'd mastered. And yet, he knew the skill was most needed now.

He and Blodwyn started slow, twirling staffs in their hands.

Mykal concentrated on the twisting of his wrists. The staff spun around faster, and faster.

"*Raa*! What are you thinking? Why are you doing this?" Queen Sarah shouted.

Queen Raaheel raised, and dropped an arm. Arrows were loosed. The sound of snapped bowstrings was a steady, thwap thwap thwap. "I have no idea how you got me to agree to sharing the crown!"

Mykal rotated the twirling staff from hand to hand.

Raaheel continued, "I'm the oldest! The crown was rightfully mine, and mine alone!"

Mykal moved his arms, and wrists, and the staff rotated faster than the flapping wings of a humming bird.

Mykal and Blodwyn's staffs deflected arrows, keeping the others safe.

Arrow shafts skidded across the floor.

"We could have talked about it," Sarah tried. "You didn't have to go to these extremes!"

The archers weren't deterred. They continued to let arrows fly.

Mykal had worked his staff into a rhythm. The iron and wood of its make-up whistled. He and Blodwyn had built an almost invisible shield, a bubble around them.

"Oh, you have no idea just how far I've gone. None." Queen Raaheel screamed, "Attack!"

Warriors came at them with swords raised, but were hesitant. There was no easy path of attack.

With the staff in his right hand, Mykal waved his left hand in front of him. It looked as if a running wild boar chopped the legs out from under them. Then it was as if a strong wind blew them away. The warriors, along with fallen arrows, and dropped swords, slid across the floor. One warrior dug his hands into stone to keep from being swept up, and bellowed in pain when fingernails snapped back. His howling was silenced when his body slammed into the wall.

Another warrior was rammed into the legs of a table. The iron bust of King Cordillera toppled. The warrior's skull split, and head splattered. The bust came to rest where actual head and shoulders once had been.

Gembert scrambled out of the tight, protective huddle on hands and knees, dove forward onto his belly, arm outstretched, and lifted a sword off the floor. He jumped to his feet, chest puffed, head high, and joined the fight.

Mykal rotated his staff this way, and that, connecting with and diverting arching, and thrusting enemy swords. Covered in sweat he wished he could remove his cloak. He never would. The shed dragon scales woven into the fabric protected him better than a steel shield. It was the beads rolling down his forehead that threatened dripping into his eyes he worried about most. Salty sweat stung eyeballs something fierce!

There was no way of checking on Blodwyn's progress. He heard his friend's heavy breathing. Gembert stayed close. He lunged, and parried, riposted and feinted like a champ. The three of them kept at it as best they could, but signs of being physically taxed showed. The labor of the fight took a toll. The grunts, and groans sounded weak, exhausted.

Queen Raaheel still had a worthy army behind her.

Mykal knew if Clairece wasn't on the floor, unconscious, they'd have a better chance at defending themselves. It gave him an idea. All at once Mykal spun around. He dropped to his knees, He places a hand on Clairece's leg, and Geneva's shoulder. He closed his eyes.

When he opened them, the two were gone.

He hadn't been sure if it would work.

Thankfully, it did.

He'd transported just them in an instant from the foyer floor up into his apartment, and onto the sofa. They were now safe for the time being.

Mykal summersaulted past Queen Sarah, turned, touched her on the back and sent her with Geneva and Clairece.

Now the three of them could concentrate on the fight at hand.

The warriors closed in on them, the circle drawn tighter and tighter.

Arrows continued flying at them with deadly accuracy.

If it were not for gyrating staffs, they would have been punctured, time and again, with bodies full of holes.

Mykal dropped to a knee, and waved his hand from across the room.

Wind came from the east side of the foyer and blew the warriors around. The armed men fell into each other.

Gembert was accidentally caught up in the sweep. Launched into the air, he came down hard on his shoulder. He grunted, and cried out. His sword clattered on to the ground, chipping away at the flat stone. When he knelt to retrieve it, he'd inadvertently avoided decapitation. The swinging sword cut through only air.

Mykal smack the head of the staff into the back of the warrior's neck, driving a now unconscious man to the floor.

"Thank you for that." Gembert stood up, sword in hand.

The warriors were getting up. Instead of being dazed, confused, they looked pissed off.

"Get behind me!" Mykal gripped his staff horizontally, his hands were shoulder width apart. "Both of you, now!"

He raised the head of the staff into the air, twisted it around, and then slammed the base onto the floor. A shockwave of color exploded: blue, red, and green light rolled out in waves around the base of the staff from the impact.

Ripples grew, and becoming hotter with each wave. The green, and blue ripples stopped altogether. Only red waves of fire flared out. Camouflaged garments worn by the warriors ignited into flames.

The men screamed. They pulled at the clothing. The material melted with their skin. Charred flesh, and rising flames filled the foyer. The putrid odor of cooked meat, muscle, and organs mixed with smoke.

Mykal knew the difference between sweat and tears. He let the beads blend and roll down his face.

Raaheel's Thane stepped forward, in front of his queen with a sword in each hand. He strutted toward Mykal, his blades cutting through air. He growled as he got closer, and also speeded up his steps.

Mykal didn't hesitate. He twirled his staff around in his hands, as he moved to meet Axel half way.

They swung at each other. The air whooshed between them. There was a loud crack as steel smashed into Mykal's staff. The initial blow was deflected. Mykal brought up the bottom end of his staff and drove it into Axel's inner thigh.

The thane backed up a step, swing down from the left with one sword, and down from the right with the other.

Mykal ducked from the left sword, dropped and rolled away from the right blade.

He heard the whoosh, and realized he'd been closer to death than expected. Mykal swept his staff around on the floor. Axel attempted to jump over the staff. One foot cleared. Mykal raised the staff, tripping up the thane's second foot.

Axel went down. Hard.

His chainmail rattled.

Mykal, now on his knees, slammed his staff over the back of Axel's head. The first blow sent swords out of the thane's hands. The second knocked the man out could. "He's not dead. Secure him!"

Winded, Mykal slowly got to his feet. Geneva rushed over, took him by the arm, assisting.

Queen Sarah didn't look relieved. Instead, she appeared startled. Her eyes were open wide, and she pointed. "She's getting away!"

CHAPTER 36

Mykal saw Queen Raaheel and two of her warriors take off running. He gave chase. He stumbled, his vision blurred. Every muscle in his body protested. The queen was getting away. He wasn't sure he could keep up. He'd called on his magic to defeat the queen's warriors. The act saved the lives of his friends, but left him depleted, deflated.

The sound of their heavy footfalls on the slate floor echoed. His breathing was fast. Shallow. He huffed, struggling to breathe.

Raaheel threw open a door, and passed through the threshold, one warrior directly behind her. The second closed the door, and spun around. He waved his sword, cutting through air, and stomped his feet as he chose a defensive stance.

Mykal launched four small, glowing blue orbs. They were the size of melons, smaller. Charged, and electric. He heard a snapping, and hissing come from them as they raced forward.

The warrior batted them away, splitting one in half. He re-gripped his sword with both hands, and re-set his footing.

Without slowing, Mykal came upon the warrior, his staffed raised over his head. The warrior lunged forward, driving his blade toward Mykal's gut.

The sharp blade would have punctured his stomach and come out of his back if Mykal didn't twirl his staff around, and counter the attack. The impact of the clashing of weapons knocked the sword out of the warrior's hand.

Mykal banged the head of the staff over the warrior's skull. Bone cracked. The legs wobbled. As the warrior was dropping to the floor, Mykal was already pushing the man aside, and reaching to open the door.

The dropped body blocked the entrance. Mykal used his foot and swiveled the warrior out of the way.

Once the door was opened, Mykal recognized the staircase.

They led to the top of a tower, the one where the dovecote was located.

More stairs.

The decision had to be made quickly. Or did it? He could use magic, transport himself to the top and surprise the queen.

He heard the child in her laughing. The sound bounced off the rock walls. It echoed all around him as the door behind him fell closed.

Or he could chase her up the stairs. He might not catch her before she reached the top, but did it matter? Where would she go? The only thing at the top of the tower was the lone dovecote.

She was trapped.

It was a dead end.

Using magic would make him weaker. Chasing her up the stairs wouldn't make him less weak. It was almost a lose - lose situation.

He gave chase.

He wanted his magic handy.

He took stairs two at a time. Running up the stairs with the long staff wasn't helping. He kept one hand on the wall, maintaining his balance. His vision clouded.

There was a chance he'd not make it to the top.

Winding, and winding around the staircase as he ascended turned the climb surreal. He couldn't tell if he was going upward, or down. Sideways, or backwards.

He'd stumbled more than once, and fell knocking his shins into the stone edge of a stair. Wincing, he'd got back up and continued.

Where the energy came from, he had no idea. His reserves were on empty.

It felt as if he'd been climbing for hours.

And then the door was in front of him.

He stopped for just a moment. He rested a hand on the closed door, head bowed. His breathing was out of control, and he felt lightheaded. He didn't want to step out and collapse. Passing out was a possibility. It had happened on the trail to the valley. There was no reason it wouldn't happen again. The circumstances were very similar.

He counted to ten.

In those brief seconds, he'd regulated his breathing.

In through his nose. Out through his mouth. In. Out. In. Out.

He threw open the door.

The dovecote was all that was presented.

He stepped out of the staircase, and searched left and right. She wasn't there. She wasn't hiding. There was no ambush waiting for him.

Raaheel must be inside the dovecote.

Trapped.

She picked the hiding spot. That made him apprehensive. What did she know that he was missing? What could vampires do that Blodwyn hadn't shared?

Could this young queen have the upper hand?

She must think so.

He decided to check around the back side of the dovecote before entering the cylindrical construction. He stopped.

Raaheel stood on the tower ledge, between turrets, facing him. Arms spread wide.

She smiled, eyes shining.

Aside from the cleft in her chin, Mykal thought something was amiss.

Her teeth.

They were different. The queen had sprouted fangs. "Raaheel," he said.

"Queen Raaheel!"

Mykal shook his head. "Your sister is queen. You'll never rule the people of Osiris. You turned your back on them. Royalty ended for you when you fed on your subjects. Come down from there. You must pay for the crimes committed."

She laughed. Head back, neck exposed. When the chortle ended, she eyed Mykal. Unblinking, she said, "It will never be that easy, mage. And this is far from over."

"Oh, it's over." He held out a hand. "Now come away from the ledge."

It was like she didn't hear a word he'd said. "We will meet again."

She was trapped. There was no escape. Mykal wasn't sure why she behaved as confidently as she did. "Raaheel..."

Without a sound, the vampire fell backward off the tower.

Mykal raced toward the ledge. "No!"

He prepared for the worst. She'd wind up in pieces down the face of the castle, splattered onto parts of the mountain. He saw her body fall, the fold of her dress flapping, as if wings. He wasn't sure if the laugh continued. He heard it though. Could the sound have been bouncing off the castle walls? The clouds above him?

Then she was gone. He could no longer make out her shape as she fell. There was no a sign of her below.

And then he heard her laugh, again.

Raaheel taunted him. Not from below, but from above. He looked up, but could not find her in the sky, or mixed in with the clouds.

He stood between the turret until long after her laugh had faded away, and then he stood there a little longer.

CHAPTER 37

Queen Sarah sat with Gembert at the table in the Long Room. She'd dispatched knights. The castle was surrounded, under her protection, and hopefully once again under her control.

Gembert sat at the table, arm in a sling.

"How are you?" Mykal asked.

"I'll survive." Gembert raised the broken arm best he could. "Thanks to you."

"Any sign of your sister?" Blodwyn asked.

"No sign at all. All we know for sure is that she and Axel are no longer anywhere inside the castle."

"Do you know where they could have gone? Any idea?" Mykal asked.

Queen Sarah shook her head, eyes lowered. "We'll not give up on looking for her. Those men that attacked us, they weren't part of my knights. Gembert's checked on the knights. They're all accounted for. I've no idea who they are, who they were."

There was a moment of silence.

The queen said, "Blodwyn? I would like to know more about vampires."

"I'm no expert. I've never run into one before. I can't say for certain your sister has succumbed to such evil ways."

"I understand what you're doing," Queen Sarah said. "But I would like you to speak freely."

Blodwyn cleared his throat. "If her transformation is complete, she is now of the night. Daylight will be her enemy. If any part of her bare flesh is exposed to the sun, she will burst into flames."

"That sounds like a curse. Why would Raaheel pursue such a change?" Sarah said.

"More than you may realize. In order to maintain her youth, she will need to consume on human blood. And often. Her appetite will be insatiable." Blodwyn added, "She will, however, live forever. She will be immortal."

Mykal shivered. A diet of human blood? She'd leave a trail of bloodless corpses behind. She wouldn't be difficult to track. Mykal wouldn't rest until she was caught, punished.

"In darkness?" Sarah said, she sounded confused by the prospect. Then she shook her head. "She is not very different from our father. He always sought the unimaginable. Good enough was never good enough for him. She's no different. Not really."

She turned around lifting something up from the table. Sarah then presented the item wrapped in thin leather case to Mykal.

"What is this?"

"Open it."

He undid laces. Inside was the book he had seen Raaheel carrying.

"I want you to find out what she did, how she did it... and if it can be undone."

The unspoken words were there. Despite the horrors that unfolded, Sarah wanted her sister back. Not the monster, but the little sibling she no doubt remembered.

"I will do everything I can to help you, your highness." He couldn't make any promise. He suspected

Raaheel was beyond saving. When Queen Sarah started crying, he assumed she knew the truth, as well.

Mykal wasn't sure how to comfort her, nor was he comfortable knowing Raaheel was still out there. He remained still, and waited.

And waited.

***

Baron Richmond, and the Baroness Henriette hugged their daughter tight. The three of them almost looked like one massive person. Elma stood with hands clasped together, and raised to right in front of her face.

"You have no idea how thankful we are." Richmond gave up on acting strong and unemotional the minute he'd opened his apartment door and saw his daughter standing in front of Queen Sarah. He sobbed for several seconds before yelling for his wife, and pulling his daughter into an embrace that threatened cutting off the poor girl's air.

"And you will never know how sorry I am that all of you have had to suffer through such an ordeal while visiting with us. With me. I hope this experience will not destroy our relationship." Queen Sarah spoke in a soft tone of voice, her confidence rattled.

"We have pledged loyalty to the Cordillera's. That has not changed," Richmond said.

Mykal, standing behind the queen, wasn't sold on the degree of loyalty. It seemed pointless calling him out at this juncture.

"The wizard would like a word with you," Sarah said, stepping aside, and indicating Mykal with a side-sweep of her hand toward him.

The wizard. Mykal didn't care for the title. He wasn't sure he could do anything about it, though.

Richmond gave his family a squeeze. He reluctantly stepped out of the embrace, and let Elma get in on the moment. When he stepped into the hall, he tugged on the waistline of his tunic, and offered up a big smile. "Thank you, wizard. I've no doubt you had a hand in the safe return of my daughter." "It was Queen Sarah's wise counsel that made this reunion possible." Mykal bowed toward the queen.

Richmond continued smiling. "What is it you want to talk about?"

"The butterflies."

Richmond arched an eyebrow. "What about them?"

"Your daughter was able to communicate with me while in captivity. That is a rare gift she has. Her ability—"

The baron held up a hand. "Are you saying my daughter is also a wizard?"

"I'm saying Clairece has magic inside her. I don't know if she is a wizard, or perhaps just a magician. And while I say, just magician, I don't in any way mean to diminish the awesomeness of such a gift. Her ability—"

"I think you're mistaken, Wizard. And I say so, respectfully. We're ordinary people."

"I know you're afraid. But her ability—"

"She is not a wizard. I thank you for your concern. And once again, I thank you for all you've done. You've made my wife and I the happiest parents in the empire."

"And I am the happiest aunt!" Elma said. Her words were muffled. It was no surprise. Her mouth was half-buried in Clairece's hair.

They went back into the apartment.

The door closed.

Queen Sarah pursed her lips, regarding Mykal thoughtfully.

"Her abilities are a mystery I would love to explore." Mykal completed his thought. Closed his hands into loose fists.

"I'm sorry about that," Queen Sarah said,

The apartment door opened. Richmond and Henriette stayed just inside, while Clairece emerged. She held the box of butterflies in her hands.

"She insists you accept this gift for saving her life," Henriette said.

Mykal took the box. "This must have taken you a lifetime to collect. I could never accept this."

"I want you to have them. I know that they mean something to you. They mean the world to me. Nothing would make me happier than knowing I was able to properly say thank you for everything you and your friends did to help me."

Mykal nodded. He turned, and handed the box to Blodwyn.

"Hold out your hand," Mykal instructed the girl as he reached up to the throat of his cloak, and unfastened the dragonfly pendant. "I will only accept your gift, if you accept mine."

"You do not owe me anything else. And this brooch is too much for me to accept."

"Like you, this is something I want you to have. Because I believe one day our paths will cross again. But if you ever need me, for any reason, I believe with this brooch you will understand how to call on me." Mykal closed her fingers over the dragonfly. He bent forward and kissed the top of her head. "You stay safe."

The family disappeared behind a closing apartment door.

"I have a feeling she will show up at our doorstep one day," Blodwyn said.

"As do I." Mykal retrieved the box of butterflies, and found he already looked forward to seeing her again.

***

Mykal closed the apartment door.

Geneva stood in the hall, hands together in front of her.

"I appreciate you walking me out."

"I wanted to say goodbye." She smiled.

They walked toward the stairs. Mykal knew his steps were slow, deliberate. "I wanted to ask you something."

"I'm listening," she said.

"We've not told the queen where you found us."

She held up a hand. "I would never tell her. The old library is our secret."

"Thank you. We appreciate that." It wasn't that they were in hiding. He just had a feeling the less people who knew where they resided, the better. Or the safer.

They walked in silence.

"Was that what you wanted to ask me?" she said.

His cheeks felt hot. He knew they were red. "It isn't."

"I'm listening."

"If you wanted to come back with us to the library, I know Blodwyn would like to have you around," he said.

"Oh really?" She said. "*Blodwyn* would like to have me around? Just him?"

"Well. I suppose I could get used to the idea, too."

Her laugh was more than a flirtatious giggle, but then she stopped walking, turned around and faced him. She took his hands in hers. "Mykal."

He hadn't been expecting the gentle touch.

"I would love to join you, and Wyn." She couldn't look him in the eyes.

"But?"

"But, my cousins need me right now. My aunt is gone. I'm all the family they have left." She met his gaze. "If the offer remains open, perhaps sometime soon I can come visit. When the weather clears?"

"I would like that."

"So would I." She stood on tiptoes, and pressed a kissed on him.

Mykal did not want the moment to end, so when the slow kiss ended, he kissed her back, wrapping an around her waist and held her close.

***

Once Gembert collected their belongings from the apartment, and final farewells were said, Mykal and Blodwyn stepped outside of the castle, and walked down past the main gate. With burlap bags slung over shoulders they stood for a moment, looking back at the enormity of the Cordillera castle.

"If we never see this realm again, it will be too soon," Mykal said. "Take my arm, Wyn. We're going home."

The swirling smoke came up from the ground and spun around the two friends huddled close together.

"I'm not sure I'll ever get used to this means of travel," Blodwyn said.

As the smoke consumed them, Mykal smiled and said, "I'd say we can walk, but it's too late."

CHAPTER 38

In an instant, Mykal's magic had whisked himself and Blodwyn home from the Cordillera Realm. The swirl of smoke evaporated around them, along with the blanket of warmth it wrapped them in.

Mykal ignored the sinking feeling as best he could, and for as long as he could, and rushed into the Library. He'd gone far too long without contact with his mother. His mind was a whirlwind. Having been unable to reach her, his sense of dread grew like storm clouds over the Isthmian. His heart pounded. The throbbing beat behind his ears. A pungent odor filled the spacious hall. He knew the scent, but denied his mind from focusing on any answers.

The cold hearth held grey, charred logs on the grate.

"She's not here." Mykal spun around, his eyes looking upward, seeing mostly nothing. He dropped his burlap bag, and Raaheel's book onto the floor. The dull thud died fast. There was no echo at all.

Blodwyn never stopped walking, from the front entrance toward the back of the library, passing Mykal. His own sense of apprehension apparent in thick creases lining his brow.

Mykal followed, his cloak kicked up by his heels. He breathed quick and shallow breaths. The clouds he felt seemed as if they were following above him. He kept his eyes on Blodwyn's back.

The door leading to the lower levels of the ruins stood open. The torch hanging on the wall was unlit. Mykal zapped the end of the torch with a point. Without missing a beat, Blodwyn lifted the now lit torch from the hook and started down the stairs. Mykal had never noticed the musty odor before; it was as if mold covered the walls in the weeks they'd been away.

It didn't mask the pungent smell, though.

That was still there, still overpowering. Mykal squeezed his eyes shut and shook his head. He wanted the negative thoughts gone.

"You alright?"

Mykal opened his eyes. They were at the bottom of the stairs. "Right behind you."

Blodwyn used the torch's flame and lit the others in the wide-open room.

Rows of shelves worked their way toward the center of the room.

In the center of the room was a large, round table. On it were stacks of books, and rolled parchments.

Sprawled out on the floor was a person.

Mykal sprinted forward, his heart beat so fast he feared his heart might explode. It didn't matter that moments ago he'd been outside in the cold, in the snow. It didn't matter that the lower level of the library was cold, and damp. He was sweating.

Cold sweats. Under his arms, and behind his knees were wet with perspiration. The beads on his forehead rolled into his eyes. The salt stung. His forearm swept across his face, mopping up as much moisture as possible.

"Mykal!" Blodwyn tried stopping him, but hadn't stopped moving, either.

It was indeed a woman. She was on her back. Strands of hair covered deep, thick wrinkles. Soft tree bark. One arm lay across her chest with long, unkempt and unsightly fingernails which resembled the talons found on a falcon.

Mykal knelt down next to the body. He looked up, and said, "It's not her."

Blodwyn dropped onto his knees. "Oh, Anna."

Mykal's chest tightened. "It's not her, Wyn. It's not my mother!"

Blodwyn cried. He didn't wipe away his tears as his fingertips traced her skin. "What happened to you?"

Mykal shook his head. "No, Wyn. No. This isn't her. This isn't my mother."

Blodwyn took Anna by the shoulders. He gently lifted her into his arms, and hugged her against his chest.

Mykal gripped Blodwyn's arm with one hand, and ran the other down his mother's hair. "It can't be her, Wyn. What happened to her?"

Blodwyn's eyes were closed. His cheeks wet.

Mykal hugged them both. "This can't be happening, Wyn. This isn't happening."

***

Blodwyn stood beside the table. His hand hovered over an object.

Mykal sat with his mother's head in his lap. "What are we going to do now?"

"This, on the table. I hadn't noticed it before." Blodwyn's eyes narrowed, and his jaw set. "She says not to touch this box."

Mykal looked at his mother's face. What had caused this type of decomposition? Had she been calling out to him while he was in the other realm?

He'd have heard her.

"Mykal."

Mykal set her his mother down. He stood, and removed his cloak. He balled it up and then set it under his mother's head. He knew she was gone. Giving her a pillow, something soft for her head to rest on, just made him feel more comfortable. "What have you got?"

Blodwyn pointed toward an open journal.

Mykal saw in his mother's handwriting—he knew her writing very well from countless hours, and days spent on lessons—was a simple sentence was scrawled out.

Mykal, don't touch or open the box!

The box.

The box sat beside the journal. It resembled an intricately carved block of wood. The detail magnificent. The wings of a flying dragon wrapped around edges. The beast soared over a village. The flames from its throat scorched a band of knights on horseback.

Mykal reach for the box.

Blodwyn snarled. "What are you doing?"

It seemed natural, picking the box up for closer inspection. "I don't see any hinges, and it doesn't look like there is a lid."

"So, how does it open?" Blodwyn bent low, eye level with the table. His fingertips traced the edge of the table.

All at once he stood up, and put his back to the box. "I'll take care of the box."

"She said not to touch it." Mykal couldn't look away from the object. There was an energy coming from it. From inside it? He wasn't sure. All he knew for certain was he had never wanted to touch anything as much as this box. He wanted to lift it, and look it over, turn it in his hands and examine the carvings closer. And he wanted to open it. The fact that it didn't appear to open made him want to solve the mystery that much more.

"She said *you* were not to open or touch it." Blodwyn rubbed his chin thoughtfully. "I will sweep the box, and the journal into a sack and get it out of the library for now."

"Why would you take them out of the library?"

"You can't see the way you look. The box is doing something to you. It is affecting you somehow. I suspect, it is not done in a good way either." Blodwyn locked eyes with Mykal. "Right now I'm more concerned with how you are doing."

Mykal's brows furrowed. "Me? How I'm doing?"

Blodwyn sighed, frowned, and looked down at Anna.

Mykal's breath caught in his lungs, as his chest tightened. With breathing stopped, and lungs burning he let his hands become fists. "I don't know what I'm going to do."

Blodwyn reached out and clamped a hand down on Mykal's shoulder. "We're going to get past this. Together."

Instead of moving closer, Mykal backed away. "I don't see how."

"What is it?"

Mykal shrugged out of Blodwyn's grasp. "I grew up thinking I was an orphan. Only two years ago I learned both of my parents were alive, and in hiding. I mean, my father died valiantly during the War. And now my mother's dead... I'm an orphan again, Wyn. I'm all alone again."

Blodwyn grabbed onto Mykal's arms.

Mykal attempted pulling away.

"No, Wyn."

Blodwyn just waited, but didn't release his arms.

Mykal shook his head.

Blodwyn said, "You're not alone. You've never been alone."

EPILOGUE

Mykal swung an axe. The wood splintered into halves and fell off the stump. He hadn't been chopping wood long, but already felt the muscles in his lower back, and arms throb.

Blodwyn sat on a log with Daniel.

The two puffed away on a pipe, blue smoke billowed from the end of the pipe, and plumed out from their mouths and nostrils.

They seemed to be taking a break, and taking in with satisfied eyes, the fruits of their labor.

The new home for Daniel and his wife was coming along nicely.

"Once this place is done, I will bring her home," Daniel said. "She's doing so much better, but I don't want her exposed to the elements up here until I've a solid four walls, a roof, a hearth that can hold a fire all night long."

"You'll have that soon," Blodwyn promised.

"I appreciate you returning to help me rebuild."

Mykal felt guilty. He knew he was the one responsible for all of their pain and suffering. Helping to rebuild their home was the least he could do. And it wouldn't be the only thing, either. Whatever they needed, he'd do his best to accommodate them for as long as he was able.

"Stew is ready! That is, if any of you are hungry?" Geneva worked inside running a plane over wood, and smoothing out furniture she had built by hand. The woman was skilled with tools. Thanks to her, the table in the kitchen was a perfect size for all of them to feast.

He did not hide his excitement when she showed up to assist with the re-build. And while he understood her cousins needed family right now, he hoped one day soon she'd come visit the library and never want to leave.

The men tapped the tobacco out of the bowls, and pocketed the pipes.

Mykal followed them toward the new home.

At the threshold, Geneva touched Mykal's arm. "How are you holding up?"

"I miss her. We only had a few years together. I'm annoyed at all the time wasted. The worst part is I feel guilty at her for dying on me." In time, Mykal hoped that anger dissipated. He'd grown up thinking he was an orphan. "I'll be alright, though. In time,"

There *was* more. He wasn't sure he wanted to share it with Geneva just yet. In fact, he hadn't even told Blodwyn.

His magic was dwindling. He could almost feel his powers weakening.

Trying to cast a simple spell was becoming increasingly impossible, and all the more draining, leaving him feeling weak and faint for hours.

Blodwyn must have suspected something was amiss when he insisted they take horses across realms, rather than magical transportation.

Mykal's excuse was that the horses needed their exercise.

It was something of a lame excuse, but Blodwyn excepted it.

Obviously, the box was at the root of the problem. It didn't take a genius to put pieces that big together. It must have drained Anna's magic, and then siphoned away what was left of her life.

It's why he didn't want to tell Geneva, or Blodwyn.

He didn't want them worrying about him.

Once the house they were rebuilding was completed, he'd maybe discuss what was happening with Blodwyn. Either way, he needed to dedicate the rest of his time to finding out the meaning of the box.

He needed to discover a cure for what the box was stealing from him.

Mykal had no idea how long he had before the box sapped away the rest of his magic, or before he started stealing his life's energy.

He didn't want to die.

Finding out as much about the box as possible might be his only hope.

"Mykal?"

He raised his eyebrows, lips pursed. "Yes?"

"I feel like you were a million miles away just now."

He was. "I'm sorry. Just thinking, I guess. What was I saying?"

"That in time you would be all right."

He nodded. "Exactly, in time, I will be all right."

"I know you will." Geneva spoke so softly; he almost didn't hear her words. "She seemed like a caring woman. I never knew my own mother. It might not be comforting, but you were lucky to have time with her before she passed."

Lucky. That was not how he felt. "Thank you."

"Come on. We should get some stew before it's all gone."

Mykal forced himself to smile. "Race you!"

THE END

About the Author

Phillip Tomasso lives in Rochester, NY, and is an Award Winning Author with over 18 published novels. After nearly two decades of working at the Eastman Kodak Company (1990-2008: the last 10 spent as an Employment Law Paralegal), Tomasso landed a job almost seven years ago working full time as a Fire & EMS Dispatcher for 911. When not writing, or reading, he enjoys playing guitar. He can keep the rhythm, but is a horrible singer. Admittedly, and also regrettably, Tomasso sings when he plays guitar. Tomasso's three grown children are his main inspiration. Currently, Tomasso is hard at work on several new novel projects. Be sure to stop by his website, and sign up for his blog to be kept up to date on his happenings, and follow him on Twitter for his often witty, if not more than often repetitive tweets. One of his favorite things in the world is emails from fans who have read his books, (and one of the saddest is receiving story ideas. He will not accept, or write story ideas if sent to him; will delete the email and pretend like he never saw it in the first place).

An Invitation to Reading Groups
I would like to extend an invitation to Reading Groups/Book Clubs/Schools across the country. Invite me to your group and I'll be happy to participate in your discussion (either in person or via Skype, or telephones with a speaker). You can arrange a date and time by emailing me at phillip@Philliptomasso.com. I look forward to hearing from you.

Young Adult Books by Phillip Tomasso

The Severed Empire
Wizard's Rise
Wizard's War
Queens of Osiris

Jay Walker Mystery Series
The Case of the Missing Action Figure
The Case of the Impractical Prankster

Treasure Island: A Zombie Novella
Nightbreed: Young Blood
Damn the Dead

Sounds of Silence

COMING SOON

Summons of the Majestic by Tim Reed

Halfway to Anywhere Volume 1

The Hematophages by Stephen Kozeniewski

www.mirrormatterpress.com